PROLOGUE

In 1961, southern Oklahoma was a landscape of hard traditions and miles of empty space. Recycled stories and wide prairies were the sustenance from which everyone drew strength and stability. Families lived in the same houses, on the same ranches and farms, and on the same streets as their ancestors before them, and no whim of Darwinian evolution was going to break that chain. And woven into the very strands of this social tapestry was a culture of silence and a graveyard folklore that followed every day and every event like a grim, relentless shadow.

It wasn't that more people died here than in other parts of the world. Life was hard, not for some but for all of us who lived its painful cycles and endured all of nature's tricks. Drought, tornadoes, and flash floods were the obvious ones, but the real tricks involved watching a man sip his morning coffee and then, after not more than a hiccup, slump over dead in his chair. No logic or analysis could predict these injustices. But we all knew the stories and most of us had firsthand knowledge of death, had smelled its damp, rotten breath and watched it perform its slithering, languorous dance through the body of someone we loved. There were ten thousand people in Jefferson County in 1961. So when the news of death arrived, it was likely somebody we had bought milk from or sold eggs to or from whom we hitched a ride across the flatlands of Route 32. Death, in this place, was as expected as rain on a cloudy day.

The overgrown baseball diamond in Grady was where my life radically changed for the first time. And that year, 1961, when I was fifteen, it would change twice more so that soon I would hardly recognize who I had once been. Grandma Leeds, we called her "Weaver," said that's what growing up meant—nibbling on the forbidden fruit and realizing that your life was never actually as you had known it.

My mama refused to call Grandpa Leeds "Woody," like the rest of us. She hated him, or maybe she hated how he frightened her, though I had no concrete proof on which to base this theory. There were all kinds of quirky things on that side of the family, like how Weaver never let Woody drive anywhere at night. She hid his cigars from him and only let him smoke on his birthday, but knew he smoked every second he was out of her clutches. Woody told me stories of how the men in his oil cartel used to lie and cheat each other out of thousands of dollars, and then one of them would just stop showing up for work one day. He painted a picture of himself as the conscience shadowing their dirty deals, and the one who reminded them of goodwill and honesty. And whether or not it was true was beside the point. I never got to know him well enough to establish either intrinsic goodness or evil, or to judge his misdeeds. Woody was just another thread in my family's fraying tapestry.

I thought, back then, that the fate of my older sister Lewella and her premature baby was foremost in my mind and heart. But little did I know that three women—Janet Lange, Nelda McCann, and Mary, would shape my life more than any other influence. It was largely because of them, this femme trilogy, that I would become a man far before nature intended.

My adolescent world was full of trilogies like this. My Daddy, a rancher, believed every story had not two but three sides—the truth, that which covered up the truth, and a whole world in between. And there were only three things to see in southern Oklahoma—the open sky, a dry dotted landscape, and the murder of crows that flew around dead cattle. Our tree house club was a trilogy of sorts, even though neither me nor Mikey Savage liked Jimmy Wilson as much as each other. Mikey and me were best friends, though this was a fact neither of us ever spoke of out loud. Issues had come between us, like Janet for one, but not enough to dismantle a friendship that had lasted ten years so far. There just weren't enough people in Grady back then to be too selective.

The most important epiphany that came out of that year was that I was not intended to have the simple life I was born for. Mama and Daddy expected—I guess everybody did—that I would grow up, maybe study agriculture somewhere, marry some local girl, and endure the life of toil and hardship endemic to heartland farming and ranching. In my life, I had known little of both, since we started out as a dairy farm and later converted it to a ranch. But by the following year, I knew that chasing ghosts and dead bodies and killers was as native to my mind and heart as herding cattle was to Daddy.

And once I knew this, there was no going back.

I had learned that lying and pretending were for the weak of character and the faint of heart. And I knew, the night Mary McCann first called out to me, that I was neither of those and that I, of all people, had been chosen to be her savior. And so it was that I would change from a gawky, bumbling teenage boy into a superhero nearly overnight.

I heard her for the first time on the Fourth of July. Hottest damn day of the summer, the thermometer read ninety-eight degrees at ten in the morning. By noon the grass was too hot to walk on with bare feet. The air inside the house felt thick and heavy, and laden with a strange silence.

No one answered my knock on the bedroom door.

Mama's pie was still baking in the oven but her round, aproned figure wasn't in front of the stove. The house was deserted. It was a Saturday afternoon and by far the scariest day of my life.

Little did I know what was coming.

The screams had stopped sometime in the middle of last night. My older sister, Lewella, had been for twenty hours trying to have a baby that didn't want to come out. Doc Fisher and his wife stayed with us all week, but even they couldn't be found anywhere now, and I knew Weaver and Woody had been here last night from the smell of his cigars in the air. With no car out front and the red scarf tied at the very bottom of the fencepost, I knew something had gone wrong somewhere in the world. In my world, on my farm. Had the baby come out backward or upside down, or worse yet, dead? Or had they taken Lewella and her dead baby into town to get her cleaned up right at Doc Fisher's clinic?

The weight of family responsibility heaved down on me like a thousand-pound gorilla. My family had deserted me, though I had trouble digesting this reality. So I kept sane by sticking to the things I knew, and on a farm all you knew were two things—chores, and how to get out of them. So I pretended to be a big city doctor and made my rounds, reminding myself the whole time that everyone had gone without telling me. Mama, Daddy, the farmhands, Lewella, Doc Fisher, and Lewella's ham-fisted boyfriend Denny. Denny was the only grown-up I knew who was afraid of the dark. Hell, he sometimes had trouble finding his way home from Hooper Circle late at night. I couldn't imagine how he found his way to Lewella's privates to knock her up in the first place. But a brother doesn't have those thoughts about a sister. At least not in 1961 in Grady, Oklahoma.

I started by taking the pie out of the oven. The hand-crocheted oven mitts Grandma Weaver made were like boxing gloves on my knobby hands. Everything wobbled when I picked it up—the glass pie plate filled to the quick, my knees, ankles, innards. I collected Mama's sheets from the clothesline and laid them across her bed, then remembered, at the last minute, that the dogs might run across them and dirty them all up again. So I folded them in a messy stack and started on the potato peeling. I couldn't imagine how Mama did all this every day without a peep of complaint. I knew she didn't like working so hard. Nobody would. But Daddy wouldn't lift a finger to help her and that's the way it was. After the tenth potato, my hands were sticky with the residue left by the dirty skins. My mind wandered. I thought about what Mikey said in the tree house at our last meeting.

"You're fifteen now, Jake. Time for your initiation."

"Into what?" I asked him, but Mikey had a habit of ignoring the questions he didn't want to answer. I found out well enough three days later, when my rite of passage came in the form of a rock thrown through my bedroom window. Mikey would never throw it himself; he'd get one of his younger brothers to do it for him, since they did anything he told them. Luckily it happened while everyone was tending to Lewella so I'd gone before anybody noticed.

The rock had a note wrapped around it that read, "Initiation into Manhood: sleep on bare ground in baseball diamond. NO sleeping bag, no shoes, no blanket."

No shoes? What kind of a sadist was he?

Mikey made up all the initiations himself, studying books on secret societies he got from the Waurika Library and the community college in Wichita Falls. Most of them involved dissecting small animals and drinking their blood out of tiny glass vials, but Jimmy Wilson threw up when he did that, so, over the years, Mikey had changed the rules some. It was his club; he could do whatever he wanted, or so we were constantly reminded. In Grady, a fifteen-year-old boy was either in a club or excommunicated from civilization. Shunned, banished, the scorn of every girl and the embarrassment of the other boys. So I learned early on about the illusion of freedom of choice.

Or, I thought I did.

By the time I finished everyone's chores, Mama's apple pie was cool from sitting in the shade of the porch for two hours. I cut myself a three-helping slice, enjoying the autonomy of no supervision, but knowing all the while that I was about to be subjected to some form of discomfort or else why would Mikey have chosen it for me? Boys didn't become men just because they wished it, after all. You had to do something courageous, survive what others weren't equipped to because of either physical frailty or mental weakness. I was somewhere in between, I suppose. My muscles were undeveloped lumps of flabby flesh, but in my eyes was the resolve of knowing I could live through anything. And then I got to the baseball diamond—and changed my mind.

Nothing much happened in Grady after dark. Most of the farmers and ranchers in our part of town had lights out by eight or nine o'clock, and if you had no one to gossip or play cards with, you sat on the front porch looking at the sea of blinking stars. The baseball diamond was only called that because twenty years ago a bunch of doctors from Wichita Falls arranged monthly baseball games with the medical students at the college. This went on for a couple of years and then the college closed down and the baseball diamond became an empty field of coarse reeds and vile secrets.

People buried stuff there for all different reasons. They buried the ashes of loved ones, dead cats and birds, time capsules, and once Lewella planted some wildflower seeds and a pack of Mama's cigarettes when she was trying to quit. I was sure worse things had been buried there, since its size made it the kind of field no one would ever choose to search for something. I learned from Denny, Lewella's clumsy boyfriend, how to ward off evil spirits. He told me to pretend I was somebody else and talk out loud. This kept the spirits away because spirits only bothered you when you were alone. I looked up into the night sky with nothing on but the shirt on my back and some worn dungarees.

After the first noise, I became a sea captain. "Ahoy mateys! Launch the life boats, we're goin' ashore." I turned around quick in response to tricks of my ears, and then lapsed back into my role-playing. I walked sideways with a limp like a peg-legged pirate, and smiled and chewed out of the side of my mouth. Having read *Treasure Island* so many times, I had it almost memorized. "Fifteen men on a dead man's chest, yo ho ho and a bottle of rum. Drink and the devil had done for the rest, yo ho ho and—"

And then my ears became fleshy demons again, fooling me, conning me into thinking things that couldn't be. At first it sounded like Lewella's screams from the barn the other night—not steady screams but intermittent shrieks followed by long bouts of desperate quiet. But then I heard the moaning. I had made no camp because Mikey prohibited any normal sleeping comforts, threatening that they would impede the onset of manhood. So I tried to follow every rule. No blanket, no pillow, no shoes or socks, no hat to cover my head or cloth to cover my eyes. No sheets or pillowcases or secret love notes from girls and nothing to be taken from the tree house. "Just you," Mikey said, "and the dark night and your twisted imagination."

I covered my eyes with my palms and left an opening between my pinkies for air to get in, but then I needed two more hands to cover my ears from the wailing sound, and two extra long arms to wrap around my body. It came from every direction. I turned to the right and it got louder. I turned again and my eardrums were about to pop. I would have cut off a finger for another piece of Mama's apple pie right then, but I remembered the last rule of the club—no food. No Dick Tracy cards or my Superman figurines, either.

So I started running.

First to the left, out toward Happy Jack Road, pounding my bare feet into the rough grass and dirt as hard as I could, like I was trying to graft the blades into the fabric of my skin. But the noise only got louder. I turned around a hundred and eighty degrees and ran toward the direction I'd first heard the sound coming from, and still it only got louder. Was I going out of my mind? Is this what it meant to go crazy, like Mama's crazy sister Juliet who went to a convent and stopped talking and prayed in Latin lying down on her belly all day long? Then, like Lewella's episode, I heard nothing but crickets and tiny animals all around the prairie floor for three whole beautiful minutes. Silence, dark, cool night air, and peace in the pit of my bowels.

Shrieking came again but lower this time, lower in pitch and volume like the person was closer to death now. I tried to find her, as I knew it was a woman. A young woman.

"Where are you?" I called out, trying to appeal to her sense of responsibility. I was a humanitarian in that moment, trying to help, to hold her hand as she screamed, while all the life essence drained from her into the cold, unwelcoming dirt. I cried as I ran and never told another soul about it. I hadn't cried ever in my life, not to myself anyway. I'd cried in front of Mama one time when she made me feel guilty for stealing candy bars from Munroe's store, and I cried on Daddy's knee while his long black belt whipped pink lashes into the flesh of my behind. But never before had I allowed myself the luxury of feeling fear or sadness and let my crying resonate into the night air like this. I didn't care what people thought or how I looked to the boys in our club—to Mikey, or Freddie or Jimmy Wilson or his brother Nate. It was just me running in circles trying to save a dead witch from the tortures of her longing soul.

A speck of the moon peeked out from the layered folds in the clouds. And I saw something, or thought I did. She was twenty yards ahead of me, so I assumed so from the nebulous smears of white and red that I saw between the spaces of tall fescue. When I moved closer, the sky got dark again but the form in the brush didn't move. Ten yards away now, then eight, and I could see it was a blanket. Was it a baby's cry that I'd heard? No—clearly the moans and cries of a woman. Whether she was young or old I couldn't tell and wasn't sure I even wanted to know. As I came upon her, the jerking back motion of my head became a nervous tick. I couldn't stop looking all around me, even though the woman in the grass and I were likely the only two souls out in all of Jefferson County that time of night. I saw her; not just looked, but absorbed fully what my eyes were taking in. Her skin was young and smooth without wrinkles, her untrusting eyes were small and dark, and her mouth was gagged with her hands bound behind her back. I wasn't close enough for her to actually see me, but she felt me coming. I could tell because the screams resumed the closer I got. When I came into view and gaped down into the bloody grass, it got quiet.

The wide, dark eyes moved back and forth and down the length of my body. The cloth gagging her mouth was wrapped high on her face, nearly covering her nostrils, but I could still see her fair complexion and beauty amid her despair. She sucked in air violently through her nose as I neared and her wet eyes glistened in the droplets of moonlight shining down through the evil sky. I bent down and reached toward her face to remove the cloth and then the shrieking started again. The sound startled me and I fell back on the hard ground. I didn't know how she made that sound considering her mouth was gagged. It was a full and open scream loud enough to wake every dead body in the Ryan Cemetery twelve miles away. I used my opened palms to try to communicate a gesture of peace, as no words would come out of my mouth, but the closer I got the louder she screamed. So I ran again, and this time I didn't stop 'til I got to a road. I wasn't sure which road it was as all the light from the sky had been blotted out by the clouds' terror, but I knew somehow if I stopped running, I would end up dead like that woman would be in an hour. God help her, and maybe me while he's at it.

two

Mikey said he found me the next morning passed out on his front porch with my shirt all grimy and balled up under my head.

I didn't know how I got there and didn't even recognize Mikey at first. But I wanted to bend down and kiss the weather-beaten slats under my head. I heard him ask his mother if we could have breakfast in the tree house. We kept a box of Cheerios in there along with spoons, knives, and a loaf of bread and peanut butter for midnight snacks. Half the time, Mrs. Savage let us sleep out there, except for a month or so after she caught Mikey smoking his brother's cigarettes. He carried a bottle of milk in both hands and motioned for me to follow him. It was the only morning I can remember when I actually wanted a bath.

He poured fresh milk over mounds of the cereal in the same bowls we'd been using all summer. Anything we put in there now tasted funny, as the bowls had been embedded with the taste of sour milk. Mikey looked me up and down, sized me up good and started eating.

"Aren't you gonna ask me what I'm doing here?" I said.

He just shrugged. "It's summer, man. What do you think? You come over here every day."

"Not that. I mean today? After last night??" I was yelling now. I felt like I'd slept for all of ten minutes.

He just stared at me like he didn't know what I was talking about. And maybe he didn't.

"I saw a girl out there," I whispered.

The edges of his mouth cracked slightly up.

"A dead girl, or close to it."

"You don't say?" Mikey chomped hungrily at the cereal and sour milk.

11

I pulled the bowl away from him, spilling globs of milk on the edge of the mattress. "I'm telling you that I saw a dying girl out on that prairie last night. With my own eyes."

"What'd she look like?"

And when he asked, in his typical uncaring way, I had a feeling he was thinking about her bra size or whether her face was pretty or not. I conjured the image back up in my mind and looked away from Mikey's sneer. "She had long, dark hair, small brown eyes, and a cloth was wrapped over her mouth and her hands were tied behind her back. She was on some old blanket and there was blood on it, though I didn't see where exactly. Just looked like blood." I looked at Mikey's bowl of cereal and almost threw up right on it. I tried to get my stomach to stay calm and my mind to focus, but then I found myself leaning my head out of the tree house, with clear strings of bile and gastric fluid hitting the rungs of the ladder and landing on the soft dirt below. Mikey was looking at his cereal like it was a pile of maggots when I sat up again.

"Don't even pretend you don't know what I'm talking about. You sent me out there. You knew, didn't you? You've been out there. Who was she? Who did it to you? One of your older brothers? And where is she now? I went back out there but there was no sign of her." I sighed and caught my breath. I was almost crying. "Maybe I belong in one of those institutions."

Mikey looked down as if he'd been caught. "I been out there."

"Who sent you?" I asked, knowing this detail would largely determine the outcome of his experience.

"Blackie," he said under his breath.

Blackie was Mikey's oldest brother. "Man," I said with both sympathy and admiration. "You must've had to spend six days out there alone."

His eyes stared straight ahead. "Let's just say I'm not scared of nothing now."

Neither of us spoke for a while, and I was sure we were both thinking the same thing. That sound, that woman. Could I have imagined it? I saw on Mikey's face that I hadn't. He'd seen the same thing, or had heard it anyway. Was she real? I thought of asking him, but decided he'd tell me when he was ready.

"Her name's Mary," he said after he finished eating, "and she sure as hell didn't die last night." His hands were fumbling with the hem on his shirt. It was too long for him, a hand-me-down. With five brothers, Mikey never had new clothes. Neither did I.

"So she's all right, then?" I asked with the naivety of someone who's seen something they shouldn't. Then I remembered Mama, Daddy, and Denny, and felt the strongest urge to run home and see if they'd all come back yet.

He chuckled. "If dead is all right, then yeah. She's long dead and gone now, but she lived here once in Grady, near your ranch, come to think of it."

I tried to comprehend this impossible scenario. "What happened to her?" I asked.

Mikey sipped the milk right out of the bottle and then handed it to me. He shrugged. "Guess somebody killed her or something."

"You guess?" I asked, incensed by his lack of information. "You mean you don't know? Who told you about her?"

He shrugged. "Everyone knows about her."

"Who?"

He gave me the idiot look. "Ma-ry! She died out on that prairie just like you were out there last night. All alone and she couldn't get up and even call for help. Somebody gagged her, tied her hands behind her back, and beat her up so bad she couldn't move. That's why they say she screams like that all night. She couldn't scream when she was alive so now she haunts the whole prairie, calling out for her killer to return."

I felt a current zigzag up and down my spine. "So what the hell did I see and hear last night?"

"Same thing everybody's seen. Her ghost."

All the blood drained from my face and the tree house felt like a meat locker.

"Would she kill the man who killed her?"

Mikey shrugged like he'd told the story a thousand times already.

"How should I know? She *is* dead, you know. Dead people can't kill the living. That's what I heard."

"So why's she looking for her killer then?" I asked, begging for some additional detail to help me comprehend this odd new story.

Mikey sighed and that's when I knew I wouldn't get another word out of him about her. "Ask your sister."

"Lewella? Why?"

"It's her boyfriend's dairy farm that it all happened on."

Now I was confused. I told him Denny's farm was nowhere near the baseball diamond.

Mikey shook his head back and forth and grinned deeply. "But they used to live on Happy Jack Road and owned that plot of land before it got converted to a baseball field."

I ran all the way home in bare feet on the dirt path and made it in close to twenty minutes. By the time I got there no air would fit in my lungs. Doc Fisher was pacing on the front porch with a glass of yellow liquid in one hand and a cigar in the other.

"Where've you been, boy? Gave your mama a near heart attack. She's had enough of those lately."

I looked up into his bleary blue eyes and knew something bad had happened, maybe last night, maybe at the same time the baseball diamond witch was haunting me. "Where's Lewella?" I asked in a small voice, terrified of the answer.

He shook his head. "Weak. Don't know nothing yet about that baby neither."

"It's not mature yet?" I asked, and the Doc couldn't help but laugh.

"Premature, you mean. It came a month too early and your sister nearly died in the process."

I didn't know if I was more afraid to look at her or go back to that baseball diamond. It was a toss-up. I heard Mama's voice in the house.

"Jacob?"

I was too scared to move.

"Jacob Leeds. Come on in here this minute."

I stood on the porch with my nose on the screen door. I could see everything, but felt somehow insulated from the unmistakable smell of childbirth, which I remembered from Lewella's last baby.

"I thought you all moved away and left me here," I said in a voice that I knew would gain sympathy from the only person who could properly give it. "So I did the chores and slept in the tree house with Mikey." It was the first of what I knew would be many lies to come.

"Come inside," she enunciated clearly as if I hadn't heard the first time. But I'd heard her all right. I opened the screen and slid in through the crack. Lewella's big, usually rosy-cheeked face was the color of milk now. Her eyes looked like they'd been dipped in red paint and lacquer and her lashes were matted down with tears. Her hair was wet and brushed off her forehead. I could tell she was barely breathing.

"Do you want me to get you anything, Mama?" I asked.

She shook her head and wiped fresh tears from her eyes. "Say a prayer and light a candle at the church next time you go."

Church? Did she actually think I went to church voluntarily? I had sort of assumed she knew Mikey and me played kickball in the schoolyard during Mass like all boys our age did. But now I had to go, didn't I? Damn.

I found Denny Simms out by the barn brushing Lewella's horse. He looked so small and pathetic with his head down and back hunched over. I would have felt sorry for him, if it wasn't for the fact that his poison seed had brought nearly two dead babies and more misery into my family. Not that misery was anything new to rural Oklahoma, or new to America even. I was born during the Second World War and we'd already been in another one since then. From outside the barn doors, I could see Denny weeping and brushing his tears into the horse's mane.

I knew it was serious when I saw Doc drinking scotch out on the front porch. In my heart I was terrified for all of them, all of us. But my head was longing for answers to all my questions about the baseball diamond. Out of respect, I thought I should announce my presence.

"Hey Den? It's Jake. Can I come in?"

Denny sniffed and wiped his eyes on his shirtsleeves. "Where you been all night?"

"In the tree house," I lied for the second time. "How about you? I came back for supper and everyone'd gone."

"Doc Fisher said Lewella had to try to have the baby in a hospital. So we drove out to Wichita Falls and got there after dark. Don't know how she held out that long but they had to have two doctors cut the baby out of her stomach."

I didn't know how to tell him how badly I didn't want to hear the rest. "She's okay now?" I asked.

Denny sniffed again. "Baby was turned backwards and Doc Fisher couldn't fix it. Lewella's taking medicine for the infection and the baby's still in Wichita Falls 'til it gets strong enough to come home," he explained.

I had closed my eyes.

"Only reason why Lewella's home now's 'cause I begged Doc. I knew only your Ma could make her well again. God knows I only make things worse for everyone."

"Don't say that, Denny. Lewella knows it's not your fault and she'll tell you herself soon as she can talk again." I was feeling charitable. Besides, I needed something from him. So maybe it wasn't charity at all.

"I got a job at the lumberyard last week," Denny said, continuing to brush the horse with his back toward me. "Today would've been my first day."

Well, there was no consoling him now. I might as well jump in, I thought. "How long's your family been at your ranch, Den?"

He either didn't hear me or was pretending he didn't. "Soon as I get that job and some money coming in, I'm gonna have Lewella a big wedding in a church like she wanted." He turned around now. "It's been so long since I done anything right, I think I might have forgot how."

"You'll do fine in that lumberyard," I said. "You got good hands for carpentry. Daddy says so."

He almost smiled at that.

It was now or never. "So how about your ranch?" I tried again.

Denny looked up. "What's that now?"

"Your family been there long?"

He tilted his head back and the sun lit up his swollen, red face. "Since about 1920. Before that a preacher and his wife owned it. It belonged to the family of the preacher's wife for near a hundred years."

"They have any slaves?"

He chuckled. "Not this far west, no. It wasn't no farm back then either. A cattle ranch. A big one's I understand it."

"Ever heard of anyone named Mary on that ranch?" I asked after a long pause.

Denny looked down and had a secret on his lips. "You don't mean Mary Prairie?" Now he laughed out loud. "I had a feeling you didn't sleep in no tree house last night."

I began inspecting my fingernails.

"Where'd you hear that old legend?" Denny asked.

"Nowhere. I was just curious is all. Everybody's heard of her. Everybody who lives in Grady, that is."

"I don't know much about it, other than some girl died out there in the pasture after getting beat up real bad."

I pulled out an imaginary shovel. "Anyone else know about it, maybe?"

"Walter van Geller, I reckon. He's the son of the preacher who owned that land."

tHRee

Walter van Geller was listed in the telephone directory. He had an address in Ringling, which was about twenty miles north on Route 81 toward Oklahoma City. There were several reasons for bringing Mikey with me, most important of which was as a cover. That way, when I didn't come home for supper, Mama wouldn't be able to call Mrs. Savage and see if I was with him, because we'd both be in Ringling by then. But Mikey didn't understand why we were going and I guess I didn't feel like telling him.

"For Denny?" he shrieked, enraged by the prospect.

"Well why the hell not," I argued. "He's nearly my brother-in-law by now and he can't seem to get a job on his own. Doc Fisher says his man Van Geller might have a job for him." Lying was the easy part now.

"But you hate Denny. Hell, you've called him worse names than any I could ever think of, and I've got two older brothers! What do you care if he gets some stupid job or not? He'll just lose it anyway on his own, 'cause that's what guys like Denny are: l-o-s-e-r-s."

Besides just spit and vinegar, there was a logic to Mikey's words that I hadn't counted on. I needed a new lie, or at least a better one.

"Mama asked me to go," I said, the wheels in my devious head like a giant spinning jenny now. "Lewella's pretty bad off, and Ma wants to have good news for her when she wakes up. Since we won't know 'bout the baby for a while yet, she thought finding Denny a job might make her feel better."

"You'd be better off flying to the moon," Mikey said under the breath.

We were almost at the Grady train station, change jiggling in our

18

pockets. Mikey ran up to the top of the steps and stood over me with a pointed finger in my face like God or something. "I reckon you're lying, Jake Leeds." He always called me that when he was pegging me for something. "You know the penalty for lying?"

I clenched my fist and shook it. "How about I give you a fat lip?" I said in my play-fighting voice.

Mikey put his smelly hands, which he took pride in never washing, on my head and then pushed me backward onto the concrete. "I think somebody's chasing Mary Prairie."

"Shut up."

"Jacob's chasing Ma-ry, Mary Mary Prai-rie," he said and laughed out loud.

I knew Mikey would tolerate nothing less than the absolute truth from then on. I sat down on the top step, admitting defeat. "It's your fault," I blurted.

"Me? What do I have to do with it? You just had the shit scared out of you and you need someone to blame."

I turned toward him. "You sent me out in that goddamned haunted field, and you're the one who got me reading all those Sherlock Holmes books last summer."

He gave me a puzzled glance. "Those things? I never thought you'd really read them. There's not even any sex parts."

"But they're puzzles and I like trying to find things out," I admitted. "I read every one of those books, twice." There. I'd said it. Or part of it.

"I thought this was about the baseball diamond witch who made you too scared to sleep outside," Mikey said.

"After that night, I remembered something I heard a long time ago, and I forget where, so don't go asking me."

"Probably from one of them Methodist faggots from Edmond."

"Maybe. But there was a girl who just up and disappeared one day from Ringling. She had a rich daddy who offered a cash reward to whoever could find her, but nobody did. So he gave all his money to that Seventh-day Adventist church and sort of went crazy looking for her."

Mikey had his head in his hands. "I wish I'd never told you."

"I think that girl who disappeared from Ringling has something to do with Mary Prairie. Hell, maybe she was the same person."

Mikey didn't say a word the whole train ride to Ringling, but I knew he was interested in my story. That's how he acted when he was interested in something, like the time I told him that Marcia Anders almost barged into the boys' locker room to kiss him on the mouth because of a dare. After the conductor came around and took our tickets, he said, "So who's this loser we're seeing?"

Mikey called everyone a loser.

"Some old preacher."

"Oh man!" He wrinkled his face. "Aren't we gonna see any girls at all on this trip?"

I knew he needed an incentive now. "How about stopping off at the school to watch the girls' ballet class?"

When he grinned, that look revealed all there was to know about my friend Mikey Savage. So I told him about Walter van Geller, about how he was our only link between what I'd heard on that baseball diamond and Lillie Mechem, the girl who disappeared from Ringling. I pulled a book out of my backpack and flipped to the dog-eared page.

"What's that?" Mikey asked and poked his head down into the musty pages.

I pointed to a photograph of the Mechem girl.

"Somebody killed her?" he asked.

"No one knows for sure. The police never found her. She just disappeared one day." I cleared my throat. "She would be twenty-three. Lewella's age." This correlation terrified me, and gave me a moment of homesickness like I'd never felt before. I wondered about the color of Lewella's cheeks and the fate of her and Denny's ailing offspring. For a split second, I wondered what we were doing on a train on the way to Ringling when my own family was being held together by tricks, string, and glue.

"Hello, boys," the man said, pushing open his screen door. He sort of smiled.

"Are you Walter van Geller?" I bravely asked, wiping my wet palms on my pants.

"You betcha." He leaned down to reach perfect viewing distance of our faces. That's how preachers found out about your thoughts—by reading them through your eyes. He had a space between his front teeth. Grandma Weaver told me to watch out for gap-toothed people, as it meant their mouths were too full of lies to fit all their teeth in there the way they should. "Now what can I do for you? Y'all selling something for school?"

He seemed more like a furniture salesman than a preacher.

"We're on summer vacation," Mikey piped in with a smirk.

I elbowed him hard in the ribs. "We're going to summer school, sir, for extra credit, and we're doing a report for social studies on missing persons."

You could have heard a cockroach crawling across the floor. All four eyes were glued to me, but for different reasons. I knew immediately that I'd earned Mikey's eternal respect by the fluency and precision of my story, not to mention the curiosity of our host. To break the silence, Mr. van Geller slipped into the house and returned with two glasses of chilled lemonade in frosted glasses. It was sweltering hot but I was used to it by now.

"Thank you," I said and slowly took in the cool liquid.

Mikey, on the other hand, grabbed the glass and slurped it down in one long gulp and then wiped his dripping mouth on his sleeve. I gave him a death stare.

"I'm not sure I have the information you're looking for, but if I can help two younguns, I surely will."

I took a deep breath, as I had to be sure to get my words exactly right. "We're studying one girl from here, and another from Grady. The one from here's Lillie Mechem. The other one I only know her first name. Mary something."

The man opened his mouth, closed his eyes and tried to talk. "Now now now now w-what class did you say you were taking?" he stammered. I'd struck a nerve all right.

four

"He didn't tell us a goddamned thing," Mikey whined on the walkway outside of Van Geller's gigantic white-pillared house.

It was true. I felt satisfied, though, that we'd not come all this way for nothing. "That's right."

"So why'd you look so happy?"

"The way I look at it, the fact that he told us nothing is something."

Mikey stopped walking. "You think he's lying?" he yelled.

"Sh!" I hissed. "He's probably watching us from his window, dummy." I grabbed Mikey's arm. "And don't turn around, for God's sake!"

Mikey still didn't understand but I was tired of bringing him up to speed. I hoped that at some point, he'd just be happy to get out of Grady for a day and stop asking questions.

"You see his face drop when I mentioned Lillie Mechem?" I asked him on the train ride back.

Mikey squirmed in his seat and pointed to an older girl who had just sat down across from us. I rolled my eyes, not because I was uninterested in girls but because I was on a mission now and girls were a distraction. So was Mikey, for that matter, but I needed a partner and he would have to do. After a few minutes of staring, he leaned in close to my ear. "It was when you said 'Mary' that he turned all white and pasty. You think he knows who she is?"

"He knows something, but he won't tell us anything else. Men like that are what Mama calls 'insulated from blame.' He's a preacher so people think he could never go against God and do nothing wrong. But I seen his face and I looked in his eyes."

"So did I," Mikey added.

"And so we know differently. Don't we?" I said like I knew the answer already. The question now was how to get what we wanted without scaring people off. And that I didn't know yet. But I could consult an expert anytime I wanted.

We never did get to see the girls' ballet class through the fortuitous hole in the wall from the boys' locker room. A sign on the gymnasium's back door read "Canceled 'til next week." So to kill some more time, Mikey knew of a mound of dead rats in a quarry behind an abandoned factory near Ringling. That amused us for at least an hour.

I saw the scarf tied low on the post as I approached Hooper Circle. Mama made supper for Daddy and me and then disappeared into the bedroom to tend to Lewella. I let the boiled ham and white potatoes get cold on my plate while I planned my next move and thanked God that Walter van Geller hadn't asked our names. Surely he was the type to have called Mama and Daddy to verify my tall tale about summer school. I had never thought much of lying, but now that I had done at least two days' worth, I knew many more would need to cover the ones I'd already told. I was becoming an addict.

Daddy dug into the ham, not bothering to cut it into bite-sized pieces. He hadn't done much farming since he got back from the war. Mama said she didn't know why and I was too scared to ask him. We seemed to have enough money to pay for groceries and other things, so maybe he would never work again. But what would he do all day? It didn't seem fair that Daddy got to sit on the porch swing all day long while I sat sweltering in school and Mama baked in that hot kitchen in long sleeves and an apron. Lewella, well that was another story.

If she lived, I guess, she and that blockhead Denny would move away somewhere and I'd see her at Christmas and Easter and we'd sit next to each other in the pews at church. The days of her introducing me to all her girlfriends when they came over to study were over forever. Maybe a lot more than that was over now, too.

After washing the dishes—and I didn't mind too much because a cool breeze blew on my back from the porch window—I took my tiny black notebook and sat on the floor under the light. On my bookshelf were mostly schoolbooks, some comic books, a dictionary, and my collection of Sherlock Holmes stories. I didn't tell Mikey but I remembered one called "The Disappearance of Lady Frances Carfax." It had been one of my favorites the first time I read it, as I tried to read stories about girls whenever I could. Since Lewella was so much older than me—eight years—and didn't live home anymore, I had no one to spy on to watch their habits, their movements, and to make observations about how they thought and what they liked and disliked. Mikey believed everyone was the same deep down. Girls, boys, old men and spinsters, kids and babies.

What I knew so far about the baseball diamond ghost could fit on a baseball card. Her first name was Mary and she died in that field. She may or may not be related to Lillie Mechem who disappeared from Ringling. Lillie Mechem had a rich daddy who offered a reward to the finder of her killer and gave the money to a church instead. There was so much work to be done and so many questions to ask, and hardly anyone to answer them.

I decided, the next morning, that Mikey's presence had probably weakened my position with Van Geller. So I took the rest of my saved-up allowance, asked Mama for a little extra, and bought my second ticket in two days to Ringling. Outside of Van Geller's house, I organized my thoughts.

The screen door swung open the same as it had the day before. "My name is Mikey," I lied. "I was here yesterday about my social studies project."

He looked down at me but said nothing. I could see a suitcase with its handle sticking up behind the door. Seconds ticked by while the July sun burned holes in the back of my shirt. I waited, resisting every urge to speak or run away. Finally, the screen door opened farther and I was soberly motioned inside. The house was dark with no lights on. Tall, vertical windows were covered with white, see-through curtains.

"I'm all out of lemonade today," the man said as if this would make me leave.

"That's okay." I appraised everything about Van Geller now and wrote my observations in an imaginary notebook. Long and spindly, with a square, almost knobby face. If it had been drawn in charcoal, the nose and chin would spill clear off the edges of the page. He had big hands with strong fingers and protruding knuckles. A fist made out of those knuckles could punch someone's eyes out. "I heard you used to own the land where the baseball diamond is now. In Grady, I mean."

The man sat in a chair across from me and crossed his long legs. "And who'd you hear that from, boy?"

"Denny Simms. He lives there now with his family."

"Where you know Denny from?" Van Geller asked. "He got dropped on his head when he was a baby. Bet you didn't know that."

I tried not to laugh. "No, sir, I didn't." I figured that using the manners Mikey failed to use yesterday might win me some points.

"I lived there a long time ago, when me and the wife first got married. We bought it from my father, Wilfred Van Geller. My grandmother's family owned it for a hundred years before that. So I guess you could say my own blood's spilled on that land."

We'll see, I thought, distrusting his use of the word "blood" under the circumstances. I cleared my throat and took out an imaginary clipboard and pen, ready to tick off the questions as I asked them. Van Geller kept blinking when I asked him questions, but I kept right on asking them, like where the farm was, how far it was from the baseball diamond, if he ever went there and then who his farmhands were.

"Farmhands?" He seemed surprised. "Why you wanna know all that?"

"It seems like you don't want to answer my questions, so maybe I shouldn't ask any more," I commented.

Van Geller shook his head and scratched it where he'd scratched it plenty before. I could tell because a patch of his hair stuck straight up toward the ceiling. "Just strange is all," he said now. "How should I remember farmhands?"

"When did your wife pass on, sir?"

The man's eyes bulged. "Twenty years ago. She died of TB."

I wrote his answer in my notebook. I was being relentless now but I'd had enough of his dark, musty house and cagey answers. "Did you get remarried after that?" I sounded like a reporter and knew it was because of two things—because I read the Grady newspaper every day and because Mikey Savage wasn't dirtying up Van Geller's house with his grimy paws.

"No," he replied.

"Did you have any female farmhands when you lived in Grady, sir? A cook, perhaps?"

Van Geller made like he was thinking about it. He looked right at me and seemed to decide right then that I wasn't gonna back off. "We had a cook named Althea and her assistant was Mary-something."

And there she was. Mary Prairie. For the second time in my life.

"What was her last name?"

He shook his head. "Damned if I remember, boy. Something Irish, like McCourt or McCain. I think, no, wait, McCann. That's it!" He slapped his leg like he was happy about it or something. "Mary McCann."

"And where is she now, do you think?"

"Well how should I know?" Now he was getting mad. "All grown up and married, I reckon."

Or maybe dead, I thought, and haunting the bejeezes out of teen-aged boys trying to be men. "Was the girl from Grady, sir?" The proper language felt all wrong in my mouth.

"Oh yes, I think so. Then Althea might have told me her people come from up north and she moved out and came to Grady herself to get away from her stepfather." He laughed. "Can't imagine how I remember it all, old as I am with all I got stuffed in the space between my ears." He showed the gap-toothed smile and I thought of what Grandma Weaver said again.

"Do you know where Althea lives now?"

"Died giving birth a few years back. Heard it from my flock."

Flock. So now I was talking to Moses? I looked out Van Geller's living room window and could see a week's worth of rain on its way to Ringling. I began to dread the long walk home from the train station, but the rain would cool me off at least. I wiped my forehead and watched swarms of flies collect on the back of Van Geller's screen door. I could tell it was about ninety-five out there.

"The other girl my teacher told me to research was Lillie Mechem. Did you know her?" I asked him, growing more lethargic by the minute.

"Knew her daddy from my church is all."

"Where'd she live?" I asked.

"Well right here in Ringling of course. Family's from here going back five generations. Now what's your project about again? Social studies?"

"Yessir. We're studying criminal justice and I chose to do my report on missing persons." It was all coming out so easily now; I almost believed it myself.

"And what's your teacher's name?"

I made damn sure I didn't flinch.

"I just want to call her and see if I can help further. I've lived in this town a long time, you know. Folks call me a historian."

But I could see in his face he didn't mean what he said. He meant to check my story and now I needed a phony teacher. If Lewella wasn't half dead at the moment she'd do it for me, and Mikey's mother might if I told her the whole long story, but it wasn't worth the risk involved.

"Miss Jessup," I said, the name just spilling out of my mouth. "And we're having classes at the community center in Grady 'cause the school house's closed for summer." Now that I didn't need him anymore, I no longer cared what lies I told him. He wouldn't call anyway, unless I asked my last question, and unfortunately it was a question that had to be asked.

"Was your church, sir, the church Lillie Mechem's daddy gave all that money to? I mean, when the police couldn't find her?" I asked, but when I looked up, Van Geller and his suitcase were walking out the front door.

Damn him, I thought. But he'd answered it just fine, hadn't he?

five

It was a start, anyway. Van Geller hit the high road and I explained everything to Mikey that night, since Mrs. Savage said Daddy and me could come over for supper 'til Lewella got well again. But Daddy didn't go. He didn't like being around people that much, people he didn't know, that is. So I talked to him out in the front yard by the old hitching post before going to Mikey's. That's where Daddy smoked his cigars in the afternoon before supper. I could tell by his face how things were, even without looking at the red scarf hanging down toward the dirt. But I still couldn't help asking questions.

I asked him how Lewella was today.

But Daddy never answered questions right away, on account of him spending extra time choosing his words. Even to Mama he never talked much about anything, and answered with only one or two words. "Same, I reckon," he replied. "No better than she was yesterday."

"What about the baby?" I persisted.

He took another drag on his cigar. "Doc Fisher's sending another doctor down here to stay with us until he comes back to Grady. Said he'd telephone us when it was time she came home."

She? In all this time, I hadn't even asked if it was a girl or a boy.

"Did they name her yet?"

Daddy just shook his head, and with that I knew our little talk was over.

"Van Geller's gone," I said to Mikey when we got to the tree house after supper. Crickets eeped from the ground under us. The air, cooled down a bit, smelled of rain being dragged for miles across the empty dustbowl plain.

"Loser!"

"What?"

"Why'd you go alone? I would have gone with you," he said, visibly wounded by my secretive act.

He didn't get it. Mikey didn't get lots of things. "He knew both of them," I said and lay back against the dirty mattress on the floor that we brought in for experimentation with girls. Our tree house also had a coffee can filled with condoms and breath mints, though I was sure none of us had ever used either. "I don't know how much of what he told me is true, but I got a name anyway."

"Who?"

"Mary McCann."

He scrunched up his eyes.

"Well you know her or not?" I asked him.

"I don't think so, but one of my brothers might. I remember hearing the name McCann."

I looked out the window. It was still light out. "Can you get a telephone directory from inside?"

Mikey climbed down the wooden steps, ran inside the house, and ran back out with a book under his arm. Mrs. Savage was yelling something after him. I picked up a notebook that was lying on the mattress and opened the cover to get a quick glimpse before he got back up the steps. The top of the page had the words, "Tit sizes" and below it a list of unsuspecting names with a letter designation beside each one. "Julie Bixby: B, Madeline Gittings: C."

"Who's Madeline Gittings?" I asked when he climbed in through the tiny door.

Mikey glared at me, then at the notebook and back and forth a few times. "She's a senior from Wichita Falls who used to go out with that asshole Frank Desmond."

I remembered Frank. He had graduated two years ago and was built like a brick wall. So much for ever seeing Madeline's C-cup breasts.

We found three listings for "McCann" in Grady. Mikey looked at his old Spiderman watch and then at me. "Nine o'clock's not too late, is it?"

Mikey and me were more than just used to walking. Hell, we would have gladly walked to Ringling if we couldn't scrounge up money for the train. The first McCann house was in the center of town on North Street. I made Mikey ring the bell while I formulated my plan.

An older, stocky woman answered the door with her lips pressed into a tight scowl. She was wearing overalls that had something splattered on them.

"Yes?" She was annoyed already. Just wait 'til I got started.

So I told her who we were and said we were looking into the disappearance of a girl from Grady.

She regarded me and then Mikey and then me again. Mikey was getting antsy just standing there waiting in the quiet dark of her front porch. He kept jamming his hands in his pockets and then pulling them out. She'd better hurry up or who knows what he might do. That's how it was with Mikey. I never knew what to expect.

"You don't mean Lillie Mechem, do you? Not her again," she added and looked into the night sky.

"No ma'am," I said. "The Mechem girl was from Ringling. We're looking for someone named Mary."

"Mary McCann, Mary McCann," Mikey yelled out. "Your name *is* McCann, isn't it? Did you lose a daughter or what?"

Sweet Jesus, I thought. Please don't let the woman whack us in the head with some shovel or something. But she didn't move a muscle. To Mikey, she raised an eyebrow slightly, and then looked straight ahead. "You got the wrong McCann. Those McCanns," and she stressed the word 'those,' "moved out of Grady long time ago. The Lyons live in their house now. Maybe they know where they went. Why you want to find them anyway? That woman's been through enough."

I was nervous with this woman, I think because she seemed so at ease with us. But she was the kind of woman who would have showed up at the White House wearing her mud-splattered overalls and her snappy attitude. "Do you know about when she disappeared, the Mary girl I mean?"

"Oh, must've gone on near ten years now. No one really talks about it anymore, except for all them ghost rumors. I myself think if I'd died the way she did, I'd want to stay as clear from that plain as a soldier from a minefield. Anything else you boys want, 'cause I got something cooking on the stove," and she closed the door at that.

I would have asked her where the Lyons lived, but there was no way I was ringing that bell again, especially now that I'd seen Mikey's temper at work. "What's the matter with you?" I asked and jabbed him in the shoulder with my fist.

"She was taking too much time. We're in a hurry, you know."

"Why? I'm not in a hurry. What the hell's your hurry? I thought you were just along for the ride 'cause you had nothing better to do."

He looked at the ground and kicked a stray rock into the bushes. "She was making me nervous."

"Me too, but when you need something from someone, you try to behave."

"Yes, mother."

"Idiot."

"Loser."

The only thing left to do, as we were already across town and too far to go back to look at Mikey's telephone directory, was to try to find the other two McCanns that lived in Grady and ask them if they knew the Lyons.

Mikey didn't like that idea.

"What's your idea, then? You got a better one than that?"

He chuckled. "Than roaming around town after dark knocking on people's doors? Shit, we're lucky that spinster didn't have a shotgun pointed at our heads."

"Okay, I'll wait here and you run home to look in your Ma's phone directory—"

"Wait, I got an idea." His face brightened. "My Pa's getting the Chevy fixed at PJ's Auto Body, and he said he'd be home late since they'd be working on it 'til all hours. If they're there, well hell, mechanics know everybody."

"I wouldn't know," I admitted. All my time was spent reading books and doing homework. I had no experience with things like fixing cars.

So I followed him down the remainder of North Street, and then we walked across a short field to get to the center of Grady. The field made me extra jittery, as I was now forever scarred by the baseball diamond incident. I vowed to never make fun of Denny again for being afraid of the dark. And then something dawned on me—maybe he had spent a night in that same field and heard what I had heard. Then again, someone like Denny would be committed to an institution if he ever lived through what I had.

PJ's Auto Body had a light on outside the front door. Mikey walked past the door and knocked on the first bay of the garage where he knew his father's car would be getting worked over. A short man with a stubbly beard hoisted up the door a few feet.

"Who's there?" he said, and cleared his voice and then spat on the concrete sidewalk.

"Hey PJ, it's Mike Savage. Is my dad still here?"

PJ opened the door all the way, looked me over, and motioned us inside. It was lit up like a hospital operating room and hotter than blacktop in August. PJ disappeared under the hood of Mr. Savage's ten-year-old Chevy and Mikey and I walked into the center of the room where his father and some young girl were sitting. It was the oddest combination, seeing Mikey's crusty old dad in his plaid shirt and denim overalls smoking a pipe and the prettiest young flower I ever laid eyes on sitting two chairs away from him. Mikey started talking to his dad, I suppose explaining the situation as he saw it or some elaborate lie to conceal our true mission. I sat in the chair next to the girl and looked at my shoes. She was about my age, fifteen, and had her light hair worn back in a high ponytail with tiny gold stud earrings on, and a bright yellow top with a low collar. I thought of Mikey's secret notebook diary and guessed she was somewhere between an A and B cup. But her femininity came from other places, like the way she pretended not to notice me by rubbing the skin under her eye, and the dainty way she held her hands with her right pinky in the air. I could just imagine her on a Southern plantation during the Civil War in one of those giant whalebone dresses drinking English tea out of bone china. I had read about these scenes for the past ten years in my extensive reading.

Sherlock Holmes, *Treasure Island* and *Gone With the Wind*—there were so many. Mikey only liked to read comic books and dirty magazines, and occasionally a book about mountain climbers or something true to life. I preferred escapism.

"Hi," I said.

I couldn't tell if she said hi or not, because my ears had blocked up in the last two minutes, along with my nose and my eyes. I was a blind, deaf mute all of a sudden, with the strongest urge to run out screaming into the street. Her name had to be Melody or something pretty like that. Maybe Melanie or Meredith. I liked the name Meredith, except the only one I knew weighed about two hundred and fifty pounds. This Meredith couldn't weigh more than a big sack of potatoes. Maybe a medium sack.

"My name's Janet. Janet Lange." She turned to look at me now. And I wasn't much to look at; I knew this because that's what fifteen-year-old boys did all night when everyone else was sleeping. We stayed up late in front of mirrors inspecting ourselves. Our muscles, lack of muscles, hair and lack of hair, looking for ways to augment our size and increase our presence the way girls instinctively knew how to do. "You getting your car fixed?" she asked.

I wanted to laugh. Did she see me drive a car into the garage? Or maybe that was her way of saying she thought I was old enough to drive. Wow. I could just imagine driving around town with Janet Lange in my front seat. "No," I said. "My friend Mikey's gonna ask PJ something. We're looking for someone, for a girl." I wanted to dunk my head into a bucket of water. If there was one thing I'd learned about girls from all of Mikey's older brothers was to never, ever, mention another girl in their presence except to put them down in front of her. So I thought of a way out. "But she's not near as pretty as you. Matter of fact, I've never seen her before." Matter of fact, she's dead, I thought to myself and looked again for that water bucket. I was as unfit for socialization with girls as Mikey. Maybe even more, if that was possible.

"Who is she?"

"Actually we need to know where the Lyons live. They bought the house the McCanns used to live in."

Janet Lange licked her lips and pulled a stray eyelash from her eye.

And then she looked at me and smiled. "I could take you there. The Lyons live on my street."

She told us, on the way down the street, that she was PJ's niece and was staying with him while her parents were away on vacation somewhere. PJ said he didn't mind her walking with us for a while, especially since Mikey's Pa was spending all kinds of money in there tonight. The Lyons lived on a nice street in a nicer part of Grady than either Mikey or me. They had some grass in their front yard and trees that weren't all bent over and dry and dying like ours and all the other homes on Hooper Circle were. Under the light of the Lyons' front steps, me and Mikey and Janet Lange all looked at one another to try to tacitly decide who was going to do the knocking.

"Shit, I ain't doin' it," Mikey said. I shot him a look for using such bad language in front of the only pretty girl who'd ever taken an interest in me. Okay, maybe not interest exactly, but attention. I stepped forward and knocked on the door rather than ringing the bell. By now it was past ten o'clock, and most folks in Grady were either farmers or ranchers and went to bed shortly after supper. A man came to the door and looked a mite friendlier than Overalls McCann down the road.

"Help you?" he said.

"Are you Mr. Lyons?"

The man smiled and had the whitest, straightest rack of teeth I'd ever seen. I was sure he had to be a dentist or something, but if he was, he wouldn't be living in Grady. "One of 'em. What you want?"

I cleared my throat and prayed that Janet would hold Mikey's attention long enough to suppress his frustration and boredom for at least a few minutes. I told Mr. Lyons that I was looking for the McCanns who used to live in Grady years ago.

"I don't know where they're at now," he said and bit his lip.

Lip biting was one of the ways I tried to hide when I was lying. Was he lying now, too? Did he know the McCanns and know about Mary and the baseball diamond?

"I really need to find them because my sister's real sick," I blurted without really thinking about it. It was true enough. I really needed to find the McCanns and my sister was really sick, close to death the last I heard. It's just that those facts weren't related in the least.

The man looked me over good, and then bit his lip again when he looked at Janet. She looked older than fifteen, now that I had a good look at her myself; Mikey had noticed too. I could tell. God help him if he so much as touched her. "Haven't seen them or talked to them in a long time, so I don't know . . ." his voice trailed off while he grabbed something from a cabinet by the front door.

"This here was my wife's address book. She died last Christmas but she might have had . . ." he started flipping pages to the Ms. "Nelda McCann. Moved north to Enid, I guess, from the address here. Did you want it or the telephone number?"

I thought about it a minute while Mikey's frustrated energy bounced back and forth between us. "Both, I reckon, if it's not too much trouble."

"No trouble. Wait here and I'll copy it down for you."

The man returned a minute later with the address book. He looked around with wide eyes and an odd, sheepish grin. "I can't find no paper in the house. Don't do much writin', I guess. You just go on and take the book with you. If you get by this way sometime, you can bring it back. I don't use it no more, since the wife died. My son, Buddy, comes by once a week to take me out for barbecue and he's the only one I see. So go ahead. Hope she's the one you're looking for."

I reluctantly took the book, yet something told me Janet Lange would not approve of this action. I looked at her and her eyes told me to give the book back. "We can remember the address," she whispered without barely moving her beautiful, painted red lips.

"I shouldn't take your wife's address book, sir. Maybe you could just read us the address and we'll remember it. I reckon between the three of us we could remember it."

The man didn't speak or move or even blink for a whole minute. The air was cool on our faces and I prayed that Mikey would just keep his mouth shut a minute longer. I didn't dare look at him. "Forty-one Alliston in Enid. Her name's Nelda McCann." Then the door quickly closed.

Enid, I thought. Anything to get me out of Grady.

SIX

I was oddly taken by the shape of Roman Laszlo's nose. It had to be a Polish nose, by the way his name was spelled with an "s" before the "z." And it had an unusual slope to it. The bridge thick and strong, nostrils slightly flared, it seemed to extend more outward than downward, but without appearing too large for his face. I knew immediately that he was going to change our lives.

His accent betrayed only that he was from outside of Oklahoma. Not a drawl and not English, exactly, but it had a European tinge to its proper diction.

"And where's the patient?" he asked with a gentle knock on the screen door. To my bewildered face, he explained he was Doc Fisher's temporary replacement. "While tending to your niece, he asked me to look in on your sister." My niece, I thought. Laszlo walked in without being asked but had such a friendly, airy way about him, no one protested. Daddy pointed toward the bedroom.

"Ah," he said, swooping into the darkened room, which was dark not just because the blinds were closed up. "You must be Grady's newest mother. And such a pretty one, too."

Well he was a practiced liar, all right. I liked him right away. Lewella's face brightened at the sound of his voice. So did Mama's. Daddy whispered for me to wait in the kitchen, but my sister was dying and I was curious about the stranger in our house. So I hid behind the door. Laszlo set a black bag on the dresser and pulled out a stethoscope. Lewella recoiled when he came close, but he touched her hand and gently lowered the sheet.

"It's all right now, young lady. I need to give a listen to your heart." He looked at Mama for tacit permission to reach down Lew's blouse.

Mama nodded after a second's hesitation. I could tell she liked him too, despite the mistrust on her face. Dr. Laszlo listened while he moved the stethoscope around Lew's white, bare chest. Then he gently rolled her over and listened on her back. His smile faded, but only a little.

Lew cleared her throat, and Mama touched her forehead with a damp cloth. "My baby dead?" she asked with her eyes open all the way. They didn't look as red as yesterday.

Dr. Laszlo shook his head and smiled. He turned her back over and fixed the front of her shirt.

"You're Doc Fisher's assistant? He said you'd be coming."

Laszlo smiled and tilted his head. "You could call me that, yes."

I could tell Lew had insulted him some, as he probably had twice the formal education of Doc Fisher. But he didn't let on a smidge. "Dr. Fisher's looking after your baby girl right now. I spoke with him last night and—"

"How much she weigh now?" Lew interrupted, knowing, it seemed, that she had only limited energy for talking in her condition.

"Almost five pounds. She's gained a few ounces already."

"What they feeding her?" Lew's voice was thick and strained. I moved closer to the crack in the door hinge to get a better look, and her red eyes caught my movement.

"Well, milk, and a formula of nutrients so that—" the Doc began.

"Jakie?" she screeched. "That you cowering behind the door like some shrew? Come on out so I can see you."

Mama gave me a sneer of disappointment and Doc Laszlo was losing his patience. I stepped out and stood awkwardly beside the bed. My hands were sweating like when I was at Mr. Van Geller's house. "You look better," I said. And she did, when you considered how bad she looked the day before.

"She is better," Doc replied, rubbing a balm on his hands. Then he rubbed them together faster and quickly laid them on Lewella's white cheeks. She smiled.

"Feels warm. Smells nice too. What is that?"

"Oh, just a healing elixir balm I concocted. Should help you breathe better."

Lew sat up when he pulled his hands away. "How'd you know I wasn't breathing right?" she asked.

"Your lungs don't sound so clear, Miss. Nothing serious, though." He sat down on the corner of the bed and held her hand inside his. Lew's eyes were wide and attentive. I noticed, then, how handsome the doctor was. We all noticed.

"You're gonna get up and walk tomorrow like a good patient."

At first she just looked back and seemed to lose herself. "You want me to go running 'round town?"

He blushed. "Just up out of bed long enough to walk to the window and back. No help from Mama, either."

Mama nodded obediently, as she was raised in a generation where a doctor's appointment was like a meeting with God.

"Well all right, then. To the window and back. What about the next day?"

"I'll be back tomorrow night and we'll discuss the next step together," Laszlo replied. I could tell Lew liked the way he said the word "together," and I knew she would have gotten up and danced a jig if he told her to.

"Gordon?" Mama said, following Laszlo out of the bedroom. "Lew's asking for you."

When Daddy went in the bedroom, it was Laszlo and me standing in the kitchen with Mama and Denny at the table. I knew it'd be proper to introduce Laszlo to Denny but I didn't want to sound too proper. I figured the sooner he knew how odd and quirky and backward we all were, the better. After a minute of awkward silence, Mama offered him some stale coffee from this morning.

"No thanks," he said. "I'll see you all tomorrow."

Now if it wasn't for Denny ruining every good plan I ever came up with, I could have told Mama my story about why I had to go to Enid tomorrow. My mind raced with ideas about getting Denny out of the house. But he was his own worst problem in a way. I could think of nothing to motivate him because he didn't care about anything. Anything except my sister. If it were Mikey I was trying to get out of the house, that would be easy. Just tell him a girl was outside with a busted tire on her bicycle. He'd be out the door faster than you could swallow. And then fate stepped in when Denny went into the bedroom.

Mama was at the kitchen table looking down at her wrinkled hands. Her eyes looked puffy and she hadn't combed her hair in a few days.

"Mama?" I said.

"What is it, Jakie?"

"I'm going up to Enid tomorrow, if it's okay with you. With Mikey and a new girl, Janet Lange."

"Taking the train?" she asked. "Trains cost money."

"Mrs. Savage's driving us," I lied. It was a risk, but I decided Mama had too much on her mind to go around confirming every story I told her. "She's doing some shopping up there and Mikey and I want to go to a comic book store they have in the center of town." I knew the more I kept talking, the less Mama believed me. I kissed her moist cheek before going upstairs.

"You're so full of shit," I said. It was only 7:00 AM and I was sick of Mikey already. In the summertime, I either slept in the tree house every night or slept at home and went over there at sunup.

"What do you mean? She didn't even know you were there. I'm more qualified than you are to talk to girls," Mikey said. "I'm older, remember?"

"More qualified? You were as nervous as a whore in church when we were waiting in front of the Lyons' house. You couldn't even open your mouth you were so scared. Besides, I'm the one who met her first while you were talking to your dad. At least I went over and talked to her."

"You said hi," Mikey replied as if this didn't count.

"What would you have said?"

He looked at the floor of the tree house. "I don't know. More than that, though. Did you even tell her your name?"

I'd forgotten that, hadn't I? Well, the way I looked at it, considering my experience with girls it could have been a lot worse than that. Two years ago I would have started talking about horse manure or the mound of rats behind the quarry.

We munched on bananas and Cheerios that Mikey brought out from the house and drank thick mugs of coffee with lots of sugar. It was only this summer that we took to drinking coffee. Jimmy Wilson got the idea one Sunday morning. He showed up at the tree house with the Sunday *Oklahoma Gazette* and coffee for all of us to see how we fared with a chance at civility. The coffee stuck. The newspaper, with the exception of cutting out all the bride photographs to add to the tree house wallpaper, was used in a bonfire by the creek behind Jimmy's house that night.

It was a standoff. Mikey and me instinctively knew that whoever brought up Janet Lange first was the one most in love with her. And that would determine the fate of so many things: the fate of our friendship at the very least, maybe even the rest of our lives. The worst thing happened—we both started talking at once.

"When do you want to pick her up?" I blurted out of the silence, and Mikey asked at the same instant, "You ready to go?"

Another standoff.

So we crawled out of the tree house together, tucked in our shirts, pressed down the cowlicks in our uncombed hair, and set off for the only place we knew to find her—PJ's. The Auto Body sign was lit up, which was surprising for a Saturday. Since we hadn't yet determined who was taking the lead on our entanglement with Janet, neither of us knocked on the bay doors of the garage.

"Oh for God's sake," I said and finally knocked three times.

Janet pulled up the bay door. I couldn't believe that her trim, delicate arms could lift something so dirty and heavy. PJ had lifted it with just a few fingers the other night.

"Hi, Janet," I said. "I'm Jake Leeds."

She smiled back and looked at Mikey. "I know."

I stared stupidly at her. None of us moved. "I forgot to tell you my name the other night, so—"

"That's all right. I asked Mikey your name, and he told me." She cleared her throat. "He said it was Jacob."

I gave a silly, flirty laugh. "Only my Ma calls me that when I'm in trouble."

"Which is all the time," Mikey added.

I didn't even bother to jab him in the ribs with my elbow this time, as he was in deeper trouble with me now. How could he have neglected to tell me this? Such a question was an overt gesture of interest, I was sure, and even more certain by the look in her eyes. I looked back at Mikey's scared face and then turned to Janet again. "So did your uncle say it was okay to come with us?"

"Yeah. He gave me money for the train too."

"We got a long walk to the station," Mikey said, exaggerating the word "long." He was trying to scare her off; I knew it, as payback for his feelings of betrayal that she liked me and not him. Janet walked between us and our hands touched a few times. She didn't pull them away. I figured we were as good as married.

By the time we got to the station, we heard everybody talking about an approaching tornado, and how more were supposed to be in its path. My mind raced. The memory of the sounds in the baseball diamond fogged up most of my brain, yet all I could consciously think of was getting back home to Grady, to Lewella, and the farm, to go through all the steps Daddy had taught me and the farmhands and the ranch foremen about tornadoes. Then again, if you were in its path, it didn't much matter how much you'd tightened your wire fences.

But I kept my mind off my troubles by intermittently glancing at the front of Janet's pink collared shirt. It had tiny, shimmering buttons down the front and was tucked into her tight jeans. They weren't all worn and stained on the knees like my jeans or Mikey's, and her shirt didn't have holes in the elbows or stains from food or smashing bugs on it like ours did. Her hair was back in a ponytail again, which drew attention to her long, feminine neck and made me wonder all the more what she looked like with her hair down. Janet and Mikey gave me their money and I bought the tickets for all of us. Mikey was the oldest, it was true, but I had always been the bravest in the whole tree house club. Freckles was scared of his own shadow, and Jimmy Wilson had no daddy and a mama who beat him, so he only came out on the days when his sister was watching him. And that left Mikey, who was an African lion on the outside and a field mouse deep down. I guess I was an African lion all the way through. Or I was before my initiation, anyway.

"Can we get drinks on the train? Uncle PJ gave me some extra money," Janet said as we found a seat in the window car.

"How come he let you go with us?" Mikey asked. Everything he said, lately, made my eyes roll back in my head. "I mean, he doesn't even know us that well."

She looked at me now instead of Mikey. It was a small triumph but it lightened the dark feeling in my heart. "He said you come from a good family and so I would be fine," she said to Mikey. Then she turned to me again. "He doesn't know you that well, though, Jake. Don't your cars ever break down?"

"Not much. We don't drive 'em much these days. Just farming all day and all night. Usually Daddy makes me help in the mornings in case some of the milking equipment goes on the blink, but I've got out of it lately."

"Why?" she asked, noticing, I suppose, that my expression changed.

"My sister's took ill. She had a baby and now she might die."

Janet's face turned white, and Mikey turned toward the window. "Which one?" she asked.

I shrugged. "Both of them, I guess. But the new doctor said the baby gained a few ounces yesterday. I guess that's good. I don't know much about them."

"Was it premature?" she asked.

I remembered how I'd put it to the doctor and how he laughed when I'd said it. Janet had the gift of vocal expression just like all her other gifts. I imagined she'd be a good singer, too. "About a month I think."

"Oh that's nothing," she said with a comforting look. "I was two months premature and I'm fine now."

"So you are," I said, and Mikey pressed his face closer to the window.

"What are you looking at?" I asked him.

"Tornado watch. What do you think? They said one hit in Jefferson

County and there were a few more seen where it started." He looked back with a mocking face. "We do live in Jefferson County, you know."

"You two been friends a long time, I can tell," Janet said and snickered. Mikey took out the wrinkled, dog-eared baseball cards from his pocket and began flipping nervously through them.

And then it came. A silent, dark stranger infiltrating our simple world the way death slides into the body through unsuspecting wounds. The progression was familiar to any native of Oklahoma— a shadow envelopes the sky with light on the far horizon. There's no sound, the air suspends, and a dense wall of undulating blackness hovers directly above, leaving the bittersweet smell of cut grass and prairie sage. The rest before the rage, calm before chaos.

"Oh God," Janet whispered and grabbed for the edge of the seat.

"We're screwed," Mikey said, his eyes suctioned to the glass. I don't know why I said nothing. Maybe I was too scared to talk, or maybe it was another moment where language just failed. What good were words when you could wake up with a train or a tractor covering your body?

I was glad, in a way, that at least if we were going to die, my family would survive. The cows out to pasture would have known first, crouching together on the ground and feeling the secret vibrations only discernible to livestock. Daddy would have seen this ritual and immediately gotten everyone downstairs. Luckily our shelter was in the basement of the house for easy access.

It was strange being able to sense the formation of the funnel without actually seeing it. The train was moving about fifty miles per hour, and I kept changing my mind about whether our speed was helping us or not. Janet had her arms around Mikey and I didn't even mind now. From the aisle seat, I watched a sand flurry fill the air on the east side of the train just like someone had yanked up a giant tablecloth. Then the howl started. The rain pounded onto the east windows with fist-sized hailstones on the other side. The hammering of hail on the roof of the train car reminded me of war, and how Mikey's oldest brother described artillery fire. The train car shook like an old washing machine now. I couldn't imagine it staying on the track. Women shrieked, babies were crying, and the men all had stone-white faces.

Then, like out of some cheap monster movie, the startling mass swooped down and glared its laughing face into view.

"Quarter mile away, maybe closer," someone whispered.

"Jesus, Mary, and Joseph," another mumbled. It was quiet on the train because everyone caught up to my thinking. Words? There was nothing to say . . . except your prayers.

The funnel thinned out, branched apart, and then braided itself together again, spraying the empty landscape with a destructive fury of grass, rain, hail, mud, steel, and wood, catching and releasing at the same time, using anything in its path to snowball its size.

"Where's the howl?" Mikey asked, looking right at me. His pupils were tiny dots. Janet looked, too, though she seemed shrunken to half her size.

I didn't know—I couldn't hear it either. The train had slowed to about twenty miles per hour and hardly shook at all now. The rain stopped, and so did the hail. Had the gods spared us? Maybe, today anyway.

seven

I could hear an old woman breathing three seats away. And it was a good hour before anyone even got up to use the bathrooms or order drinks. A little boy across the aisle eyeballed the three of us with a scared, blue terror. His white socks were crumpled down around his ankles, showing bare skin the color of snowfall, and his hands were braced on his knees like he was about to start a race. Everyone on the train looked like this. Vividly aware, yet mentally frozen by the horror that struck us. With the rest of my allowance money, I got colas for Janet, Mikey, and me, but those two just sat with the cups in their frozen hands, staring straight ahead. The customary gentle rain that always follows a tornado spilled off the top of the rail car now and made a comforting white noise to quiet the communal heart palpitations and anxiety. I wondered about Lewella's baby, and Ma and Daddy and Denny's job at the lumberyard. But in the middle of all this wondering and worrying, even with all that happened in the last week, I was more desperate than ever to find Mary Prairie's killer.

I knew what she looked like now, though only through clairvoyant hindsight. At the time that I was hearing it, the night of my failed initiation, the only thing my mind could do was try to find a way out of the field. But now, close to a week later, I remember seeing something through the tall brown stalks and scrub brush. Right before the first round of screaming started, right around the time I was pretending to be a pirate, I saw a shape in the grass, partially hidden by brush and loose clothing and camouflaged by the dark and shadows of the moon. The hair was long and black and the skin was tanned by the dustbowl sun. It had been Mary's skin. Her hair, a black shiny mane, was visible through the spaces between grass and reeds, between past and future.

The way I saw it, there were only two possible scenarios that led to her fatal beating in the baseball field—some older man forcing himself upon her or else a chance, random attack by a madman stranger. And in a town the size and dimensions of Grady, I decided against the madman stranger idea. So that left one question in my mind. Who was the older man?

I stuck close to Mikey as we deboarded the train.

"I feel like kissing the damned ground," he said. I watched him peering around and over the train and I knew exactly how he felt. When you've seen the side of a funnel cloud up close, you think it's around every corner. This paranoia was more than just a part of Oklahoma folklore.

"Did you tell her?" I asked him.

"Why should I? This is your witch hunt."

I just rolled my eyes at the irony. Janet followed us out of the station and waited for us to formulate a plan. "Do we know where we're going?" she asked.

"Where's that address?" I dug in my pocket and pulled out a wrinkled piece of paper I'd written it on. "Forty-one Alliston Drive, Enid." I went to the reservations desk at the station and asked for directions to Alliston.

"Three blocks north on Franklin Avenue and then ten blocks west on Main, south on Alliston," I announced. I knew Mikey hated those kinds of directions.

"Just say left and right, why don't you. Who has a damn map in their head?"

I looked at Janet. "Mikey's scared of getting lost in the woods."

Janet smiled politely, but I could tell she was uncomfortable hearing about other people's follies. "I used to be scared of horses," she said.

"No escaping them here, I guess. Too bad you don't live by the ocean or something," I replied, not really knowing what to say. I was feeling more at ease around her but still felt awkward around anyone other than teenaged boys.

"So I tried it."

We both looked at her.

"I didn't like being scared, and I knew I was only scared 'cause I didn't know any better."

"What happened?" Mikey asked.

She looked at the ground. "I got up on this great big Morgan once, and sort of never got off."

Mikey wrinkled his face.

I understood her, though, or more understood her body language. "You win derbies now or something?"

"Two so far. There's another one coming up in September that I'm practicing for. I just got a new coach so I might have a chance. Never know."

We concentrated on the walk now and no one seemed to care that it was still raining. Our eyes scanned the street for tornado wreckage but didn't find any. Had it not come into town at all? No cars piled up eighty feet high? No collapsed buildings? In the silence, I tried to think of something I could say once we got to the house. Hi, I'm Jacob Leeds. You don't know me but I wanted to ask you about a ghost in a baseball diamond. Yeah right, I thought. Maybe I'd let Mikey do it this time.

I knew it was the right house even before I saw the number above the front door. The faded welcome mat was turned over and angled sideways toward the steps. A thick film of plains dust covered the windows. No lights were on. And I could tell no lights had been on in a long time. White paint had chipped off the edges of the shingles and a sad slope leaned the house about ten degrees to the right. Its very spine was collapsing, maybe just like Nelda McCann's. Mikey and Janet stayed out in the street as I walked up the concrete steps. And I found myself knocking on the door instead of pressing the bell. I guess I wanted to gently ease my presence into this house without any undue alarm.

After all, I wasn't leaving without some answers. The front door was already open and an old screen hung sideways from the worn hinges. The sun, partially visible now, bled shears of light through the screen that made a mosaic pattern on Nelda McCann's living room carpet. When I gave in and rang the bell, a waif drifted toward the front door in a white robe and slippers. She seemed disoriented by the chiming sound, though uncertain and uncaring of who rang it.

"Mrs. McCann?" I asked.

She cleared her throat and stared.

"My name is Jacob Leeds." Pause. "I need to know about Mary."

Her eyes were fixed on something far off in the front yard. "What about her?"

Well, what about her, I repeated to myself. How could I answer this question? While I was thinking about it, she motioned me inside and shuffled down a cavernous hallway toward the kitchen. I looked back at Mikey and Janet. They were sitting on the curb throwing stones into the street.

Nelda McCann's carpet leading from the living room to the kitchen looked as if it had never been vacuumed. Dust coated every surface. She was putting on a fresh pot of coffee. I could smell the aroma traveling along the trail of stagnant air in the house, like that air welcomed the smell, like it hadn't carried any smells throughout the rooms in a very long time.

"Did she live here?" I bravely asked.

But Nelda couldn't answer this question. Not with her eyes, not with a nod of her head, and not even with her hands. Some people, like Mama, answered questions by clenching her fists. A tightly clenched fist meant absolutely, positively no. But a gentler fist, especially the kind where the pinky sticks up slightly from the nest of other fingers, implied all kinds of possibilities. Nelda's knobby hands needed a year's supply of Bag Balm and Corn Husker's Lotion. While she stood all shrunken and shriveled in front of the stove, I thought of Lewella and wondered when she would ever walk again and run and scream like she always had. What was it about life and pain that gnawed into the marrow of your bones? I didn't want any coffee, but her indifference to whether I drank it or not made me reconsider. I can't really say why.

"Mrs. McCann—" I started.

One of the wrinkled hands slapped the air above her head. "Never was much of a wife to that cheatin' husband. Call me Nelda."

I felt more than just impatience now. Mikey was out by the curb telling Janet all his funniest jokes, probably convincing her to stay the hell away from me by telling her all my most embarrassing secrets, and besides, the house felt like someone had died in it. Maybe it wasn't death, exactly, but the complete absence of life. I didn't know much about the female species in general, let alone a lethargic fifty-year-old woman. But I grew up believing that every action should follow some sort of conscious plan. Okay, I decided. No holds barred.

"I gotta get back to Grady, ma'am. Can you tell me or not whether Mary lived here?"

She remained at the stove playing with the tie on her terrycloth bathrobe.

"Well how about telling me if you know anything about Lillie Mechem."

Now Nelda turned, a quick jerk to meet my gaze and then slowly turned back. "She and Mary were thick as thieves, those two. You never knew what they were gonna cook up. Good girls, though, the both of them."

I guess what she meant was except for the disappearing and the dying. "So Mary and Lillie knew each other?" I asked. "How did they meet if Lillie was from Ringling?"

"Four-H. What else is there in Ringling, 'cept a dirt road and a bunch of churches? It was Lillie's uncle who brought her to the meetings and conferences. Her daddy was always off working and making money, so the uncle, some old preacher, used to drive her there. She met Mary and then the uncle started picking Mary up for the meetings, driving all the way up here way out of his way. Guess he had nothing better to do."

My hand was scribbling in furious speed in my head. My notebook pages filled with words and thoughts, flashing past two at a time. I could barely keep up. Mary? And now Lillie, and—

Nelda McCann brought a cup of coffee to me and sat in the only other chair at the table. "So they live in Ringling now?" I asked, trying to be coy.

"Who?"

I took a deep breath. "Mary and Lillie."

"They're off at school at that community college in Tulsa."

"It's summer break, Mrs. McCann." I hoped this might draw her out. Out of what, though, I wasn't sure.

Now she looked right at me with one good eye and another that sort of looked at the side of my head. Her eyes were a pretty light blue, hidden under big googly glasses. "You want to make some money?" she asked.

I was too terrified now to answer, as our conversation had strayed into uncharted waters. I didn't know what I was doing there. Would it be too rude to run outside to the safety of Mikey and Janet? I guess I nodded, somehow, because now she was pointing out the back door.

"I need someone 'round here to mow the grass, clean out the shed, and walk the dogs."

There was no shed in back and I didn't hear any dogs. The house would have smelled like dog. Was she making up excuses to keep me there?

"Boy your age could always use some money."

"Yes ma'am," I affirmed.

"You be here in the mornings by ten o'clock and I'll put you to work every day 'til you go on back to school come September."

"You mean ride the train every day? I don't think I could afford it."

She stood up and the tie to her bathrobe got stuck under the wobbly leg of the kitchen table. The robe flew open at the bottom, showing her bare knees. They were the skinniest legs I'd ever seen on a girl, not that I'd seen any girls' legs except maybe Lewella's and the girls in gym class. She pulled a set of keys off a hook by the telephone and tossed it to me. "Truck's out back. Take it if you want."

She stared at me again, gauging my intentions and looking into my past. For three years I had been trying to find a job to save up enough money to buy an old truck. And here, in the dingiest corner of Enid where I was searching for two ghosts, they were both falling in my lap at once. I was either the luckiest boy in the world or cursed.

"You old enough to drive?" she asked.

"Reckon so, ma'am."

We drove across her front lawn and knocked over her mailbox on the way out.

Every fifteen-year-old boy dreams of joyriding in a hot car. And what constitutes a hot car isn't necessarily something brand spanking new or stolen. Nelda McCann's twelve-year-old Chevy pickup was neither, but it was three quarters full of gas and had four tires and an engine. Sure, we were old enough to drive, in theory, but I didn't even have my permit, let alone a license. Over every bump and skid, Mikey and me couldn't wipe the smile off our faces. Janet's white knuckles clung to the dash.

I don't know how, but I found my way back to Grady from Enid. It involved two highways and a bumpy, all-dirt county road winding through a secret side of Ringling. On the eastern edge of Grady, I started worrying about being seen driving somebody else's truck.

"What could happen?" Mikey yelled.

"The sheriff could see me, for one. And how about one of our parents, or teachers, or one of the doctors taking care of Lewella?" I was just talking without thinking now.

"Just tell the truth. Some old lady gave you a job up in Enid and when you told her you didn't have a car, she let you borrow her truck to get there and back. It's true, ain't it?"

The truth didn't seem the least bit real, let alone a credible excuse.

"So what's the deal with her? Is she the mother?"

"I think so."

"She said so?"

I sighed. "No. She didn't answer even one of my questions. But I know she's the one—and just can't talk about it yet."

"Yet?" Mikey gave a phony laugh. I hated that laugh. "It happened ten years ago. She'd be over it by now, I reckon. You sure she didn't say nothing more about it?"

"Mary and Lillie Mechem were friends from 4-H," I said as I pulled into PJ's Auto Body to drop Janet off. Mikey seemed to understand the gravity of what I was saying, and that was only the half of it. Because I was almost certain that Nelda McCann knew a preacher in Ringling named Walter Van Geller.

eight

The red scarf was tied higher on the fence post when I got home, and I could tell it meant that Lew had walked by herself to the window and back. And I knew that for Roman Laszlo, she would have walked across the Badlands in bare feet. It was Daddy who usually tied the scarf in the mornings when he went out to the empty ranch riding around from marker to marker, checking on the pastures, inspecting the wire fences, coordinating with the farmhands, and talking on the telephone to other farmers and ranchers lining up who we'd sell our stock to after the gathering. He told me once that Grandpa Leeds stole the tradition from his great-granddaddy, who during the Civil War used to inform the neighbors about who won the latest battles—a red silk scarf tied to the top of the fencepost meant a Confederate victory, and tied to the bottom meant the Union had won. I always thought this was ass-backward, if you thought of the fencepost as north and south. Grandpa Leeds's house was near the train station, so he always heard first about the latest battle stories and victories. This was the first time I learned that my people came to Oklahoma by way of Arkansas.

Daddy carried on the scarf-tying tradition but adapted it to his talent for reading the sky. Depending on the cloud patterns and colors lit up by the sunrise, he would either tie the scarf on top to mean good weather for farmers, or tie it on the bottom, meaning inclemency was on its way in one form or another. For farmers like us, inclemency meant either hot dry weather, which made the cows too lethargic to graze, or else tornados, which kept them all inside the barn. Sometimes, as I learned from experience, inclemency could mean relationship discord rather than just meteorological patterns. After the past week, I accepted the scarf high today. I didn't care what it meant.

"That Denny Simms is a mite luckier than me," Laszlo said, standing over Lewella and monitoring the thermometer in her mouth. I saw him alternate his gaze from Lew to the pink and red dusky sky outside the west window. Mama and me, sitting outside the bedroom at the kitchen table, rolled our eyes at the comment.

When he pulled the thermometer out, she sighed, saying, "What's he got to show for this good luck o' his?"

"You," Laszlo replied and motioned for her to roll over. He gently lowered the sheet and lifted her blouse up from the bottom, pressing a stethoscope against her bare skin.

"What for? I ain't much to look at."

Laszlo stood back from the bed and grinned with just his eyes. "Not today, maybe, but you got the potential for beauty. I'll bet you were pretty at your high school graduation. And before you had this baby. I'd bet you were pretty then, too."

I could tell by the silence that Lew was crying in the secret way she could without actually showing tears. "How should I know?" she tore back at him. "Denny never told me. Just followed me all over town like some mangy, stray mutt looking for scraps."

Laszlo was writing something in a black book. With his head down, he said, "You might be sick, but you sure got a pretty way about you, Miss Lewella."

Mama and me, without any acknowledgement, seemed to get it right away. Something was happening in the other room between my sister and the new stranger in our lives, the kind of thing that I imagined was happening between Janet and me.

"Where's Denny?" I asked Lew after Laszlo had left.

Mama and Lew looked at each other, then Lew looked out the window and Mama stared at her shoes. "I threw him out," Lew replied, playing with the buttons on her blouse. She sat on the edge of the bed now and put her bare feet on the floor. They looked much smaller than I remembered. Actually she looked about half her normal size. "Denny doesn't like such a young doctor treating me. So I asked him if he preferred that I stay in bed for the rest of my life, and he said yes."

I figured the less I told Mama and Daddy about my quest and the new job I had accidentally fallen into, the less time I'd have to waste explaining myself. Mikey and Jimmy Wilson were waiting for me at the tree house, so I took the trail of a coward and left a note on Mama's dresser. It read, "Got a job for the summer in Enid—staying in tree house tonight, start work tomorrow—home for supper."

I took the shortcut through the burnt creek flats to get to Mikey's. The rough reeds against my bare knees reminded me of the old baseball field and how Mary Prairie's screams were forever engrained in my ears. I heard her in my sleep, and in my dreams my mind conjured her image in icy detail: strong body, long stringy black hair, and the way her body looked like it was running from you. It's not like I was happy to do chores for some grieving mother, but like it or not, Nelda McCann was as close as I'd come to finding Mary's killer, and I wasn't stopping now. Not for nothing.

As if I didn't have enough on my mind, I found Mikey and Jimmy wrestling on the ground beneath the tree house. God, I thought, that's all I need is Jimmy Wilson tonight, Jimmy who does nothing but gossip about other boys and talk about the tit sizes of every girl in school. He bored me, and the truth was that I never liked him, even in the beginning. But Jimmy's uncle had beaten him up so bad a couple of times, he had to go to the hospital in Wichita Falls to keep him breathing. So I guess this fact made me tolerant of his flaws. From far away, it looked like he and Mikey were fighting for real, but I saw one of them smiling as I neared the tumbling mass and knew it was fake. A little closer now and I could see that Mikey's nose was bloody and Jimmy's face had scratch marks on his freckled cheeks. They were like two Rottweilers struggling over a slab of raw meat. It wasn't like the organized boxing matches Daddy had taken me to a few summers ago. This fight was one big clinch, raw flab and muscle against the wall of bone and fury. At one point I stepped forward thinking I could pry them apart with my hands, but I gave up pretty quick.

"Hey!" I yelled, to distract them if nothing else.

"Stay out of this, Jake. I can take care of myself," Mikey said in a voice clearly not his own. I heard the screen door creak open and then slap shut against the wooden frame. It was Mrs. Savage. Here we go.

"Mikey?" she yelled in the thin, whiney voice that all women had in the face of brute force. They didn't understand. How could they, after all? It was like how any teenaged boy felt when he had to hold a baby in his arms: an alien world as unfamiliar as it was unwelcome. "Come on, now," she said. "That's enough!" came her second attempt. Both of them stopped moving, unclenched themselves from each other's bodies, and fell back exhausted and sweaty against the hard ground.

"Idiots," I mumbled and pushed past them and climbed up to the tree house.

"What was that all about?" I asked Mikey a few minutes later. He was blotting his bloody wounds with the bottom of his shirt.

"Jakie's chasin' a dead girl," Jimmy said and cackled. Mikey shot him a look.

"You told him?" I yelled and slapped Mikey in the head. But I guess he'd had enough of a beating already.

"I didn't tell him nothing. He asked me where we were and—"

"Shut your hole," I snapped. "You'd better go now," I said to Jimmy. "Me and Mikey need to talk."

Jimmy got up and put his feet on the ladder, and then turned around, giving full view of his red face and swollen lip. "I already know, and I'm gonna tell."

"What are you, a girl?" I asked. "Go tell whoever you want. I don't give two shits."

Jimmy had gone down the ladder and was limping home when I looked back at Mikey. His eyes were closed but moving in their sockets.

"Wake up," I said, pounding him on the shoulder.

He jerked. "What?"

"Blackie still work for the Waurika Police?"

When he turned over, a damp, sickening odor came from the mattress on the floor. "So what if he does? He's still a loser even if he wears a uniform and carries a gun."

55

"He has access to police reports. Right?"

"I guess. I know he's always complaining to Mama about all the paperwork he has to fill out."

"Then maybe he'll track down the police reports for when Lillie Mechem and Mary McCann disappeared. Could you ask him for us?"

Mikey snorted. "Hell, I'm not asking him nothing. You know how he is. If my head was on fire, Blackie wouldn't lift a finger to put it out."

I needed to return to the field. It felt good driving in Nelda's beat up old Chevy with all the windows down and the night air blowing on my face. It made me think of Janet and how she looked with her pony-tail down and her hair blowing all around in the truck on the way back from Enid. So before I got on Happy Jack Road, I turned left on Route 32 and drove to PJ's. It was eight o'clock but the light was still on. I could picture PJ on his creeper beneath some old clunker with Janet sitting in that grimy lobby with a magazine between her pink, painted fingernails, as out of place as Miss America at a cockfight.

I parked Nelda's truck a ways down the street so I wouldn't have to explain it to PJ. Even before I knocked, the garage door on the second bay rolled up. PJ had a cigar in his mouth. "Jakie," he said. Then Janet stepped up behind him and smiled at me.

"It's Jake, PJ. How are you?"

"Just fixed up an old ragamuffin car to run like a Cadillac. Want to take a spin?" he asked, and looked back and forth between Janet and me. Men like PJ knew everything without being told.

"How about me giving Janet a ride home? I mean, if it'd be all right with you."

"You drivin' your Daddy's truck?"

"Yessir." Lie number forty-seven. I was keeping track now.

"Be just fine, then. You ready to go, darlin'?" he asked and put his hands on her shoulders. When she nodded, he took the cigar out of his mouth, wiped it with his hand, and kissed her on the cheek. As he pulled away from her, he peered at me with squinted eyes. I had the same thoughts as we were walking out to the truck together. Imagine. Me and Janet Lange lifting off into the night together in an unsupervised vehicle. I could never tell Mikey about it, ever. No matter what happened, he'd twist and contort the truth to make something different out of it. I'd never let that happen to Janet.

She wasn't acting happy to see me but I could tell that she was. She carried her purse on her left shoulder so her right hand bounced up and down on her right side. Our fingers touched at one point and I grabbed the rest of her hand and she didn't pull it away. I felt her smile even though I couldn't see it.

Boys like me got a chance with Janet Lange once in a lifetime, and only by some freak twist of nature. I tried to think of something to say.

"You're driving pretty good now," she said. "Did you practice when you got home?"

"Nah. I parked the truck out by the edge of Hooper Circle so no one would see it and I only went in for a little while. Just long enough to see my sister."

"Did she look better today?" she asked.

"Not really, but she's got a good doctor who comes by every day to check on her."

Janet reached to turn on the radio and sat closer to me when she leaned back. There weren't seat belts in the truck so I was being extra careful not to get distracted by her. I'd memorized the way to her house already. She mentioned her address once, and I went home and checked Daddy's map to find out how far it was from Hooper Circle.

"So you going to Enid again tomorrow?" she asked. Our legs were touching now on the bench seat of the truck.

"I told her I would, so I reckon so. It's another dead end. She can't tell me what I need to know."

"Maybe she can, just not right away. Sometimes it takes your brain a while to warm up."

"Like she'd have to trust me first?" I asked, impressed by the depths of her logic and reasoning. I'd just assumed that she was too pretty to be smart.

She shook her head as I turned the corner to her street. "No, more like someone who's not too used to talking has to talk a while before the right words come out the right way."

57

It was dark and the only streetlight was busted. I parked a hundred yards down from her house in front of a clump of wild, overgrown cottonwoods. For a while after I clicked off the motor, we just sat there in the cool, dark night with the edges of our legs touching and trying not to move. My breathing was shallow because I was too afraid to scare her away. I'd never been this close to a girl before. Not one who wanted to be close to me, anyway.

She seemed to like the quiet because she leaned her head on my shoulder and the back of the seat. But I knew there was a very narrow window now during which I had to make a move. I wasn't even sure what that meant, but I'd read plenty of articles about the mechanics of intercourse in Denny's dirty magazines that he hid in a haystack out in the east barn. Even in the quiet closeness of Nelda's truck, being so close to her I could smell the perfume she'd dabbed on her wrists and the shampoo in her hair. But I still couldn't get Mary Prairie out of my mind. At least until Janet sat up, took her hair out of the ponytail, and swished it all over her face. The perfume smell of her shampoo flooded the air around our heads and burned the corners of my eyes. I moved closer to it. She didn't back away.

I wanted to touch her, all of her, more from curiosity and education than a sexual urge. After their first wet dream, most of the boys in the tree house club masturbated ten times a day. I, on the other hand, was more interested in the emotional effect that girls had on me—fear of speaking, fear of rejection, uncertainty, inhibitions, and outright panic. I kissed Janet Lange for well over a minute. I know because I was counting the seconds in my head. My hand was posed awkwardly on the front of her shoulder, and I could have easily moved it down to her chest or else behind her to reach her bra strap, but I wanted her to go away wishing I'd done more to take advantage of her. I wanted her to trust me and be surprised that I was a gentleman, even though that was probably a lie too.

Now we were lying down in the front seat of Nelda McCann's old truck, the mother of Mary McCann, a dead girl, and here I was nailing the prettiest girl in the whole county. It didn't seem right, somehow, that I was simultaneously investigating a murder and experiencing so much pleasure, but my body refused to let me protest. Denny told me once that a man is endowed with a brain and a penis, and blood can't flow to both of them at once. So much for curiosity and education. After I unhooked her bra strap, I leaned up and looked at her face to make certain, at each step, that I had permission to go on. And I had it, all right. Until the noise came at the passenger side window. When I jerked my head up, it was stabbed on the crown with the metal door handle, and then I saw the woman's face.

"Someone's there," I whispered to Janet. We both straightened up, followed by a flurry of refastened zippers and buttons and hooks.

"Shit," she said. I couldn't believe she'd use a word like that. "It's my aunt. I better go. Call me tomorrow."

"I don't have your phone number," I said.

While she put her hair back in the ponytail, she reached out for my hand and squeezed it. "I'll be at Uncle PJ's shop tomorrow," she whispered, then looked up to meet the unfriendly eyes at the window. "Meet me there after you get back from Enid."

NINE

At every curve in the paved road and every bump on the dirt roads, the axles loosened even more, threatening with each successive revolution to spill out across the dry soil. But I didn't care about the jiggly ride or how loud the engine cranked in Nelda's 1949 Chevy pickup. I had already dropped off Mikey, I'd kissed Janet Lange, and now I was alone driving free on the slick tongue of night in my own truck.

Dreams were made of nothing better.

The air was cool, almost chilly, against the bare skin on my arms. At the same time that I wondered if Janet's arms had been cold lying on the front seat of the truck, I wondered if Mary McCann's arms and legs had been cold lying in that empty baseball field. I could only guess that fear and panic coursing through her veins and the pain of her injuries made her colder than ice. I knew, from the few times I'd been injured in my life, that injuries hog all the blood in your body so there's none left over for the rest of you.

I could feel I was getting close; to what, though, I wasn't sure, and I was even less certain I wanted to know. Blackie Savage, Mikey's oldest brother and the meanest boy I ever met, was one thing to me now—access. He was a Waurika cop, had been since he graduated high school, and he could get into where old police reports were kept. And in a town like Ringling or Grady, if a young girl disappeared, someone had to have filled out a report. It was as logical as butter with your grits and milk with your coffee. Somewhere, in some police station of some Oklahoma town, there was a police report telling why two young, healthy girls just vanished.

The old radio in the truck was tuned to one of the three white noise static stations in the empty space between Grady and Waurika.

Ninety-nine bottles of beer on the wall, ninety-nine bottles of beer, take one down, pass it around . . . That was another of Denny's scared-of-the-dark tactics. Start singing or pretend to be a pirate. Well, I'd already done the pirate thing and look where it got me.

On the edge of Waurika at the end of Route 81, there were overlapping signs for Kiwanis, the Elk's Club, 4-H, and the Junior League, that spoke of a kind of civilization that Grady inherently lacked, a civilization based on an actual population of people rather than just livestock, a real demographic rather than just legend and folklore. Three young men all clad in matching black jeans, black Stetsons, and shiny black boots stumbled out of a bar called "Jay's" and round the corner on the next street was another bar. This one had no name, and that's why Blackie Savage liked it. He could disappear there, be anonymous with his bad attitude and his overt drinking problem. He could start fights with strangers, pick up other men's women, and his sins would die right then and there. What would people do, anyway? Hey, did you hear about Blackie Savage and that woman from Ryan? Where it happened? Well, I don't know. Some bar in Waurika. Yeah right. There were ten bars in Waurika and only one that attracted men like Blackie. I saw his pointy head at one of the two pool tables in the back of the bar. And sadly, the bartender didn't say a peep to me as I walked in. I had it all rehearsed, too. Sure, I looked young, but I was really twenty-three and studying at the community college in Wichita Falls and my girlfriend's brother lived out here and I needed to ask him when my truck would be fixed. And if the bartender asked the name of my girlfriend, I had already worked out the name of a real girl who went to high school here. So much for preparation.

"Hey, Blackie," I said, loping up to him. You never knew, with Blackie, whether he was about to shake your hand or whack you across the face with the knobs of his bulging knuckles.

Leaning over the billiard table with his arms wrapped absurdly around the cue, he turned and looked at me squarely. "Didn't think you were allowed out of Hopper Circle 'til you were eighteen."

"Hooper," I replied, and that was Blackie all right. Getting one in wherever he could. Of course he couldn't have it any more backward, as I'd been to Enid and back, rode on a train, survived a flash tornado, and nearly laid the prettiest girl in Grady in the last twenty-four hours, but who was I to argue with a Savage, especially this one?

A girl came by with a tray in her hand. She smiled at me and I could tell she was estimating my age. "You old enough to be in here?" she asked. Then she looked at Blackie for affirmation.

He looked down at me from his six foot two inches and returned his gaze to the table. "Old enough to be talking, I reckon," he replied to her. She moved away quickly, as most people did around him. I couldn't see any sparks flying off his body, but his face had a ghoulish shadow beneath the skin. You could feel it standing near him.

"You off duty now?" I asked him, sticking close to the table, as what I had to say was confidential.

"You see me wearing a uniform?"

"No."

"What do you want, Jake? Spit it out. And how'd you get here, anyway? That little runt Mikey with you? Bad enough I have to see him every weekend."

Close family, I thought to myself. Then again, lately mine wasn't much different. It was now or never. I had to summarize all my thoughts about what happened the night of my botched initiation into manhood in a way that a cretin would understand. "I need to see a police report."

"For what?" he said and hit the eight ball so that it hit the back rim, bounced off the side, and disappeared into the left corner pocket.

I swallowed the fleshy mound in my throat and would have cut off a limb for a glass of water right then. "I'm searching for Mary McCann."

"Who?" he said, still pretending to ignore me.

"Mary McCann. She disappeared, some years ago I guess, in the old baseball diamond down in Grady."

"Mary McCann?" He looked me over good, obviously amused by what I'd said. "You mean Mary Prairie? What do you want with her, for God's sake? She's been dead, what, ten years?"

"I want to know what happened, Blackie." I moved closer to him and closed my mouth after I said it, which made my face look meaner.

I knew this because I'd rehearsed this look in the bathroom mirror. "If you won't help me, th—"

"Then what?" he said with the evil look on his face now. It was the Blackie shadow, the red-shining skull bleeding out through the skin. I saw it and wanted to run but something inside me, some new part of myself that had lived through dead girls, sex, and tornadoes, kept me still, facing him with my blank unrelenting face.

"Then maybe somebody else will," I replied softly. I could tell he was impressed, or at least intrigued by my courage.

"You wanna see something, Jake? You all grown-up now? That what this is about? That's nice if you're trying to follow in my foot-steps and be a cop or a detective someday, but I don't think you have the stomach for it. You might be brave, from time to time, but it takes more than that."

I didn't want to be a cop, or at least I'd never thought about it before this instant. I just needed access and information. I had a feeling I wasn't going to get either. Not tonight anyway.

I followed Blackie out the back door of the no-name bar in Waurika and stepped into an alley lit up by lights attached to the very top of the old, brick building. It had that warehouse look to it and was probably a bakery a long time ago, judging by the constant yeasty smell inside the men's room. Blackie was ahead of me now—I followed his long legs and white T-shirt through the type of alley I'd only read about in books. It smelled like rotten food and decaying flesh, though I saw no evidence of these smells behind all the buildings. There were trash bags stacked up high against one of the back doors, and one old man sleeping on top of them, but all the dumpsters looked either empty or full of card-board boxes. As we got closer to the other side of the street where I had parked the truck, I heard sirens and saw the red lights of an ambulance reflecting off the alley floor and the backs of the brick buildings. The sound got louder and I heard a commotion of voices. Blackie glanced back at me and gave a "you're in for it" grin. He flipped his hand, tell-ing me to follow him into the crowded street. Five or six policemen were standing in a circle, arguing about the details of how some man got into the first floor apartment and some emergency medical personnel were hovered around a body lying on the ground. I took deep breaths into my lungs, even though this alien world smelled awful. But I wanted to smell it, smell death and neglect and decay, just like how Blackie wanted to show me a part of the real world now, now that he'd seen that I was becoming a man. I didn't know what any of this had to do with Mary Prairie, but I'd get around to asking him again before I left. I was as determined not to leave as Blackie was determined to scare the starch out of me. To hell with him. Blackie Savage was just some dumb old stray dog that had been chronically neglected and underfed all his life. So that meant he was always hungry and perpetually in a bad mood.

"Over here," he said, waving me into the elite semicircle of uniformed men all looking at the ground and shaking their heads.

"What?" I shouted, hoping he'd just tell me without making me look. When I got two feet away, Blackie reached his long arm back and snagged me by the collar of my jacket. And there it was, this bleak vision to which I was cruelly affixed, Blackie grinning beside me as he appraised my reaction.

Before speaking, I took a second to appraise my surroundings. Main Street in Waurika, Oklahoma, the seat of Jefferson County, 10:00 PM in a side alley that on one side led into the big antique store and on the other an abandoned furniture store that vagrants sometimes slept in when they could jimmy open the back door. The door to the antique store was hanging askew off its hinges as if someone had laid their entire body weight against it and shoved with every ounce of strength, as if they had been desperately trying to escape.

"Looks to me like Lila Pagett," one of the officers mumbled while crouching down to get a good look.

"What do you think, Jakie?" Blackie asked me.

I looked at her limp body, seeming to bleed all its mass into the hard concrete, the plump middle and bunchy sweater that was gathered in all the wrong places, brown polyester pants, and tiny, pointed shoes that looked all wrong against her height and girth. I breathed the way I learned to in a book about scuba diving—slow, rhythmic breaths, to keep me from vomiting. One, two, three, four, one, two, three, four. It wasn't really the sight of a dead body that provoked my gag reflex, but the odor of death, of body fluid leaking into the hard, smelly, oily, back alley ground and the accompanying odor of the grim reaper flooding the street with his long, grimy cape, jamming his sickle into the hard earth to claim his prize.

"What happened?" the cop said to Blackie.

"Robbery, I reckon. The place is all trashed inside, and the glass on the gun cabinet's all busted open and most of 'em are gone."

"I knew her," I blurted out, hoping no one would hear me.

The other cop glanced at me and nodded his head toward Blackie for an explanation of my presence.

"This here's Jackie, a friend of that little pigeon turd, Mikey," Blackie said and let go of my collar. "You buy lots of antiques, do ya? Don't seem like your kind could afford such things."

You neither, I thought, but kept my mouth shut. Until the other police officer took three steps toward me and spoke. "You knew this woman, Jake?"

I cleared my throat and tried not to look as small as I felt. "I bought some books here a few times."

"Books?" Blackie laughed. "Figures you'd be the reading type. What books?"

"Sherlock Holmes, mostly."

"Well you mustn't be scared off by the sight of this, then, reading all those murder stories."

"I ain't scared," I replied, losing track of the lies. Blackie stared me down hard, visibly annoyed by my sudden composure. I couldn't believe it myself, really. The only explanation I had was that this corpse was already dead and wasn't making any noise. One ghost was about all I could handle in this lifetime anyway. Blackie's brown eyes bored through my skin and bone. I knew what he was thinking, knew he was plotting some other plan to scare me and make me sorry I'd come barging onto this protected turf.

"You gonna help me, Blackie?" I said, trying not to blink away from his stare. But finally I did, and once you've broken a stare, there's no going back to it. He watched me slowly retreat back down the alley. I went back into the bar and walked out to Nelda McCann's truck parked in the street out front, and waited.

For a minute or so, there were no sirens or screaming or huddling people or cars screeching onto the sidewalk. Just the wind blowing through branches and the eep of summer crickets. And then the fast clomping of Blackie's boots. God help me now.

"Damn you're a pest, Jake! What you want, anyway?" he said, leaning on the driver's side. I was sure he was gonna hit me through the open window.

"A police report."

He took a cigarette from the rumpled pack in his shirt and lit it like he'd been smoking all his life. He probably had. Then he patted down his pants pockets, his jacket pockets, and nodded. "You think I got them all in my pocket or something? Those are locked up in the police precinct. What you thinking, now?"

"Not the new ones; I need an old one. Ten years ago, maybe more. Where are those kept?"

"City Hall, I expect. Have to go through the sheriff to get permission to see them, and I'm afraid you're just too young, Jakie. Little Jakie out so late at night, driving some stolen truck. You got a driver's license for that?"

I was damn sick of Blackie Savage by now and I didn't care about hiding it. "No."

"No license?"

"Nope. No registration either."

"Where'd you get it then?"

"Some old lady in Enid I'm gonna be doing some work for."

Now he laughed out loud in that phony, toothy, haughty sneer. "Work?" More laughing. Son of a bitch. "What work could you possibly do to help an old lady? Polishing her bookcase?"

I was staring straight ahead, not letting him reel me in. "Yard work, mostly. Light carpentry."

"I'd really like to see what you could build, Jakie." Blackie reached his long arm into the truck and pulled out my hand. It took all my restraint, but I didn't pull it away. "Look, now, lily white like an old lady's hand that's never touched nothing but potatoes and flour."

I started the truck. "I got what I wanted," I said, still staring straight ahead. "Night, Blackie," and I sped off.

ten

Now I had really done it. Stepped too hard on the gas pedal, nearly ran over Blackie's boot, and peeled away from the curb so fast that smoke filled the air. Blackie jumped from the truck coughing and ran to his squad car. I could see the blue strobe gaining on me.

When Blackie got his mind fixed on something, it was like trying to tear wild dogs away from fresh roadkill. Well, I thought, I'd been wondering how fast this truck could go. It was now or never.

Unsure whether any of the truck's controls were in working order, I calmly observed the speedometer rising to sixty miles per hour. Sixty-five. Seventy. I heard my mother screaming in my ear. "What the hell are you trying to pull, boy? You want a ticket? Go to jail, maybe, in case you haven't learned your lesson yet?" And even though jail would be like a day off from school compared to an ass-schwamping by Blackie, my foot kept pressing the accelerator. I saw a vision of my parents and Janet Lange and the few neighbors we had on Hooper Circle all gathered round a small, white coffin. Mine.

The blue flashing lights came closer.

As soon as I passed the 52-mile marker, I remembered the ditch and the tangled web of gnarled tree trunks knotted at the east end of it. Of all the ditches in Jefferson County—and Mikey and me had explored them all at least a few times—Lucy's Ditch was the longest: nearly a quarter mile gully where the Oklahoma flatlands had separated probably during a tornado or heavy storm, or maybe during a string of summer rainstorms.

Lucy's Ditch was my only chance against Blackie Savage, against the only man I had ever been truly afraid of. With my leg stretched all the way to the floor, I sped up to almost ninety miles per hour. Rattles, taps, and clanking sounds emanated from every possible place on the truck and inside the engine, but I kept driving. I had to get far enough away from Blackie so I could stop the truck, turn off the lights, and hide in the far end of Lucy long enough for him to drive past me. I'd never been much of a planner. This was the price. Here we go, I narrated to myself. Eighty-five miles per hour, eighty-eight, and with that, the blue lights behind me seemed barely visible . . . ninety! I knew the ditch ended just before the fifty-three-mile marker and I saw the sign coming up fast. I jammed on the brakes with both feet and held tight to the steering wheel so I wouldn't fly out the windshield. The truck buckled and shook, but I was careful not to brake too hard to make a screeching sound or skid marks on the road. It stopped beautifully, almost peacefully, cooperating with my plan. Nelda's truck was my friend now, perhaps my only friend. I drove off the road onto the sloped shoulder, veered to the right and turned the lights off just as I turned onto the dirt road. Lucy was just in front of me, a desolate, gaping hole in the prairie; ready to digest anything that dared open up her mighty jaws.

The motor and lights were turned off. I crouched now in front of the truck with my eyes peering back into the bluish blackness, waiting for the grim reaper to exact his revenge. I knew my enemy, Blackie Savage. I knew he didn't care that I'd almost run over his foot, and that I had the gall to come marching into his "no-name" bar to pump him for information. Blackie's revenge was because he didn't scare me. Fear was his element, his tool, and I had robbed him of this fundamental hunger.

I was far enough off the road so that when he drove past, he would need to have his head turned to the right to see Nelda's truck. The blue lights crept up farther, and I withdrew silently into Lucy's warm, brown womb, and ensnared myself within the tangled tree stumps, waiting to see his black cape and sickle.

Waiting.

Nearly an hour past without my knowing it, though how I was able to actually sleep in that horrific tomb while being chased by a rogue cop is forever beyond my comprehension. Sherlock Holmes believes

that human behavior is subject to the constant whimsy of unstable per-
sonalities. I read that in more than one of his books. I liked Holmes
because he was civilization's penultimate hero. Deeply flawed on the
outside—blatant drug addict, antisocial, rude, explosive temper—but
on the inside the most patient of all specimens, willing to sit in the
cold dark and wait, insidiously, painstakingly, for his enemy to make
one fatal mistake. Maybe Holmes was the inspiration for my bravery
tonight and for allowing my mind and body to succumb to temporary
sleep while the very fate of my life and survival was in question.

I didn't know, now, whether Blackie had driven past me, or if
he had set out on foot to try to find me in the vast darkness of rural
Oklahoma. I looked up into the sky and saw a panorama of stories.
Deep black with a billion blinking stars and a sash of horizontal light
bleeding through the thin tapestry. Was it an asteroid belt, or a band of
rogue meteors? I wished that Janet could see the sky like this, but was
glad she knew nothing of what I had done and how close I came to
the darker side of civilization tonight. After allowing my adrenaline to
seep into the solid, cold earth for a long while, I was no longer afraid.
Blackie would either be waiting for me when I crept up into the truck
or not. I heard a distant sound, not the rumbling of a car motor or even
distant thunder, but something else as I padded across the dry soil to
Nelda McCann's truck parked behind a cluster of cottonwoods.

It wasn't until I got home, brushed my teeth, and climbed into my
own bed that I realized what it was, the midnight whining I heard in
the field near Lucy's Ditch. It was the haunting cry of Mary Prairie's
soul in unrest. As if Blackie Savage wasn't enough, now I had a ghost
chasing me.

The back of the house where all the bedrooms were was still quiet and
dark. The strange smell that came out of Lewella's room right after she
had the baby had gone away now. Maybe she would be all right one of
these days. Maybe we all would.

Daddy and Denny had the hood up and the carburetor off of Nelda
McCann's truck when I got up the next morning. Good thing I had my
story already worked out.

I could hear their unspoken conversation from the kitchen. Daddy never liked Denny much, but he always gave people a chance to prove their worth to him. Not that Denny had done that, so far anyway, but Daddy tolerated him all right. Denny was standing back while Daddy leaned down into the bowels of the engine. The image of tearing a Band-Aid off quickly came to mind as I walked down the front steps.

"Morning," I said, and waited for it to start.

Neither of them said anything at first. Just looked at the sky, their shoes, and back into the engine of Nelda's truck.

"This Mikey's?" Daddy asked me with a raised eyebrow and a gentle nudge of the head. I could tell he was trying to do something unnatural with his voice, something he had trained himself to do, maybe while talking to my mother.

"Nah," I replied. "A woman up in Enid lent it to me so I can drive there every day and do work for her."

"Work?" Denny laughed out loud at the irony. "You're just a kid. I'm the one needs a damn job. Get one for me, why don't you."

"What work?" Daddy said, stepping away from the truck a bit. He crossed his arms now and I knew the small talk was over.

"She just had surgery, I guess, and can't move around too—"

Daddy's palm went up. "How'd you find out about this in the first place?"

"Janet Lange knows her," I blurted without thinking about it. Damn it. Now I had implicated her in this little scam.

"PJ's daughter?" Daddy scratched his head.

"Niece. She goes to my school. Mikey and me met her just the other night, and she told me about it."

Daddy leaned back into the truck and the face-to-face interrogation was over. Denny sat on the bumper and sipped coffee from his thermos cup. "You doing handyman work for her? Some old lady?"

"Pretty old," I said. "It's a long drive but I know a shortcut through the flats that takes about twenty miles off. Y'all reckon the truck'll make it?"

Daddy turned around to size me up. He smiled, then, in a way I had never seen before. "Make it where? You going on a long trip or something?"

Enid, Enid, I thought, how many times did I have to say it? The ground was dry and sandy, and had a layer of white dust under my shoes. "Just driving north to Nelda McCann's house every day."

"That her name?"

I nodded.

"Should last a short spell. On Saturday I'll change the oil and replace a few belts and hoses, fix one leaky seal, and fill up the gas tank."

I met his gaze but quickly looked away, as I could tell he was about to give me that strange smile again, an entirely unfamiliar demon look that did not, could not possibly come from my father. Something was very wrong here, in our driveway of Hooper Circle, with dumb Denny lurking in the background and Daddy fully braced in his new, spurious being, as if to say "I'm not who you think I am but try not to resist." After all, when was he going to ask me about my driver's license? We had already been talking about me driving sixty miles twice a day to an unknown destination, unknown to him anyway. Was he satisfied with the meager explanation I gave him? Not likely. And if he wasn't going to ask me about it, I felt sure Denny would do something, if possible, to ruin my few fleeting chances at freedom for the rest of the summer. But Daddy didn't say a word and Denny was doing something in the barn. I didn't understand any of them anymore, not since Lewella went and had herself a sick baby and almost died in the process. We were still, at that moment, unmoving, unbreathing, stuck in some gluey, viscous time zone that only existed between three people in Grady, Oklahoma. I felt the same sense of impending doom that I felt on the train just before the terrible twister revealed its ghoulish face.

eLeveN

mama mumbled something from behind the front porch screen. Her voice seemed surreal, almost haunting. I could see the universe as I'd known it folding in on itself. Then she yelled, "Breakfast, anyone?"

I felt invincible at that moment, reassured, like I could do anything I wanted with the fate of the entire planet in my palm. If the universe could allow Mama to interpose trivial house-talk into the bizarro world out front, the possibilities were limitless.

Daddy said, "Driving lesson, Jake. Now."

So much for breakfast.

In a second, he'd closed the hood of the truck and secured me in the driver's seat like I'd never even been in a car before. I drove us out to the fenced-in field south of Hooper Circle behind where our cattle grazed. The cows huddled in thick knots along the dry landscape, preparing for whatever weather pattern was on the way. Daddy always said that the cows felt the vibration of storms through their hooves. Today, though, he sat beside me on the torn bench seat of Nelda's truck with his long arms folded. Thinking, observing, judging my every tick and mannerism, my form, habits. I sat up tall and stretched my legs down to the pedals, slowed to a complete stop at the stop sign leading to Main Street, and flipped on my turn signal even though it was broken.

Say something, I silently begged. I continued down Main Street in the slowest fashion I could muster while a murder of crows made a demonic halo under the graying sky. I turned my head left to look for dead cattle.

"Could end up dead doing that," Daddy snapped. "Look away for one minute, about anything could happen."

"Yes, sir," I replied, so he'd be sure I noticed his bizarre behavior. We were not a family built on formalities or custom. Mama and Daddy avoided manners around the house, but were quick to give a licking to anyone who failed to behold society's mores in the company of strangers. So anytime Lewella or me used yessir and nossir language around the house, it meant Satan had been summoned from the gates of hell and there was no escape.

Daddy offered nothing more; he just sat there with his invisible clipboard like a health inspector walking through a sewage plant. So I drove, slowly, carefully, down Main Street, painstakingly turned onto Hollis Avenue, and ended up down the road from PJ's Auto Body. Panic set into my bones at the thought of Janet Lange and Daddy flanking me on each side, staring awkwardly at the asphalt and talking about the heat, as most strangers did anywhere in Oklahoma this time of year. I looked up and down the street for turnoffs, but there weren't any.

"Pull up, while we're here," Daddy commanded in his scariest voice ever. "Not there, here," he added as I tried to turn into PJ's driveway. My heart raced within my chest.

I saw the third garage door snake up and PJ appeared under it with grease covering both hands and a cigarette burning in his lips.

"Guess he didn't make the connection between oil and fire," Daddy commented.

"He's always doing that," I said for no good reason other than to fill the silence.

PJ shuffled to the passenger side of the truck, where Daddy had his elbow on the window jamb. Daddy nudged his head up at his approach. "Peej," he said.

"Howdy."

"Thought you might have a second to look under the hood. My eyes don't see what you see."

At that, PJ peered in at me, then at Daddy, trying to size up the situation. Both men stared at each other in a moment of contempt and solidarity, as if they had both cheated on their wives with the same woman. I had a feeling this moment was important, but I couldn't tell why. Daddy got out of the truck, left the door wide open, then circled around to where PJ stood and took hold of his hand. I felt like I was watching a bad play, the worst of plays, with stilted dialogue and choppy movements and pauses and silence in all the wrong places. The rhythm felt all wrong.

Janet came outside as PJ lifted the hood. She motioned me in. Daddy watched this out of the corner of his eye. I expected him to yell for me to stay there and absorb the tension between he and PJ, but when I looked back he just winked.

"Hi," Janet said, sidling up to me with a warm hug. I guessed we were as good as wed by now.

With one eye on the shop window and another on Janet, I held her shoulders and planted a kiss swiftly on her pink painted lips. I felt a movement in my body as I did this but had learned from Mikey how to conceal such things from girls. In that secret way only women have, Janet saw the look of fear in my eyes.

"That's your Pa?"

I nodded.

"You in trouble 'cause of that truck?" She looked guilty, remembering her role in its acquisition.

"Not your fault even if I am." I sighed and plopped in one of the two chairs in PJ's front office—a grimy, four-walled room decorated with calendars, plaques, and automotive posters with grease stains in all the corners. "He's just losing his mind is all. I swear today his mind's been taken over by aliens."

She laughed lightly, but saw I hadn't even cracked a smile. "He's just upset about your sister, I'll bet. Men don't know how to handle that type of catastrophe. They can be soldiers in the Army and shoot off burglars in the dark of night, but they don't know the first thing about caring for the sick. He's just scared is all."

"My Daddy, scared? I don't think so. He don't act like he's scared of nothing."

"That's what scared looks like, to a man like him. Betcha I know more about men than you do."

I turned to look at her, and drowned in a vision of beauty and purity intertwined. Her smooth skin, pink lips, and golden hair looked much too young for the makeup and earrings she wore, but I didn't mind, for I knew at that moment that Janet Lange had put them on for me only. And that was something Mikey Savage would never be able to take away.

"Where're your parents anyway? Why you spending so much time here? Crime for a girl like you to be all stuck up in a grimy body shop."

"Away. Up in Tulsa talking to some lawyers I guess. They didn't tell me much."

"They got a land deal going on or something?"

Janet shook her head and bit her bottom lip. She looked worried for the first time since I'd met her. I wondered if I should change the subject. "You know about that?"

I didn't, really. "Mikey said your family owned a few ranches is all. I figured there's a lot of buying and selling going on. You know." I prayed she did, prayed I hadn't screwed up already.

"Something like that. Nobody tells me much about it, and I guess Daddy's kind of like yours. You know, sort of quiet and mysterious, and when he's not that way he's downright scary. My ma says he's nicer with a few drinks in him so she has his drink on the table before he even gets home. He swigs it soon as he walks in the back door and by the time he's done there's another one on the table."

While I listened to this outpouring of family scandal, I knew every family had one, someone like Mr. Lange, someone who didn't know the limits of their own tolerance and others' tolerance of their behavior. I watched Daddy mostly smoke cigars and rock in the front porch chair while Mama washed the dinner dishes. I had no real conception of him as a relentless consumer of alcohol. Then again, that was the idea with secretive people. You never really knew about them but you were never surprised, either.

Just as I anticipated, PJ "finished up" in less than ten minutes, which shows that Daddy never really intended for him to do anything anyway. He motioned for me to come out just as Janet slid her white hand onto my knee.

"Head toward Ryan, why don't you. I need a few things at the hardware store."

75

I did as I was told, as it seemed obvious now that I was taking commands from an alien being who had taken control of my father's mind. His body looked the same—tall and lanky enough to hide the spare tire around his middle and well enough endowed with bone structure that his thinning hair didn't detract from his looks. Yet, I still didn't recognize him. I didn't dare turn on the radio, or even ask what it was PJ was doing under the hood. So I asked the only allowable question in an effort to soften his icy heart. "How's Lewella today?"

"Haven't seen her yet. Fine enough, though. Getting good care from that Dr. Laszlo, and Doc Fisher still comes by sometimes."

Anytime Daddy brought up Doc Fisher's assistant, he said "that Laszlo" as if there were three of them in town. "Denny doesn't like him."

"Denny don't like anybody, and especially a man who's taken an interest in his woman. Can't blame a man for feeling slighted by someone better than him."

"I guess not." If he'd told me the sky was falling at that moment, I would've agreed with him.

And then he said, "I saw Blackie Savage last night," just as I started turning the corner to our neighborhood.

twelve

By now, Lewella was walking around the house once a day, an exercise that left her panting and sweating with Mama attached to her hip with a damp rag and water basin. Dr. Roman Laszlo drove out to Hooper Circle twice a day. He would have come three times a day. Hell, he would have slept balled up in the corner of Lewella's room if Daddy let him. I sometimes caught Denny crying out in the barn. Everything was going to hell in a handbasket. I hadn't even seen the red scarf in two weeks.

I was in the kitchen clenching my fists when Daddy came in and poured the remaining coffee sludge into a clean cup. My mind, a tangled mess of possibilities, tried to create one solitary thought or feeling that I could cling to, but instead combined with fear and anxiety. My palms were clammy. When he sat down, I imagined his fist slamming onto the kitchen table, demanding to know what in the hell I'd been doing in Waurika near midnight three days ago, which would send Mama running in from the bedroom with Lewella or Denny or Laszlo on her heels. The way I figured it, the less I said about it the better. I poured some coffee for myself, too, and garnished it with three sugar cubes for extra fortification. I felt braced for the interrogation.

Daddy hummed as he tapped his lean, strong fingers on the tabletop. I felt infuriated by this betrayal, by being led down this path to believe I had an ass-schwamping coming and all he could do was hum some stupid radio tune he'd heard on the way to church. The door to Lewella's bedroom creaked open. Mama came out looking more tired than I'd ever seen her.

"Almost didn't recognize you," she said to me and put her palm on Daddy's shoulder. She looked back and forth between us, and sensed the tension like a good mother always could. "Where you been, Jakie?"

Daddy jumped in and said, "Jakie's got himself a job up Enid." His voice was controlled and mocking. I hated him right then.

Mama put her hands on her hips, which made her flowered house-dress bunch up around her plump arms. "Enid? How you gonna get up there and back every day?"

Oh God, I thought. Please let me die right now. Right here in this kitchen under the yellow overhead lights with my dirty hands fumbling on my lap under the table. Die. Now, please. I'll give up comic books and Sherlock Holmes for a month.

"Jake? Are you riding the train or riding up there with someone? Mikey maybe?" Mama looked at Daddy for the explanation that didn't come. Daddy's fingers still tapped the table while he slurped the coffee from the bottom of the cup. Mine was getting cold. But cold coffee was the least of my worries.

"The lady I'm working for lent me an old truck. Daddy looked at it and PJ looked at the engine. Is it all right, Daddy? Is it safe for me to drive?" Well, now I was playing him in front of Mama, but what choice did he leave me?

Daddy cocked his head back and smiled at me. "Sure, Jake. It looks fine." Now he looked at Mama. "And we've just had ourselves our first driving lesson."

"Is that so? How'd he do?"

"Fine, long as you remember what I told you." He peered at me out the corner of his eye. I didn't know what he meant, but I could tell this line of talk was more for Mama's benefit than mine.

"I remember." I squirmed in my chair. "Can I go to Mikey's before dinner, Ma?"

"Sure, it'll be another hour at least."

Daddy shot her a look.

"I'm sorry, Gordon, Lewella needed me and—" she let her voice trail off into the silent kitchen. Mama dragged her palm across her wet brow and then fanned herself. "We're going outside tomorrow," she said with a proud smile.

"Lewella? Really?"

Mama nodded and I got up from the table.

"Jake," Lewella boomed from the bedroom, "stop leaving your clothes in a heap on your bed. Dr. Laszlo's a very busy man and I want everything to look just right when he comes here to take care of me." She appeared in full form under the hall light now, which illuminated the lines of color streaked on her lips and cheeks. She was wearing her prettiest dress and stockings and high shoes.

"Aren't you a sight for sore eyes," Daddy commented. "Denny taking you out tonight?"

Lewella looked nervously at the floor and so did Mama, the one who was witnessing Laszlo's crafty misappropriation of her daughter.

"Just thought it was high time I did something with myself is all. I finally feel up to it. Dr. Laszlo said if I felt all right, he'd take me into town tomorrow to see the baby."

I'd never seen Lewella smile like that, and I suspected it wasn't the baby that caused it. That's when Daddy got that lost, alien look to his face again, like he was losing all of us one by one. Lewella to Laszlo, me to Enid, and who knows what he thought about Mama after all these years. I wasn't even sure Mama knew herself.

"Hey."

"Hey," Mikey replied, slugging me in the shoulder. "Where've you been?"

I wanted so badly to tell him about Janet, but I saw the "Blackie" look in his eyes. No good conversation ever came out of that look.

"Nowhere. What's with you?"

Mikey shifted his weight from one stockinged foot to the other. And his fly was down.

I instinctively looked up at the tree house and saw a small, whitish, distinctly feminine foot sticking out the door. I snapped my head toward him. "Well?"

"Well what?" The Blackie look turned into a guilty look.

"Spill it."

Mikey took two steps toward me. I could tell he'd skipped his bath

the night before. Maybe the night before that, too. "Helen Jeffers's little sister, Carmella," he whispered. Though I'd never met Carmella,
I remembered Mikey's entry of Helen's bra size in the special notebook—C-cup. Carmella giggled and started humming something
twenty feet above our heads. I shot Mikey a look.

"What's the matter with you? You like boys all of a sudden?"

Well if this didn't lead to disaster, nothing would.

"Come on up," Mikey said with a deliberate wink.

I looked toward his house.

"Nobody's home. Come on." He stressed the last word.

When he got all the way into the tree house, I didn't move for a few
seconds. I just listened for any of the customary sounds of sex—lips
smacking, clothes rustling, deep breathing, zippers, snaps, moans. But
I didn't hear any of that. Maybe she was undressed and Mikey was
staring at her breasts with his mouth open. The most likely scenario, I
decided, and headed to the side of Mikey's house.

"Hey! Jake, where you going? Get up here." He stared down at me.
"Now, Jake."

I shook my head the whole climb up the stairs, and reaffirmed the
essential, intellectual distance between Mikey and me. Here I was,
fifteen, with a vehicle, a job, and independently, single-handedly
investigating a murder. And Mikey was getting greased in the tree
house.

"Hi," I said and tried to look interested in Carmella Jeffers. She had
a roundish, doughy face that didn't seem to match her long, knobby
legs. I saw she had on a pair of shorts and sandals, and a loose cotton
shirt with buttons down the front. It was misbuttoned, and in the con-
text of an unsupervised tree house in rural Oklahoma, this fact meant
only one thing—that it had been buttoned up quickly.

"How much?" I asked her, and Mikey jabbed me with his pointy
elbow.

"Jesus, Jake, have some manners. Would ya?"

"Manners?" I laughed. "A girl you don't even know is flashing for
money and you talk about manners?"

"Only a dollar," Carmella said with a scintillating smile that showed a piece of bread stuck between her two front teeth. It was white like the soft, white bread Mama bought at the Main Street bakery in Ryan.

"Get a dollar, Jake, for God's sake!" Then he turned to the girl. "He's a little slow. Don't mean he doesn't like you or nothing."

"You just want to peek at *my* dollar's worth, don't you? You've already had yours," I protested, but knew there was no getting out of it. Here I was, nearly married to a strange soul named Janet Lange, beautiful and pure, yet paying for a C-cup peek-a-boo with the little money I had. I pulled a folded dollar bill from the left pocket of my pants, and the bready smile appeared again. Carmella Jeffers's fingers unbuttoned the front of her blouse and Mikey quickly zipped his erection back into his baggy pants. I heard the squeak of the zipper, though halted and quickly followed by a scream.

Mikey let out a howl loud enough to wake all the church ladies in Tulsa. He moaned and rolled to the side with his hands covering his crotch. I was sure the grungy mattress would be blood-soaked, so I peeked down there but couldn't see past his hands. The screen door of Mikey's back porch cracked against the doorframe.

Footsteps. Someone came running out and I saw my life pass before me. Take stock, I told myself. You're in a tree house with a screaming boy and a girl with her shirt off. Goodbye job, goodbye family, Janet, and goodbye Nelda's truck, which would be by far the biggest loss of all.

"Button that, quick," I hissed at Carmella. Mrs. Savage, surely recognizing the sound of her own boy's cries, tore up the rickety steps and shoved her girth through the narrow doorway. She landed on the grimy mattress beside Mikey.

"What on earth happened?" she said, blinking her teary eyes at me.

And that's when I realized I wasn't one of those quick-thinking people. Mikey, if he were me then, would have blurted "Jake was about to jack off looking at Carmella's tits when he zipped his pee into his shorts." And I was sure Blackie Savage, in the same situation, would have instantly conjured a credible scenario of some medical anomaly. But I just bit my bottom lip and prayed she would forget I had even been there.

"Jake? Jacob Leeds? Tell me what's going on up here."

And all I could think of was, "Mikey got a bad pain in his stomach."

"His stomach? That's not what he's holding. Why's he holding his privates? Carmella, you know anything about this?"

"No ma'am," Carmella quickly replied. "We were getting ready to play cards when he started screaming and holding his belly. I don't know what's wrong with him."

Mrs. Savage squinted her eyes at Carmella, then at me, and rubbed Mikey's back real slow to calm him down. It was part of that secret training only mothers get when they have kids. Her hand was moving so slowly but there was a fire lit in her blinking blue eyes darting left and right. "Well I don't know either but I reckon it's got nothing to do with cards and something to do with what's inside your shirt, little miss. Guess you'd better go on home now and hope I don't call your Mama."

"Yes, ma'am."

"Jake, be a good boy and help me get him in the house."

There was no way to carry him down the spindly stairs, so I went ahead of them and stood on the top step. "Wrap his arms around my shoulders," I said to Mikey's mother, us both as deeply entangled as the other.

tHIRteeN

In the dream, Blackie's mouth moves all by itself. And there's a Whitey in there, too, but not altogether separate from the Blackie Savage of all my nightmares. The Whitey character, and I don't mean dressed in a diaphanous robe with a halo or anything, stands a few feet away from the real thing and whispers in Blackie's ear, a ghost-like form of the conscience he doesn't have in reality. A glueyness follows all Blackie's movements as if we are moving within an aircraft in outer space. Hand to head, hand to face, and then fingers curling into a fist. His approach toward me is lunky and labored, with one foot tumbling precariously over the other, barely lifting enough to make progress. The arm and fist extend toward me and the actions closely characterize what I know of this devil named Blackie Savage, but the mouth keeps moving, speaking, licking, and chopping up words that clearly aren't his own. Fee, Fi, Fo, Fum, Love, Spun, Home, Drum. Whitey's words, entering the dark cavity of Blackie's brain through his ear, are the narrow sliver between life and death, as I know, from more than just rumor and folklore, that Blackie could rub me out in one punch. The air around me grows blurry now, like we're mere illustrations being erased by the angry artist. Blackie's dark pant legs smear into a mashed mess of brown and gray, now his innards smear outward as if squashed by a giant shoe—a sea of red blood and brain matter cloud my view until the cape of Whitey's aura cleanses everything both inside and outside.

I slept on the front porch, since it was so hot and no breeze came in through the screens. And I didn't realize that the dream was a premonition 'til I felt the porch slats digging into my spine through the sleeping bag. The sky was still dark as I headed north toward Enid. I could just picture how gloomy Nelda's house would look in the dove-gray fuzz of early morning. Hell, it looked like a mausoleum even on a bright, sunny day. Daddy and Denny had gassed up Nelda's truck, and the little red line twitched up near the big "F." I was betraying them, Daddy, Mama, all of them, in a way, with this new truck and new job and my secret agendas that took me all over Oklahoma in the middle of the nights. Lewella had been near close to death three weeks ago, and some rich, European doctor was in the process of stealing her out from under our noses. Yet here I was, windows rolled down, the cool, moist air licking the skin on my arms and face, blowing my wet hair around my head. Laszlo was moving into our lives and I wasn't even there to defend her. My own sister.

Nelda McCann was hunched over a bed of weeds in the patch of earth lining her front door. I parked the truck and moved tentatively along the sidewalk, up the three brick steps and then on the slate walkway toward the front door. In a way I didn't worry about startling her, because in my heart I wasn't convinced that she was really alive, in the usual sense. When I was three steps away from her, I opened my mouth to speak, and the glassy edge of her dark voice caught me red handed.

"Gonna rain today. Good for the soil."

The sound of her was like sandpaper against my eyeballs. But at least she cared about something. She stood up with less effort than I would have expected from her creaky, neglected bones. She wore the same gray slippers, and I could see the collar of her grimy blue pajamas peeking out under the thin, pink striped bathrobe. Inches away now, she looked and smelled clean like she'd showered and used soap and everything, but I knew she hadn't brushed her hair in months, hadn't put cream on her face like Mama and Lewella did every night like their lives depended on it, and the hard lines of apathy chiseled into her cheeks were beyond the challenge of rouge and lipstick. I had the same feeling for her that I did for Lewella—the rarest of wildflowers forced to bloom in an unkind, hostile environment. Denny made Lewella's environment hostile, and Laszlo, under the guise of her savior, would only exploit and change her into someone she wasn't meant to be. And Nelda, God bless her, was beyond saving. And to me, that meant the ultimate challenge. Find her daughter's

84

killer and, in the process, resurrect a zombie from the realm of the undead. Weirder things had happened.

"You hear me?" she asked.

"What? Rain? We're in Oklahoma, Nelda. It rains here every day."

She slanted her glassy, hazel eyes at me. I responded to her like I was talking to Mikey or Freddie, not a grown-up. Usually I caught myself in time.

"Sorry it took me so long to get back up here. My Daddy was making some repairs on the truck—"

"Just keep it. I don't need it for nothing, since I don't go anywhere but here." She smiled then, showing a gray sheen on her teeth from decades of smoking Marlboros. But I hadn't noticed any ashtrays in her house and the carpets didn't smell musty.

"What repairs did you need done today?" I asked.

She walked in the house, holding the screen door out to me as I followed. "I made some fresh iced tea."

Iced tea at eight o'clock in the morning? "Thank you," I said, and took the glass she handed me.

With her back to me, she said, "Could use another shed out back. Got all that goddamned land and nothing on it but haystacks with no cows to feed off of it."

"Alfalfa?"

"I guess. Wasn't never much of a farmer. Put them bales in the back of the truck and take them if you want. You got cows down in Grady?"

"Some." I sipped the tea and struggled to swallow it. She must have poured a hundred spoons of sugar in it. "What would you put in a shed?" I asked her.

I looked out back through the dusty window over the kitchen sink. "That whole pile of stuff could go in it, maybe. The lawn mower, rakes, tools."

"I got a friend who could help me build it. He's built lots of things at his house," I said of this imaginary friend. Mikey Savage couldn't build four walls out of Lego blocks. And then an idea came to me as Nelda McCann nodded at my idea. "What about around the house?

Maybe you want someone to clean out old stuff that you don't use or don't want around anymore."

The hazel eyes blinked quickly and darted to the right as if responding to an apparition. They blinked faster now, thinking, analyzing the validity of my suggestion, and wondering about my ulterior motives. I didn't care if she knew I was after Mary-memorabilia, as I was convinced she was crazy enough to not be an obstacle to my objective.

"The man'll be coming again. Tonight, maybe. Was here this morning and said he'd be back."

God help me, I thought, wondering how our conversation had so suddenly changed. This degree of lunacy was quite out of my league. How do you respond to a woman talking to ghosts? "What does he want?" I found myself asking.

Nelda looked up from her tea and squinted at me. "The milk bottles. What else would a milkman want?"

There hadn't been milk delivery in Enid for ten years, as all the grocery stores carried it fresh. And now I just felt stupid. I stood up, and the chair awkwardly scraped against the kitchen tile. Nelda studied me, almost like she was trying to remember who I was and why I was in her kitchen. I walked slowly through the house and lingered in the hallway near the living room to see if she was watching. Her head was tilted to the right again, like she was listening to that same ghost. *Kill him*, the ghost was saying. *Take your long, spindly fingers, wrap them around the boy's throat and squeeze his neck 'til his eyes pop out.*

"I'll need some money to buy lumber," I yelled into the kitchen from the living room. And then I saw what I wasn't supposed to see— the wall behind the piano. The picture itself revealed nothing about the missing woman in my life or the truth about who killed Mary McCann—Nelda with two other women, a man, and a very old woman in the center of them—obviously, by their communal beak noses and beady, hazel eyes, it was Nelda standing with her two sisters, brother, and mother. But the content wasn't what was remarkable. It was the size. There was a bare spot of wall about the size of a bookmark to the right of the picture. The color of the ecru paint paled slightly in comparison with the paint on the rest of the living room walls.

Another picture had been there. A larger picture that was taken down and moved somewhere else.

Where was it? Under the bed? In the back of the hall closet? I scanned with only my eyes around the interior. Nelda, unmoved from the kitchen table, moved her hands now and bobbed her head in the direction of the ghost, deeply engaged in their netherworld exchange. So I crept around the house, stepping only on the carpet nearest to the wall to keep the floors from creaking. Hunched over, sometimes on all fours like a cat, I looked, scanned, and memorized features that could be used later when Nelda was out of the house. There were closets on both sides of the hallway—small, two-door cubbyholes on top and larger, shelved cabinets down below. Each of the three bedrooms had small clothes closets with not much storage space, but each had shoe boxes stacked on top of the shelf over the clothes rack.

But what about the door in the kitchen?

I could get her out. I had to. It was the only way I'd find out what I needed from her, about the daughter she couldn't acknowledge, the dead girl who existed only in her nightmares now. What did women love more than anything? And I could barely say the word "woman" when referring to Nelda without smirking to myself, but she was a woman, had been once, a real living, breathing woman who fell in love and got married and had babies just like every other woman in the world, and probably had worn lipstick and high heels and cared about things like how she came across to men and what kind of mother she was to her children. So flowers. That was my secret ingredient for bringing Nelda McCann back from the dead. As for Mary, that was another story.

I watched her go out back and let the kitchen screen slap the door-frame. She was mumbling to herself when I got there.

"How much lumber you think you'll need for a shed?" Her hands were in the pockets of her bathrobe.

"Depends on how big you want it."

"Don't matter. Up to you. There's cash in the coffee can on the counter," she said and walked back in the house.

fouRteeN

I took Mikey with me to Enid the next day. I wanted to call Janet instead, but I couldn't imagine a girl helping me carry lumber.

"Worth it," Mikey said.

"No way," I replied, of the comparison between Carmella Jeffers's underdeveloped breasts and an ass-schwamping by his mother.

"You saw. Didn't you?"

"No, and she went away with my dollar, too. A whole dollar? For that?"

Mikey fake-gasped. "Oh, like you've seen better. Only in dreams and magazines."

"Grandma Weaver says if I don't read twenty books a year, I'll be stuck in Grady for the rest of my life."

Mikey's brain twisted around the notion of reading, a notion he rarely considered. "Does she read twenty books a year?"

"Not anymore. She's almost ninety. But she lives in Tulsa," I added, to prove my point.

It was cooler this morning and we only had the windows down halfway. From the hill near Waurika I could see eighty miles in each direction. The sky came in four colors—dark, scary gray on the western horizon, white and overcast to the north, and the eastern sky bled an enticing blue down into the hazy, layered cloud cover of down south. I could almost taste the rain on my lips before it fell. Mikey tapped his fingers nervously on the door. He wasn't good with silence. "Who played the Magnificent Seven?"

I sighed. "Steve McQueen, Bronson, Wallach, Vaugh, Brenner . . ."

His round face lit up suddenly. "But who directed it?"

"How should I know? You sure as hell don't."

"So?"

Normally, and I laugh at that word because Mikey's family was anything but normal, we would have played the TV quiz game the whole ride north, but we had both acknowledged a rift in our friendship. From his perspective, I had stolen Janet Lange, and on my end I'd kept my Blackie-brush-with-death from him as well.

"Where's the lumberyard?" he said after a while.

"West side."

"What's it called?"

"West Side Lumber." I glanced at him and smirked.

After I parked the truck, I pulled out a drawing of the proposed shed to be built in Nelda's backyard. Not exactly a schematic, but for fifteen-year-olds, it would do just fine. We stood back as the truck engine sputtered.

"That truck's a beast. Surprised it even runs."

"It's a demon," I corrected him.

"The demon. That's its new name." Mikey scratched his head and studied the drawing. "We can make this?"

"Why not? We have all the tools and money we need. You can hammer nails in, right?"

He nodded slowly, and in that moment, I lost all faith in his construction ability.

"And you can read, right?"

"Why?" His eyes narrowed.

"You'll read the directions and I'll do t—"

"Uh uh. You read and I'll hammer. And I won't need no directions for that."

"That's good because we don't have any yet."

"What's the dimensions?"

"Five feet wide, eight feet deep," I estimated.

"Shit, we could make that in a day."

With the money I took from Nelda's coffee can, we bought enough lumber to frame in the shed, along with nails, bolts, screws, and braces.

"How much you get for this anyway?" Mikey said.

"For what?"

He started banging on the door of the truck. "For working here, that's what."

"Ten dollars a day, and I work whenever I want. Not to mention this truck."

"Demon." After more awkward silence, he cleared his throat, which I knew meant he was going to ask something unpleasant. "So what am I looking for?"

"Look, if you don't have the stomach for this, I'll just drop you off right now."

Mikey's jaw tightened. "I'm just asking what I'm supposed to find is all. You're doing all the fun work out back and I'm sifting around in some creepy old lady's basement."

"Look," I began, "this is just a backup plan. I'll get her out of the house and then we can take the whole place apart. Both of us."

"You don't need to do all that. Girls hate anything to do with a big old noisy mess. Five minutes of us hammering and she'll be screeching out the driveway."

"She never gets dressed, let alone leaves the house."

"What's she a vampire or something?"

I had no real understanding of a woman in mourning, or of women in general. Sure, she was a means of finding the truth about Mary Prairie and about Lillie Mechem and that snake, Walter van Geller. But I realized only now that she was something more than that, too.

We found Nelda standing on a mound in the backyard, resting her eyes on the broad, flat expanse of the field behind her house. As I approached, it reminded me of the baseball diamond where Mary had first spoken to me from the dead. Mary, Nelda's daughter.

"Hi Nelda," I said, sneaking up on her for the second time that day.

Mikey nudged me. "You call her that?" he whispered.

She turned around slowly, as if drawn out of a deep trance by our juvenile mutterings. "Who are you?" Her eyes swept past me.

"Mikey Savage, ma'am." Mikey wiped his palm on the leg of his pants in case she wanted to shake it.

Instead she looked him up and down without moving her head. "You the construction crew?"

He looked at the ground. "Jake's gonna do most of the work." Pause. "He helped his dad build a garage and a barn once. Didn't you, Jake?"

Nelda turned back to the small mound to resume her silent vigil. I motioned for Mikey to start bringing the lumber out back from the truck. Watching Nelda, I considered the irony of all my questions juxtaposed against her inability, or unwillingness, to answer them. Like trying to chisel through a concrete wall with a rock hammer.

"What do you see out there?" I asked.

"Ghosts."

When she looked down and kicked a spot of dirt under her foot, I noticed she was wearing shoes instead of slippers, and pants instead of pajamas. Then I saw her hair. Clean, brushed, parted on the side in a man's style, but still evident of an effort being made to better herself. Something in Nelda McCann had changed, and some part of me knew I had caused it.

"They call to me sometimes," she said.

My stomach tightened as the words formed in my mouth. "You mean Mary? Does she call to you?"

Nelda's eyes opened wide. "Have you ever lost anything?" The eyes stayed on me for a few awkward moments, like the rest of her life depended on my answer.

And I tried to answer, tried to form some kind of coherent response that would be acceptable to an unstable, mourning woman. I shook my head finally.

"My mother's buried in that field. And my brother, two years later."

"And what about Mary?"

Nelda brushed an invisible mosquito from the air in front of her face.

"Is she buried here too?"

"Where the hayfields stop, that's the end of the property line."

Again, I found myself wondering who she was talking to and whose questions she was answering. "Who lives out there?"

"Michaelssohns. Nobody left there now but an old uncle who drinks too much and sets his beds on fire. Gonna burn himself up someday."

"Maybe he's indestructible." The words slipped out before I could catch them.

"Some people certainly are," she said.

Some people certainly are. I wondered about asking anything else, about my blind quest to get information that I wasn't meant to have, or maybe information that ultimately I would not want, that no one in their right mind would want.

"Do you know where Mary is now?"

Nelda nudged her chin forward. "North. Somewhere."

Great, I thought. Now we're talking about religion. Please don't mention God and sunlight pouring down from the sky. But she didn't mention anything. Just cocked her head sideways and squinted her eyes down to slits, listening, reaching, longing for that shadowy visitor again. It was a man. I knew this much for certain. A tall man, maybe, by the position of her head when he spoke to her. Someone she revered. Was it Mary's father?

fifteeN

We took the long route back from Enid through a twisted web of dirt paths, county roads, easements, and ditches along the north side of Beaver Creek. Already hot and sunburned, the air through the opened windows only made us hotter. Nelda allowed us to eat whatever we could find in her kitchen, which today revealed nothing but crackers and peanut butter. I stopped at the only diner I knew of in Waurika, across from the antique shop Lewella took me to once.

"Stop here and get burgers I guess." I was trying to act casual, and not make a big deal out of how grown-up I felt with my own truck, money in my pocket, and a companion, if you could call someone like Mikey a companion.

"I could eat the whole cow right now."

"Why? You didn't do nothing but sit around in the shade all day."

Mikey's head snapped toward me and his right fist jabbed my shoulder. "Loser."

"You are," I said.

He let it go at that. We seated ourselves in an empty table near the windows, and some old man at the counter turned around and watched us while he lit his cigar.

"Where's the menus?" Mikey said. They had six kids in his family, so I knew he hadn't been out to eat much. Neither had I, come to think of it.

"No menus," I said. "Just got burgers."

Mikey bit his lip and played with the salt and pepper shakers. I sensed the old man at the counter moving toward us. Oh God, not today, I thought.

"You boys been working outside on a day like today?"

"Yes, sir," I answered. I didn't look up, trained as I had been by Grandma Weaver to pay respect to elders. I had a feeling we were in for something.

"Where 'bouts?" The cigar was hanging out the side of his mouth.

"Up Enid. Just some construction."

"On a crew?"

I cleared my throat and prayed Mikey would stay quiet for another few seconds.

Mikey looked at me. "We're looking for Mary P—"

I smashed my heel down on his right foot under the table. He yelped quietly, and I angled my head up to the man. He was tall and gangly, with a wrinkled face and short, gray hair. "Just getting something to eat before we head south, sir." I made sure I said sir again, not to be ingratiating, but as a symbol of deference. After I said it, a waitress set two plates in front of us.

"What the hell are you doing?" I hissed after the old man disappeared.

"What?"

"Why don't you just say 'Oh we're looking for a goddamn dead girl'?"

"Shut up, loser. You're just embarrassed."

"About what?"

"The truth."

"What do you know about it?" Heat pooled in my ears.

"That you're in love with a dead girl."

"No I'm not. I'm in love with Janet Lange," I shot back without thinking. Mikey sat back in his chair and slung the half-eaten burger against his plate. There. The truth. It was out, and worse yet, it came from my own lips. Had I really said it or just thought it out loud? After a measure of silence I watched a Cheshire cat grin slide into his sweaty face.

"You walked right into it, didn't you?"

I did.

"I've lost my appetite," he said and walked out. I left two dollars on the table. Still a forty-minute drive back to Grady, I got an idea of how to mend the sudden broken fence in my life. After all, it was on the way back.

Mikey stared straight out the windshield, but I saw his eyes move when I took an odd turn.

"Where in the hell you going now?"

"Ringling."

"For what?" His voice was acid.

"I got some walkie-talkies behind the seat."

He shook his head. "I don't feel like playing Superman."

"We're going on a stakeout." Now I'd piqued his interest.

"What, that creepy old priest?"

"You gotta be home by dinnertime?"

"Nah. My ma took the twins to my grandmother's house."

Mend a fence in ten seconds. A world record.

I drove us to the far side of Ringling where we parked Nelda's truck in an empty lot. It was getting late—near dinnertime, and people were already starting to shut down for the night. Mikey gave a ceremonious yawn, a symbol of his fatigue from working so hard on the shed—my fault—and of his thwarted burger consumption in Waurika, also my fault. I knew he wasn't Blackie, but I was going to pay for my insolence just the same. After all, he was a Savage. He started looking out the window.

"I parked far off so he wouldn't see the truck," I explained and handed him the walkie-talkie. When we got to the street just north of Walter van Geller's, I stopped and lowered my head. "There," I pointed.

"Why're you whispering? He lives two blocks away."

"Just being discreet is all."

"What's that?"

"Discretion. Means careful. That's how Sherlock Holmes sneaks around all the time without getting caught. By being discreet."

Mikey scoffed and a bubble of saliva accidentally flowed out of his mouth. "With that big old cape and stupid hat and pipe? Anyone could recognize him."

"Inverness Cape," I mumbled. "And it's a deerstalker hat and it's not stupid."

The corner of Van Geller's street was covered with thickly leaved trees, making it impossible to scope out a vantage point.

"There!" Mikey pointed to a small, empty lot across from Van Geller's in between two large, L-shaped houses.

"You take that then," I said, "and I'll go around the back."

"I'll never hear you on that thing," he replied, looking at the walkie-talkie.

"I won't be saying nothing. Just creep over there and stay hidden 'til I come back."

Mikey's face wrinkled. He didn't like this idea; I could tell. "How long are we gonna wait here? I mean, what if we don't see nothing?"

"Then we'll do it again tomorrow. Get to the lot from 'L' Street so no one sees you," I said and took off to find my own spot. "I'll radio you in an hour." And to him, an hour was as good as a month.

From the front, Van Geller's house was an expansive, inviting cottage style with a white painted front porch, rocking chairs on each side of the door, and a round, braided carpet at the top of the steps— the kind of porch people wanted to sit on with a glass of cold iced tea on a hot summer day, the kind of house where you pictured yourself soaking up a sunny afternoon with the leisure of a man in control of his life. But Walter Van Geller was not a man of leisure, nor was he in control. I had looked in his eyes—so had Mikey—and I saw a man clinging to bare strips of bark with outstretched claws, trying to hang on with his last bits of lost sensibility, bordering on the very nature of desperation. Walter Van Geller knew me and I knew him.

But what was he hiding?

By the time I got to a grassy spot behind a metal drum in a back-yard bordering Van Geller's property, I heard the scratchy din of the walkie-talkie.

"Jake? Jakie? You there?"

"What do you want?"

"What are our code names?"

I changed positions to keep the radio hidden but still kept my eye on Van Geller's back door. "Okay. You be Lois Lane."

"Shut up, loser!"

"Who do you feel like today?" Parasite, I was thinking.

"Mogul."

"Fine," I agreed. "I'll be Maxima. See anything out front?"

"Nah, all the shades are pulled down. Maybe he's not home."

He's home, I thought.

A whopping thirty minutes went by with no radio contact—it was more than I ever imagined. Lying on my back, I took in the silence and the gentle sway of leaves in the nonexistent breeze and tried to put things together in my head. I had always been one for writing things down and keeping records and making outlines and plans of things and projects. I'd kept a diary for most of my life, though nobody, not Mikey, Mama, not even Lewella, knew a thing about it. There was a spot in my closet, in the dark part where the light never shined, where I'd spent a day cutting a perfect rectangle in the wall with one of Daddy's jigsaws. I glued the ends so it popped in and out easily without leaving a mess on the carpet, and it served as a perfect hiding place for written secrets.

The coolness of the moist earth penetrated the back of my head as I lay prone in an old lady's backyard, radio resting on my chest. Okay. What did I know so far? Hardly anything, was the truth of it. Mary Prairie, aka Mary McCann, was a real person who died suspiciously some years ago, the exact number I didn't know, nor did I know by whose hand she died. Her insane, hermit mother in Enid had no pictures or memorabilia of her in the house. Nobody knew who killed her, but it seemed that local folklore had accepted her death as any other in the history of southern Oklahoma, without need for any explanation or justification. And Denny told me himself that the baseball diamond field where she died is technically on his property and that Walter van Geller is the grandson of the preacher who owned the property before 1920.

Clouds clustered in the blue-gray sky above my head, slowly coagulating into a dark formation that promised rain and high winds. My brain was a Spinning Jenny right then, hell-bent on finding a connection or even the smallest lead to give me hope that someday there might be justice for people who are wronged. I wasn't holding my breath.

I sat up and peered through a bunch of willow leaves and branches at the back of Van Geller's house, thinking. I was thinking about how Van Geller's family had once owned the ranch where Mary was killed, and how this piece of information fit neatly beside another piece of information—that he lived in the very town where a young girl named Lillie Mechem had disappeared without a trace. The connection was tenuous at best, but it made me feel better to know that the two deaths had at least one person in common.

The radio crackled on the ground beside me. "Maxima. Come in, Maxima."

"I'm here, Mogul. Report."

"A car just pulled up. Get your ass over here quick."

"Where are you?" Mikey radioed in when I was at the end of Van Geller's street.

"Half a block away," I said, thumbing the red button while I walked. "What's going on over there?"

"Nothing yet, wait, no nothing."

"What?"

Mikey sighed. "They're moving around in the car, like their heads are moving."

"Whose heads?"

"Now they're sitting far apart."

"Who, Mikey?"

"How should I know? Two old ladies with scarves on their heads. Maybe they're laughing or something."

Or crying, I thought. As I walked under the trees on the opposite side of Van Geller's street, the car in front of his house stopped me dead in my tracks. I must have made some sound or gasp into the radio.

"What? What's the matter?"

The car. A shiny, yellow 1960 Chevrolet just like I'd seen in magazines and in store windows. "It's the Batmobile," I said, and then felt like a five-year-old. After all, I was fifteen and well beyond my initial Batman fixation. Mikey was standing in the open field across from the house, his head only partially hidden by the thick branch of an ancient oak tree. When he saw me, he nodded his head and then fell back under the tall blades of grass. I crept into the field from the backyard of Van Geller's diagonal neighbor across the street. In one part where the grass was cut low, I crawled on all fours. The field was small and perfectly square, ornamented by a single lone tractor in the back and two small haystacks.

I camped right beside Mikey, and when I knelt down I detected a foul smell coming from his direction, not sure if the foulness was from unwashed skin or unwashed clothes. I cringed and shut my eyes for no more than a split second, after which I felt a jab in my ribs from Mikey's elbow. He had his finger over his mouth and gestured toward the Batmobile. We had to be at least twenty-five, maybe thirty feet away, and now one of the women in the car was standing on Van Geller's porch, hunched over with a kerchief on her head. The spindly legs sticking below the plain dark skirt looked familiar, but not shapely enough to be Lewella's and not plump enough to be Mama's. I tried to think of any other women I knew who would be visiting a creep like him this time of day.

Behind me, I heard something rusting in the grass. Then I heard the clanky sound of metal hitting metal and, when I turned around, I saw an old man climbing up on the tractor. Please don't turn it on, I thought. The engine hammered against our eardrums as we ached to hear even a word of conversation.

The woman on the porch held her empty palms at her waist as in complete resignation, while Van Geller, who appeared out of thin air, towered over her like an angry Cossack. He shook his head, and as he opened his mouth, the tractor came near us. The grass was so tall, I wondered if the driver could even see us. He was driving in short lines across the length of the square patch of land, and by my estimation he would reach us in seven laps. Mikey had a panicked looked on his face, but he knew conversation was pointless while the tractor grated behind us. The woman behind the wheel of the Batmobile sat perfectly still with her head aimed straight ahead, and the other woman, older by how much I wasn't sure, argued with Van Geller quietly in the privacy of his front porch. Her squarish, orthopedic shoes fidgeted on the braided rug outside the door; her small white fists clenched in and out and Van Geller, with his large laughing eyes, looked back with quiet contempt.

"Here she comes," Mikey mouthed over the tractor's cacophony.

Now it was only four rows away from us. And as I turned around to gauge our proximity to the monstrous, rotating wheels, Mikey grabbed my chin and angled my face toward the woman walking around the Batmobile.

It was Nelda.

When I got home, my bedroom was pink. Someone's grimy hands had ripped all the Batman comic book covers off the closet door, and the Superman posters, baseball card collector's editions, and painted all four walls baby-skin pink. An outrage. The trim was painted white to match the new crib in the corner. Denny made it, I could tell, and not because he was the father but because it was so crooked it barely stood up. My bed, they told me, was in the barn with my dresser and my shoes and all my equipment. All I could do was sit at the kitchen table and sulk.

Within sixty seconds, a tall glass of chocolate milk appeared in front of me, along with Mama's sad, red face.

"Can you forgive us, Jakie?"

"It's Jake, Ma. Nobody else calls me Jakie but you and Lewella and it makes me sound like a baby. I'm fifteen. Heck, I might as well go out and get myself a real job and an apartment. I'm old enough, I reckon."

"Not such a bad idea," Daddy said from the corner. Funny, coming from a man who hadn't worked any real job in ten years.

"Gordon," Mama scorned and raised her hand in the air. "Now Jake, this is just temporary, you know, on accounta that baby coming home today for the first time." She leaned in close and I could smell a mix of dough and lemon soap. "This is a big day for your sister. That baby needs her own room for the time being, just until Lewella and Denny get their own place."

"Nearly found one, didn't they?" Daddy chimed in again. His voice was sandpaper on Mama's ears.

"Oh Gordon, you know they can't afford the old Bunker's place. They were just getting an idea of the market."

"Why can't they live on Denny's ranch? His parents are too old to take care of it themselves." I sipped the chocolate milk. It was so cold and sweet, my teeth ached after I gulped it straight down. "Don't matter," I said. "Where am I gonna sleep?"

Mama pinched her lips together like when she tried to convince Daddy she needed a new dress. "We've got a nice new cot in the basement we could put in Lewella's room, or—"

"Cooler in the basement I think," Daddy said, rocking in that creaky old chair, smoking the same old pipe and spewing the same garbage that had come out of his mouth all my life. I loathed him more every second, it seemed, since the beginning of my quest, though I couldn't imagine what connection he had to it other than obstructing my progress any way he could. I remembered, then, that he'd seen Blackie Savage at one point, though I'd never know what they talked about.

"I'll drag my sleeping bag onto the porch. Cooler out there anyhow."

"Even cooler in that basement," Daddy persisted. "You got nothing to be scared about, son."

I wondered, then, if they gave the death penalty to minors for killing their parents. "Who was it owned this house before we bought it?"

Mama and Daddy exchanged a quick glance.

"Did you say someone died down there, Mama? Someone's grandfather or something, and the owners before us found him lying on top of a clothes heap?"

An agonizing silence followed, the kind between family members when they try not to say what's on their minds. "I reckon that porch'll be just as cool as the basement anyway. That's settled then."

A car was honking outside. I went out first and was sure to let the screen slap the doorjamb. Daddy hated that sound.

"She's here, she's here," Mama shrieked. She and Lewella thundered out of the house with Denny on their heels. Daddy stood behind the screen, watching from the dark claw behind his face.

Dr. Roman Laszlo stepped out of the shiny car wearing clean, pressed pants. His starched, white shirt was slightly unbuttoned and a few tufts of black hair poked through the opening. Lewella walked up to him slowly, eyes wide, like he was one of those evangelical preachers that cured blindness by the palm-on-the-forehead ploy. She was blind, all right.

"You ready?" Laszlo teased, winking.

"Gimme that baby, doc. God knows I waited long enough."

It didn't cry or nothing, not when Lewella held her or when she passed her to Mama. Then, in Denny's orangutan arms and large, flat hands, it looked all wrong. Mama and Lew stood close by, braced for disaster as he fumbled the oddly shaped package into a position both of them could live with. The baby's head dangled back at one point and I could feel all Mama's breath leave her body, but he lifted the tiny head with two fingers and leaned down close to its face.

"What's that?" he said, pretending to have gotten a secret message from the two-month-old creature. "Is that so? Well let's see what they all think."

Mama wiped her tears with the hankie perpetually stuck in the right sleeve of her dress.

"Says her name's Faith, seeing as she almost died and all."

"All right then." Lewella looked prouder and happier than I'd ever seen her, at least since Denny had started ruining her life. She took the baby and knew just how to hold it so it could feel her heartbeat and surround itself in her scent, the way baby ducks imprinted their mother's face after being born. Faith was facing behind Lewella toward Mama and me now. Even though Mama had barely touched Faith yet, I knew she couldn't live without her. I also knew that baby was gonna drive an ever bigger wedge between Mama and Daddy.

Daddy came out the front screen with his shotgun in one hand and a box of shells in the other.

"What in the hell are—"

"I'm going shooting. I'll be back before dinner."

Lewella searched my face for an explanation.

"Guys like him get weird when they get old," I said.

Mama's finger extended. "Jacob."

"What Ma? If Daddy can't be happy about something like this, he ain't never gonna be happy about nothing."

"That's old news." Lewella bit her lip and touched the thin sheath of hair on Faith's head. Then her eyes landed on the real love of her life. "Doctor," she said, "how rude of me. Come on in for some iced tea. You must be tired out from the long drive."

"Not so bad," he replied with a naughty smile. "It's only ninety today."

Standing there at the edge of that family circle, I felt more and more squeezed out, like somehow Laszlo was taking my place, or, worse yet, taking Daddy's place as the implied head of the household. Denny hung his long, awkward arms at his sides, knowing, it seemed, that he hadn't been chosen for the elite team. Neither had I for that matter.

The mosquitoes and gnats ate me alive that night, with my hot, exposed face clad in bug repellant peeking out of the sleeping bag. The combination of eighty degrees at midnight with no discernible wind proved beyond my patience. So I took off on foot in the dark silence, out of Hooper Circle, and felt like I'd just broken out of prison. I had visions of Daddy and Blackie Savage slipping out of the barn shadows holding twin rifles and aiming them in my direction. So I ran. I had enough wind to jog for ten minutes to PJ's Auto Body Shop and from there cut through a bunch of backyards, hopping fences. I even climbed halfway up a crooked old tree at one point, if for no other reason than to celebrate being out and alone at midnight, liberated from a family who'd cast me out and replaced me with an newborn baby and a city doctor. My sneakers gave good tread for tree climbing, and I got up pretty high at one point, precariously perched with my arms and legs dangling off a thick branch. And when I looked down on Grady, my eyes landed on Janet's house. I knew I hadn't come out here for nothing.

I cased the yard first, making note of the proximity of Janet's aunt's bedroom to hers. They were ideally situated on opposite sides of the house. So I started with three pebbles against the window.

No response.

I threw the only other one my fingers could find in the dark. I could see her face without even seeing it, her shiny hair and the pink glow of her cheeks. I pictured us rolling around on the damp earth below her

bedroom window, trying hard to muffle the sounds of heavy breathing and rustling clothes and flesh and zippers. I already knew what it
would be like with Janet because I'd done it with her a hundred times
already, if only in the confines of my head. It didn't matter, though.
Fake sex was the same thing as real sex if it's with someone you love.
Janet loved me, didn't she? She had practically given herself to me in
my truck not too long ago, until—

"You. You there! What do you want?"

My stomach clenched in a concave shape at the gritty voice.

"You!"

I just stood there, too scared to move and even more scared to
look up.

seventeen

"Idiot."

"What?"

It was dark, but I could see the glowing whites of Mikey's eyes. "Do you think I don't know her voice by now?" I said. "I'm sure it wasn't her. Must've been her creepy aunt," I said, and reminded myself to tread lightly.

"How'd you know what her aunt sounds like?"

When she knocked on the truck window while I was pulling Janet's clothes off, I thought. "I called over there." I spoke softly so he'd think telling him was a real concession.

"What, like once?"

"Yeah, once." Good, I thought. Be defensive.

We assumed the typical position after that, lying side by side on the grimy old tree house mattress, elevated twenty feet off the ground between the gnarled branches of a maple tree. Since I was post–heart attack, I had my head down and Mikey leaned up on his elbows using a flashlight to read the latest Batman comic.

"What do you think Nelda was doing out there anyway?"

"At Van Geller's? Hard to say."

"Either you know or you don't know." Mikey's arms were crossed.

"Well, how should I know for sure? I've worked for the woman for three weeks and I'm no closer to knowing either her or her dead daughter than I was when I started."

"He gave her something. Like a piece of paper."

Money, I thought, but I didn't dare say it out loud. "I know. We'll look for it next time we work on the shed. She's way too absentminded to even think about being sneaky. So whatever he gave her'll probably still be on her desk if we go there tomorrow. And the desk's right near the front door, so you know, easy access." I flashed a devilish smile at him, but he was back to looking at the comic book.

"First season, first five," he said, meaning I had to name the first five episodes of the first season of the Superman series.

"I'm too tired."

"Loser."

"You are," I snapped. "You didn't get caught outside some girl's bedroom after midnight. You just sat up here all night playing with yourself."

"Shut up," he said. Now I'd really wounded him. "What if I wasn't alone?"

"Right. Like you snuck Carmella up here with you? You would have gotten it stuck inside your zipper and she'd have fallen out of the tree house."

Mikey aimed the flashlight beam at my face. "Why'd you say that?"

"Because disaster follows you everywhere. It's the curse of the Savages."

The flashlight went out and Mikey put his head sadly on the pillow. Time for some quick thinking, surely not my best asset. "Superman and the Mole Men," I said. If that couldn't draw him out, nothing would.

"Wrong! That was the pilot. Doesn't count as the first season."

I feigned distress, rubbing my eyes and looking at the tree house ceiling looming just over our heads. "Okay, first season was . . . Superman on Earth."

"Right—"

"The Haunted Lighthouse—"

"Right—"

"Shut up, will ya, and let me think. Case of the Talkative Dummy, Mystery of the Broken Statues, and . . . um . . . I forget. The Monkey-something."

"*Mystery*. The Monkey Mystery. Loser," he added, under his breath.

It was beautifully silent for a while. No wind skirting through the leaves and tree branches, no Mikey-snoring, and no Mrs. Savage screaming at his twin younger brothers for talking after lights-out. The sound of crickets on the ground beneath us lulled me into the first moments of relaxation I'd felt all week. Maybe in a month.

"Aha! Here's one that I bet you forgot. Who played Lois for the first two seasons?"

"Go to sleep," I moaned.

"What are you a goddamned old lady? Come on. Answer it. Unless you just don't know."

"Phyllis Coates," I said, rolling my eyes.

"Jimmy Olsen?"

"Jack Larson."

"Perry White?"

"John Hamilton. Any retard could answer these." To Mikey, these words could incite war.

I heard him opening the cigar box standing upright on the ledge in the corner. Now I was in for it.

"I'm too tired for a quiz. Let's do it when we wake up."

"Too tired or maybe just . . . scaaaaaaaaard?" he sang. "Freddy's done this one, so's Jimmy Wilson. Guess they're both just smarter than you."

"They'll be twenty-five by the time they graduate. Shit, they've been kept back two grades already."

"Lie," he yelled, though I couldn't imagine why he'd be sticking up for those two. "Jimmy never stayed back and Freddy was only kept back once and then he studied real hard and he's back up to tenth grade in the fall."

"Great, we'll just call him Brainiac from now on."

"Asshole."

"You are." I wanted to smack him, but instead my head fell hard against the pillow.

In my dream, a mutation of both Daddy and Blackie Savage was holding a rifle in each arm and chasing me through the haunted baseball field. I turned back to look at him/them and the creature had Daddy's thin white face superimposed on Blackie's lunky frame. Then after I ran some more, I turned again and saw the opposite, but Blackie's head on Daddy's body looked even more fundamentally wrong, like an infant wearing a jack-o-lantern on its shoulders. All Blackie's teeth were missing and his mouth was formed into a large "o" where he called out to me over the flat, grassy plain. "Ohhhhhhhhhhhhhh," he/they chorused behind me in a horrific, ghostly timbre. We were outside in the open but the sound echoed like four walls had closed in on us. Closed walls in a room that kept moving south with the rhythm of my feet. My feet moved slow like trying to run through water or moving through outer space. But I was no astronaut. In the dream I was just my own vulnerable self, out running by myself in the darkness, being chased, once again, by an entity of unknown origin. This time when I turned, I saw that Blackie had vacated the body and it was only Daddy, but now PJ was beside him. PJ? From PJ's Auto Body? And they stopped running and started pushing each other, and then arguing, though their screams and yells were something out of a horror movie. I was too scared to move, but even more terrified to stand still. Something was coming up on me through the tall grass. By the sound of it, someone was dragging something behind them, like a blanket, or a body. Part of me felt the moist mattress under my face and knew I was in the tree house, but the gluey part of my brain clung to the dream and the baseball field and its quarry of demons. The grass parted now, and Blackie stood before me, his own head properly intact, and behind him was a blanket. I bent down to inspect it and saw a streak of dark red blood and long black hair. I moved slowly, circling around the still form, and saw the perfect, angelic, tormented white face.

A soft wind blew on my face and carried with it the faint scent of peppermint. It wasn't the cold, grainy wind I felt from the opened window in my bedroom at home. This wind was warm, and it hummed.

Janet.

My eyes, thin slits, saw her leaning over me and immediately my thoughts went to Mikey lying on the mattress beside me.

"Heard you wanted to see me." When she smiled, I saw a hint of pink gloss on her lips.

I turned over. Mikey was snoring, and I remembered, then, that you could vacuum the blankets on his bed without waking him. "Your aunt told you?"

Her eyes widened. "Yelled is more like it. My mother got an earful at six o'clock this morning."

Today was Sunday. I'd never hear the end of this. "I didn't mean to get you in trouble."

"Are you kidding? Girls never get in trouble."

She was sitting precariously close, and I felt sure that if she kissed me, some internal radar in Mikey's body would shake him from sleep. "I'll bet you don't," I said, just to throw words into the air.

"And I'll bet Mikey gets in trouble every day. Seems like trouble sticks to boys like him."

She leaned in close again and I felt something shift in my body, a guilt really, that blocked off any libidinous impulses and instead returned me to the fact that Mary McCann would never have someone like I had Janet. Never again would she flirt with a boy from school or someone from her neighborhood, and until I found her killer and brought them to some sort of justice, I would abstain from any kind of pleasure with Janet. She reached up and did something to her blouse. I couldn't tell if she unbuttoned it or just adjusted her bra strap, but she seemed to be preparing for something. I had to act now and prevent disaster.

"I'd better get up. I hear Mikey's mother clanging around the kitchen."

Janet jerked back with suspicious eyes. "I didn't hear anything."

I glanced at Mikey, and his head was rolling back and forth like it always did when he woke up. Janet was still sitting on the edge of the mattress closest to me, and to Mikey, this would only mean one thing.

"Hey." Now he sat straight up.

"Hey."

"Good morning," Janet said.

"What are you doing here?" Mikey said and glanced back and forth between us, looking at our eyes and at our clothing. He stared at the bulging front of Janet's thin yellow blouse for a few seconds too long. She crossed her arms in front of her.

"Hey asshole, get a good look?" I whispered.

"What? If she doesn't like it, she can tell me herself. She don't need you fighting for her."

"I don't like it," Janet said with the first look of defiance I'd ever seen on her.

He gave a pathetic "sorry" and started reading one of his comics.

"I came over to see what you wanted."

"What *I* wanted?" Mikey's eyes widened. "Jake's the one who threw rocks at your window at midnight."

Janet looked at me. "But my aunt said the boy outside my window said his name was Mikey Savage."

"I'm a coward, what can I say? I froze when I knew that she saw me and I couldn't think of what to do or say."

Janet lowered her eyes.

"She's pretty scary, you have to admit."

"Yes, she is."

"Jeez, Jake, that's worse than anything I'd even do."

I couldn't look at him. "I knew I'd be sleeping here, so I said your name so Janet would come over here in the morning. Which she did."

"Which I did," she affirmed, but Mikey wasn't buying it.

"I like the coward theory myself." He moved toward the door, pulled up his socks, and tucked his shirt in. "I gotta go inside for a minute."

Janet smiled as soon as Mikey left, and I tried not to think about my severe misfortune—Janet waiting to kiss me in the tree house and Mikey sulking over corn flakes in the kitchen.

"I'm back at my house now, and my parents are going out tonight." Pause. "I thought you might want to come over."

"Don't you have any brothers and sisters?" I couldn't imagine anything different.

"My Ma couldn't have anymore kids."

"I'd like to, but I'm not sure when I'll be home. Besides, my sister's baby came home from the hospital yesterday and they might need my help."

Janet left shortly after that and I could tell I'd hurt her feelings. But as I looked out the tree house door, I knew I had bigger problems. Standing at the back door screen were Mikey and his brother Blackie. Blackie had his arm on Mikey's shoulder.

eighteen

Blackie must have been off duty that day, because he wasn't wearing his black cowboy hat. Of course most sworn police officers in this country weren't strictly prohibited from wearing any kind of civilian hat, but I had already learned the lesson about rules that apply to only certain people. The only rule Blackie Savage lived by was the one that claimed his exemption to all rules. All he wore was a pair of torn, grungy dungarees with his big, flat feet sticking out and a Mets T-shirt. Somehow he seemed slightly less dehumanizing without his steel-toed boots. Blackie looked down at Mikey and nudged him out the screen door.

"What's with you, runt? You wet the bed again?"

Mikey's jaw was clenched tight as he studied my face. "He stole my girl."

"Who?" Blackie laughed. "Him?"

"And he crashed through some girl's window and blamed it on me."

Something told me not to argue, to let him say his piece and maybe, by some freak chance, Blackie was in a negotiating mood and would give me my turn.

"That true, Jake?"

My face worked as I searched for the correct expression. Guilt? No. Disinterest? Definitely not. So I feigned a look of mild annoyance. "No."

"Who's the gi-rl?" Blackie asked in a singsongy voice.

"Janet. You know, PJ's niece."

Blackie shot his head back and smiled at the sky. "So Jakie, you steal her out from under Mikey's nose or what?"

"She's not mine to steal. And I threw a rock at her window and woke up her aunt is all."

Blackie came outside and stood in the center of the yard between the back door and the tree house stairs. "Looks like this calls for a good, clean fight."

Blackie Savage—Conflict Resolution Expert. "I didn't do nothing and you know it," I addressed Mikey. "You're too lame to own up to the truth of it."

"Yeah? And what's that?" Mikey's face was red and swollen. "Dumb ass." I thought he might actually cry.

"You're just mad because she likes me better than you. Aren't you?"

Blackie crossed his arms. So much for my defense. "Jake," he said and dug his bare heel into the sand to draw a line, "stand here and don't move. You each get one punch and then it's over. You two retards have been friends since you was babies. At least find a worthy cause to break you up. Not just some dumb, skinny girl."

Mikey's eyes teared. "She's not dumb, Blackie. And, well," he sniffed, "I love her." Tears rolling. "And he's trying to steal her."

Laughter spilled out of me like jelly beans from a glass jar. I tried to hold it in but the harder I tried, more came out of me. I laughed so hard I fell back on the hard ground and pointed at Mikey. Then when my head was pointed up at the tree house, I felt something hard on my nose and everything went black.

I woke up a second later and felt something running down my nose—blood. Mikey paced around me like a hungry cougar, still wiping tears from his eyes, and he bent down to tie his sneakers. I tried to scramble my limbs to a standing position, but before I could get the flats of my sneakers on the ground, he kicked me hard in the ribs. He tried it a second time and I squirmed away too quick. But there was no running from him. This was a Blackie-endorsed ass-schwamping and my only possible escape would be death.

Doubled over, I felt another kick in my left side. Mikey was yelling for me to get up. Stand up, he kept saying. Get up, loser. Loser, loser, get up. Now. Now. I knew if I looked at Blackie, he'd be smiling.

"Hey! What's going on out here?"

It was Mrs. Savage. And that was the first time I ever believed in God.

NINeteeN

Note to self in next life: don't form any human attachments. It made a pretty bleak picture: no parents, siblings, grandparents, no girl to come home to every night, no friends to hang out with. But I was sure the pain of loneliness was nothing compared to the knowledge of true alienation. I didn't need any of them. Needs and attachments were just illusions. No one was really, deep down, connected to anybody else except through a weakness in the mind.

It was hard to settle into the hard seat of Nelda's truck with my body banged up from Mikey's haphazard assault. He'd never be a prizefighter but he did what he wanted to do—weaken me in front of his sadistic brother. To Blackie, that was worth the price of fifty cartons of unfiltered Camels and all the German beer he could ever drink in his life. To see someone like me writhing on the hard ground, squelched like a common cockroach, was his life's greatest dream. Even doomsday couldn't touch Blackie.

It was still early, just past eight, and I felt like I hadn't eaten in weeks. When I looked in the rearview mirror, my face looked too bad to stop in anywhere and eat. Without any water with me to clean up, the red swelling on the right cheek and the caked, dried blood in my nostrils made me unsuitable for even the café in Ringling. Highway 81 to Enid was so flat I could see the back of my head. Miles of green grass covered the land on each side of the road, and the scant trace of a funnel cloud hovered overhead to the east. God no, I thought.

Miraculously, I reached Enid in one piece in less than an hour. I'd been driving eighty, secretly waiting for Blackie to put on those big blue lights and pull me over. The light would be off in Nelda's kitchen. She hated lights in the morning, as they demanded her eyes wake up before they were ready. She said that once, though it wasn't like the kind of communication I had with Janet, or even with Mikey sometimes. Her small, shifty eyes and skinny neck combined in awkward movements every time she spoke, and each thought was articulated with perfect diction and no eye contact. That was the curse of the undead—she had no attachments to things or people. To Nelda, a couch wasn't something you plopped down on after a long day at school or a grueling day at work—it didn't carry the scent of Grandpa Weaver's Cuban cigars or have stains on the undersides from spaghetti sauce and red wine. To her, a sofa was a place to sit. Maybe something soft to rest her bony frame on, but not a splinter more or less.

For Nelda McCann, life had become a series of mathematical equations. Moving from her smoking chair at the kitchen table to the back patio required exactly twenty-five steps, and then another fifty to go back and pour a fresh cup of mind-numbing coffee and return to the patio. She breathed, she blinked, she bathed on occasion, and once in a while she changed her clothes. But forget about looking in the mirror, noticing what she was wearing, matching the color of a shirt to a pair of pants.

She greeted me the same way she always did—with a careless wave of her head toward the street. I found her in the field in the backyard again, angling her head down this time, like the invisible man in her head was lying beneath her on the ground. I told her I needed to look around in her basement to see what tools she had there.

"Do you believe in ghosts, Jake?"

It was the first time she had ever said my name. Before answering her, I stood back to look at her, and noticed she was wearing all black—polyester pants and a black long-sleeved shirt—completely inappropriate for summer in Oklahoma. Her small, inscrutable eyes were focused on something far off: something invisible to my eyes but that didn't stop her from looking. There was a resolve to the way she was standing, too. Normally she kept her arms slack at her sides, like she didn't care whether she got pierced in the chest with a sharp object or not. In the three days since I'd been gone, something here, in this house, had changed.

"Should I?" I asked.

"You either live in this world or out of this world. And when you lose a child, if you loved that child, you're locked out of that same world of normalcy, of eating and sleeping, and dreaming and hoping, and you spend the rest of your days walking among the dead. Because you can never give up that hope and silent prayer that someday the clocks will turn back and fate will restore that one missing, vital link. A parent can never let go." Then she looked right at me. "So tell me, do you believe?"

"You mean in ghosts, Nelda?"

No response.

"Well, I've seen one. Does that mean I'm crazy or something?" I thought better of the word "crazy" a second too late. And I could see, by the way her head fell back a few inches, that the word stung her sensibilities.

"It means welcome to the underworld."

Because Nelda wasn't burdened by the customary urge of human curiosity, I knew I wouldn't need to worry about her snooping down the basement steps while I rummaged around in her personal belongings. And speaking of rummaging, I could probably snoop in the drawers of her desk by the front door. I had a vested interest in this, as Mikey and I had found Walter Van Geller first, or at least long before we ever made the connection to Nelda. So, in that way, she sort of owed us an explanation of what she was doing at his house three days ago. It was weak logic, but I was alone, cast out and desperate by now, so what did I have to lose?

Death was visible in every square inch of Nelda's desk. Its grainy, oak exterior poised for giving splinters, and three weighty piles of bills and paperwork were stacked across the surface. On the very top was a miniature stained glass lamp, one of those shiny-wood, rounded radios, a brass mantel clock, and three empty spots where picture frames had once likely stood. I swallowed, thought of the baseball diamond, and yanked open the top left drawer.

Partially stuck to the hinges, I had to bang the drawer with my fist on one side, the fist I used to throw my first punch at Mikey's jaw. I wriggled it left and right and it finally opened a few inches. With my hand underneath it, I guided it out and found small pieces of metal strewn along the bare wood bottom. Then I heard something behind me near the front door.

"Looking for something?"

I don't know where she came from, but I could swear I saw Nelda in the backyard field not ten seconds ago. Was she a goddamned ghost now, like that creepy man that visited her? Were they a whole family of ghosts? And for some odd reason, I felt as calm as if I'd been sleeping.

"Yes, Nelda."

I could see, from her reflection in the kitchen windows, that she'd crossed her arms. And in some moment of freakish courage, I slowly turned around. "What were you doing at Walter Van Geller's house?"

"Who?"

My heart thudded against my ribcage, less from the fear of Nelda's wrath and more from the accumulated anger at her reticence. Time was running out. School was starting in less than a month and once it did, that would be the end of Nelda and Enid and her beat-up Chevy truck and my paying job. So I ignored her. I jacked open the drawer on the right. A small envelope stuck up at an odd angle, hastily put away, like it had been wedged on top of something thick. My fingers touched it but I turned to Nelda before removing it.

"This?" I said, threatening her with my courage. "What's this?"

"Nothing that concerns you."

I pulled it out. It had the words "Nelda McCann" scrawled in blue pen. "Is this what Walter van Geller gave you when you went to his house? Is it?"

She was unmoved by my demands. Her face looked serene and open, the way it did when she was listening to the invisible man who spoke to her in the back field. "I don't," she stopped to clear her throat, "I don't know of anyone by that name."

Fingerprints. I thought of fingerprints then, with one of my hands touching the envelope. I thought about asking Blackie (was I out of my mind?) to see if Van Geller's fingerprints were on the envelope to

117

prove that he gave it to Nelda. And there I was, suddenly, a fifteen-year-old detective, a modern Sherlock Holmes wearing torn Levi's and a dirty T-shirt. Some homage to Conan Doyle.

Okay, so my detective mind started working then, analyzing the symbolism of Nelda's response. "I don't know anyone by that name" was what she had said. So she cared enough about something or someone to conceal the truth from me, which showed that I was of some importance to her. And deceit and concealment require a certain amount of forethought, care, and planning. Was Nelda McCann alive after all? Had I misjudged her vacant expression and apathetic demeanor? I had a feeling Nelda had more than just a few surprises up her sleeve.

She wouldn't take her eyes off my hand in the desk drawer. The brass clock ticked slow seconds between us, and though I couldn't hear her breathing, I could see her chest rising and falling in quick breaths. I gently pulled my hand from the drawer and closed it. Before she could say a word, I disappeared through the kitchen door that retreated down the dark basement stairs.

twenty

Some things are better left unexplained. That hollow purgatory of illusion followed me down Nelda's steps like a sleeping shadow. It had no discernible shape, smell, or form, but I felt it just the same. It slid against my left elbow, a silky whisper of cold breath, as I turned the corner into the basement's main room. I could hear Nelda in the kitchen, yet I was being followed.

Was it Mary?

Maybe it was Nelda's mysterious ghost. And maybe I wasn't getting enough sleep lately.

"Is it you?" I called out, careful to keep my mouth aimed toward the water heater in the far corner. "Are you down here, Mary, hiding from a life that betrayed you?" I swore she could hear me because the shadow moved when I said the words. I had my arms outstretched like sleepwalkers in those old horror movies, but not because my vision was impaired. My palms were faced upward in front of me to tap into the vein of the unseen. Maybe, through palpation, I would sense or feel the edge of form where air morphs into something else, something quiet and dark, invisible and lonely.

I knew there were things in this world that *couldn't* be seen, but only felt, sensed, smelled, or perceived through the fog of peripheral vision. Beings that latched on to the hem of your coat or the soles of your shoes, and followed you, watching, and waiting—not to harm you but for your own moment of discovery.

I kept my eyes on concrete things that I could explain, normal parts of every person's basement in Enid in 1961. There were shelves of glass jars crammed full of white slimy things on the wall. Could have been pears, or maybe turnips. In front of the shelves was an old, headless mannequin, wearing a pleated, white petticoat and a pin-tucked yellow blouse. More rows of shelves were on the east wall, but these held store-bought goods in the weirdest combination: cans of condensed milk next to tobacco. Evaporated milk, bittersweet chocolate, brown sugar, and beets. Then, I counted them, thirty-three cans of green beans, lima beans, and asparagus. Stacked floor to ceiling was a wall of grains in uniform, five-pound bags. White rice, garbanzo beans, and lentils. Bottles of cola had been arranged under the stairs beside a dark, pirate-looking chest. From ten feet away you'd never see it, but when I crouched down and touched it, it creaked. I was afraid it would fall apart if I touched it, or maybe I was more afraid of the consequences of peeking at something that was clearly not my affair.

But conscience and curiosity—the Blackie and Whitey that snipe at each other from each of my shoulders—were at war. Open it, one of them whispered. No, don't! Yes, open it. Don't. My fingers reached out for the lock mechanism even before any forethought had time to take root in my consciousness. I had no flashlight and saw only a cavern of darkness inside. I picked up the chest with both hands, shook it, and metal jangled on the bottom. The small shards of shrapnel in Nelda's desk drawer upstairs came to mind, but this time I found a bunch of stray keys inside. I picked them up—there were nine—and stuffed them in my pockets: an ancient explorer armed with the accoutrements of scientific discovery. Still, I had no flashlight. My empty eyes and hands only probed me deeper in fear.

But I couldn't stop my feet from moving. From a vantage point in the center of the basement cavern, I saw a door to my right, a high platform behind me on which stood an old-fashioned, tub-style washing machine, and to my left, a corridor. Something about the concrete floor and the deep cold that bled up through my sneakers reminded me of death. There was so much of it in this house embedded in the walls and the ceilings; even the scent of decay tangled in the carpet fibers upstairs. My mind did not want to go down the corridor, but my heart, that organ composed of iron resolve since that night on the baseball diamond, had other plans.

My pupils were sufficiently dilated to see the bend in the walkway.

A heavy, black apparatus covered the wall on the right and the left side had stray boxes, empty wooden crates, and wooden dowels angled against a corner pocket. A window above my head, caked in fifty years of dust and oily grime, lit a path to the end of the walkway for me. In front of the tall door, I jiggled the keys in my pocket, but it opened with the slightest shove of my shoulder. A large version of my bedroom closet, it had high ceilings with two more windows near it, and more shelves, but these were filled with nails and tacks, screws, bolts, and a large open coffee can full of just wrenches. Someone, probably Nelda's husband, had made a wall-to-wall sawhorse that functioned as a table, complete with a vise on one side and jigsaws dangling from ceiling hooks over it. It made me think of Vincent Price in *The Pit and the Pendulum*, which Mikey and I saw four times at the theater so I had every scene committed to memory. Instead of Enid, Oklahoma, I was suddenly transported to sixteenth-century Spain and I was Francis Bonnard visiting my sister's castle to discern the reason for her untimely death. But who was the demented scientist here? Mary's father/Nelda's husband? Did Nelda even have a husband? Of course the tools had belonged to some man, somewhere in this family's past, but who had been possessed enough to make a wall-sized sawhorse? My fingers touched the edge of a shelf. I looked up into the cavernous ceiling and wondered if someone had been making doors. What else would require the use of such a long table? A coffin, perhaps?

Then I wondered about Nelda, whom she was talking to, and where she was. I pictured her crouched down inside one of the upstairs closets with her ear pressed to the floorboards, monitoring my movements, listening for the sound of doors opening or keys plunging through old, crumbly locks. I heard a noise above my head just then, but it was only the sound of a glass jar wobbling on the shelf I'd been touching. A door came into my line of vision by accident. My eyes had not sought it out, and no other part of me had sensed it. My focus just arrived there. Three steps out of the room and back onto the winding, concrete-floored corridor, I squinted at the shape of the lock and fumbled with the keys in my front pocket. They were old and long, and they dug into the skin of my hips.

"Get out of there."

Silence.

"Go on, get out. Get away from there!"

Every strand of hair on my body stuck out at a ninety-degree angle. My palms were instantly soaked.

"Get down, boy. Now. Get out, come on, off, off, there you go now—"

It was Nelda's voice.

"Geddown. Geddown from there!"

She was talking to a dog. God help me.

"Leave the dog alone." A man's voice now, low and monotone.

"It's in my yard," Nelda said.

"Dogs are curious. Curiosity's not always a good thing."

I couldn't see Nelda or the man, but I could tell his words had stopped Nelda dead in her tracks.

"Neither is meddling in someone else's affair."

"My affair. Just like yours."

There was a long pause then, during which I found two metal drums hidden in a darkened corner. To my advantage, they were positioned diagonally under the window. In an instant, I climbed on one and lifted a wooden crate on top of it that brought me almost to window level. The window was too grimy to see out of. It barely even looked like glass, but when I spit on the hem of my T-shirt and rubbed hard, I scraped off a small circle. I could see Nelda, standing the same way she was standing when she caught me rummaging through her desk drawer—arms folded, lips tight and contracted. But she was breathing heavily and moving her head slightly left to right. Was she crying? With expert movements, she lifted one hand and wiped a single tear from her right eye. But from my position on the drum, she seemed to be talking to an oak tree.

Where was the man? And, more importantly, who was he?

"She belonged to both of us, don't forget," the man said.

"People don't belong to anyone but themselves. We agree to stay with each other for a short time, a trifle, before we leave this world."

Nelda turned her back now, and I caught the man's shadow moving across the ground. Then I noticed there was another metal drum. Quietly, I climbed off the wooden crate and moved it to the next drum, steadied my weight on the top, and angled my head up near the peek hole.

"You've got to stay away, Nelda. There's no reason for it. Not anymore."

Nelda laughed, then, a laugh crammed full of fear and hate. "You don't know anything. Why are you here, anyway? Did your 'elders' tell you to visit me?" She mocked the word "elders" through clenched teeth.

"*Ak akostinincho.*"

Ah, finally, a glimpse of the man's back. There was a mane of black hair down past his shoulders and a stretched-out white T-shirt hanging down over his thick waist. His dungarees were torn along the cuffs and a wallet was stuck in the back pocket. He had a solid, blocky build. Maybe five feet, ten inches, 190 pounds.

"None of your business anymore. So there's nothing to understand." Nelda walked toward the house and the man stood perfectly still. Unless I could somehow detach my head from my body, I'd still only see the back of him, but it was enough for now. I'd made my conclusions.

A rumbling under me caught my attention. My body weight angled the crate back and forth against the thick steel drum. I pressed my left foot into the drum's surface but it was too late. A loud screech jerked the man's head toward the basement window as the crate cracked off the drum and fell on the concrete floor. My knobby knees hit the drum and it echoed so loud I was sure I'd woken all of Nelda's dead ghosts.

twenty-one

Worse yet, I caught sight of the man's torn pant legs beside the cellar window.

My hands cushioned the thud of my body sliding off the drum, and my flesh slapped against the raw concrete. With my cheeks pressed into its coldness, I looked up and saw the holy grail of Nelda's past—another door.

The pant legs vanished from the window and I had no idea where the man was now. With my luck, he was probably following Nelda inside and preparing to hunt down the varmint squirming around in her basement. Nelda wouldn't protect me from him, whoever he was. I knew that. Her only allegiance was to her dead daughter and the host of secrets surrounding her.

It was a regular door: the kind you'd find on an upstairs bathroom. I expected a tall, looming medieval thing that echoed back centuries when you slammed it. I pressed the knob's center button to lock it behind me and tugged on the dangling chain in the center of the room. A light switched on, flickered, and then went off. I jumped back toward the door and cranked the knob to unlock it.

Nothing happened.

Jesus, I thought. They're gonna find my shriveled body in here five years from now with my nails ground down from trying to claw my way out through the bulkhead. I felt my heart sink into a kind of despair that I'd read about in books—sinking down from the bright light into an abyss of cold, dark nothingness. My arms broke out in goose bumps, half from the cold and half from the bald terror of being locked in a basement full of livid spirits. I could feel the hives forming on the smooth skin of my face and neck. My nose clogged while tears flooded my vision of darkness.

I had no one now. No family, no Mikey. Nelda and the yardman would find me snooping down here and I'd probably end up like Mary, cast out into the netherworld to haunt the fields and prairies of the heartland.

I heard noises upstairs in the kitchen—Nelda making her twentieth pot of coffee. This sound somehow returned me to a sense of safety and familiarity. Women in kitchens with coffee. It all seemed very right and wholesome, and maybe I wasn't completely off track after all.

My mother made the strongest coffee west of the Mississippi, and did it without the slightest hint of mental preparation. Her people worked in the oil fields in eastern Wyoming. On her mother's side was a long lineage of Cody ranchers. Coffee, to them, was a necessity not unlike hot food and shelter, and as indigenous as Big Sky. Grandma Weaver taught us how to make cowboy coffee out of an old aluminum pot, and to keep the grounds out of our cups, she poured a flash of cold water into the pot just before pouring. Mama made coffee, eggs, toast, and bacon for all four of us in no time. But Nelda's footsteps were slow and tentative. I heard her rubber-soled slippers shuffle along the linoleum as she filled the pot at the sink. Nelda's brain wasn't working right, and until it did, her coffee would remain too weak like the rest of her.

My eyes started to adjust to the dark for the second time that day. And I knew the rule about dark places: the eyes only could adjust to darkness if some bit of light filtered inside. I knew this from the stories Mikey told me about how when he was little, Blackie used to lock him in the trunk of his car for hours at a time. Then, if he stopped screaming for a minute or two, Blackie would sometimes let him out and bring him to a broom closet and lock him in there for a while. Then, the incentive for not screaming was that he'd be released into a slightly bigger space. This practice persisted every time Mikey tried to talk to Blackie. One time, when Mikey borrowed some of Blackie's toothpaste from the downstairs bathroom, Blackie locked him in the trunk of his car overnight with nothing but a flashlight and a box of Twinkies.

When I opened my eyes wide, I could see how the small room was compartmentalized, with big things stacked on top of other big things, and all the small things bunched together against the wall. Old-fashioned popcorn popper, fireplace grate, and all kinds of boot scrapers. Something curved caught my eye. The shape of it suggested one of those old Crosley radios from the '30s with the rounded tops and cathedral-style speaker openings.

But this was no radio.

I slid my sweaty palms over the surface, and it felt cold like stone. All my body weight combined couldn't lift it off the floor, but the top separated from the bottom when I dug my nails into the center crevice. A trunk.

The sun must have come out during my brief exile in this dungeon, because I could see better now, not like I was reading a Sherlock Holmes or comic book near my bedroom window, but enough to see my way around. In my panic, I'd strayed from the door, and I could see now that the trunk had been hidden behind some big boxes and wooden crates.

I had to think—establish a plan of taking these artifacts with me for further research, like Sherlock Holmes who always managed to remove a tiny sample of forensic evidence from every crime scene, whether it was a partial fingerprint, a single hair, or a blob of ink on fine writing paper. The light seeping in from above illuminated the edges of a pile of photographs, tossed haphazardly into the gaping container—all of them turned over and facing downward. Odd, I thought, that someone had taken the time to flip them over after carelessly flinging them inside the trunk. I squinted to get a closer look at the images—they were babies, mostly, and some toddlers and young children. The backs of the pictures showed scrawling penmanship obviously etched by someone's left hand, with three lines each of writing. Name, date, and presumably parents. Squinting further, further, leaning my head closer to the thread of light bleeding in from the wall seams, it occurred to me that I was leaning toward sunlight while listening to the steady drum of . . . rain.

Where was the light coming from?

A flash of panic snaked through my body and turned adolescent flesh into sinew. I folded an armful of the photographs into the front of my pants, ran blindly through the dark hovel, and shoved open the bulkhead doors. The right one, heavier because of the thick cross brace along the center, got stuck on the hinge, so I used my hands and the top of my head to push open the other. It made a hard slap against the wall, but I didn't care to wait around for Nelda's reaction to this. And who knows where the longhaired man was by now—probably outside the basement door. For all I cared, they could go to hell, every last one of them. I was tired of running, feeling scared all the time, and always looking over my shoulder. It was time for some answers. Now, before it was too late.

twenty-two

I couldn't help but wonder about Mikey. He'd be at Freddie's house with Jimmy Wilson, hiding downstairs in that crummy basement laundry room where his father kept a stash of *Playboy* magazines behind the file cabinet. All this over someone like Carmella Jeffers. I love her, Mikey said. And the notion of him actually loving anybody was even more ridiculous than him saying it. Not that he was beyond love, or aloof to it necessarily, but to love meant having an intelligence about feelings and emotions. That was Mikey's missing link.

I knew how it would go now, or at least for a while. If I so much as talked to him, he'd sic Blackie on me like his private pit bull—the two of them having the only alliance ever in their lives with me as the unlikely, and unwilling, catalyst.

The path from Enid back to Grady was a perfect straight line— Route 3 through Kingfisher and Canadian counties became Route 81 just shy of Oklahoma City, and 81 spilled right into Jefferson County. I had the state map laid out beside me on the seat. With alternating glances between it and the road, I could see that Grady was also a straight shot west of a place called Sand Bluff in Choctaw County.

My obsession with Mary McCann, over the past twenty-four hours, had modulated to Indians. Choctaw County was mostly Indian, I guessed, and my only tangible connection to it was the word Sand Bluff scrawled across the back of each of the photographs I stole from Nelda's basement. I hadn't looked at them real good yet, but something kinked up in my gut as I flipped through the black and white images—some kind of otherworldly thing, not like ghosts but more like the acknowledgement of the presence of evil. The evil in Nelda's basement, I feared, was more than just ghosts of her dead relatives.

From Route 81, I got on Route 53A toward Comanche, where that little creek was that Mikey and me fished from so many times. We had the same argument every time, deciding about whether it fed off the Wildhorse River up in Stephens County or Waurika Lake. Like all our arguments, nobody won and they each dissolved eventually. Sometimes after we fished, we'd hitch a ride into Comanche where they had a pretty good comic book store. Not all comics, of course, but a better selection than anywhere else around. Then we'd get a burger on the way home at Ringling Tavern where the owner didn't mind feeding us for free.

I didn't know why I was going to Comanche Creek, as we called it. The closest thing I had to fishing tackle was a ball of twine in the back of Nelda's truck. But I knew of a bait shop on the edge of town near the livery stables.

Best Bait had the front door propped open with a rickety wooden chair. Even before I stepped in, I caught the foul smell of day-old fish and knew I'd be smelling it for the next few days.

"Doc says he died in his sleep," I heard someone say at the front counter. I kept walking toward the bait shop in the back of the store.

"Who?"

"You got your ears on backwards, Henry? Who'd you think? Ranch Nettle."

I turned around and saw Henry shaking his head. "Ranch Nettle wasn't the kind of man to die quietly in his living room. Way I heard it, he had an altercation with someone at the stables late last night."

"Who told you that?" the woman asked him. She had a rabid voice and bright orange lipstick.

Just as Henry was about to answer her, a barrel-chested man in a plaid shirt approached the counter. "What would you like, boy?" All the old timers called us "boy," meaning Mikey and me.

"Canadian night crawlers," I said.

The man peered at me over the top of his glasses. "You got your tackle already?"

"No sir, I forgot it. I was sort of hoping I could borrow a rod and reel from someone, or maybe you rent them by the day?"

The man's lips puckered. "You got money to be renting gear? Boy your age?"

"Yes sir."

He uncrossed his arms and set his hands flat on the counter. "You want them nightcrawlers by the pound or the dozen?" He paused and checked my expression. "You all alone today?"

I nodded.

"Dozen'll do you fine then, I should say. Fifteen cents, and another fifty for the rod and reel."

I jiggled the change in my pocket and knew I had enough. "Anything biting today?" I held out the money.

The man stayed quiet like he had a big secret waiting to spill out. "Go on and take 'em now. Just have everything back here by closing time and we'll call it even."

I could neither explain nor reconcile the man's sudden kindness, but I took the bait and tackle and went off. Maybe hearing about the dead man had instilled some sense of temporary charity in him that he couldn't ignore. Henry and his orange-lipped mistress were still talking about the dead man on my way out. I suspected I'd be hearing about Ranch Nettle for the next few weeks. That's how death was in these parts—fodder that gave people something to hash and rehash over the dinner table, at the fill-up stations and country stores. Sometimes I wondered about people's preoccupation with rites like birth and death, and why they couldn't learn to appreciate the long period between them a little more.

I parked Nelda's old clunker beside a wire fence a short walk from the creek. Mikey and me usually hitched a ride to this same mile marker, as that's where we caught ten fish one Sunday afternoon last fall. It was a lucky place for us. Maybe it would be for me, and maybe it would just remind me of things I didn't want to think about, like Mikey and Jimmy Wilson, Lewella and her new baby, and dead girls in baseball fields.

Spotting a knot of cottonwoods in a bend in the dirt path, I made camp in a shady part and threw my line in the water. There was another clump of trees a half mile away, and even though I couldn't see the truck from here, I knew it was near them. My heart started beating normally just then, for the first time since I left Grady early that morning. I'd fished enough to know that it was too hot to catch anything this time of day, so I reeled in my line and lay back against the cool grass. The cottonwood leaves fluttered in the wind like little scraps of crinkly paper. My eyelids fell, while a flood of random thoughts overtook me. It was the first moment I'd had to really think about the longhaired man in Nelda's yard and her secret stash of pictures.

I opened my eyes again and a day or a minute could have passed. Only the sky, darkened into tufts of soggy clouds, betrayed the distinctive smell of night. Fishing pole on the grass by my side, I had now committed petty larceny, as the bait shop would have already closed. The hot calm of mid-afternoon lifted into cool, angry gusts dragged across the flat prairie. Some kind of activity at the nearby clump of trees caught my periphery. I thought the small grove of Lacebark elms was half a mile away, but in the almost-darkness, it looked farther. The truck was beyond the fence by those trees, and I remembered the pitted earth and grates and crevices I'd jumped over to get to this spot. Navigating back would be treacherous in the dark.

But I had bigger problems now.

I heard Blackie's voice in that grove of trees up ahead of me.

Blackie? Out at night on the empty prairie near Comanche Creek? What would he be doing here? Then again, what was the logic in anything Blackie Savage set his mind to? None, that's what. If I thought of him like some omnipresent, Great White Shark of Oklahoma law enforcement, his behavior had a twisted sort of logic. A shark doesn't think about things or agonize over every thought and try to project the potential consequences of its actions. It does one thing and it has perfected this singular behavior over 400 million years—it feeds. And in Blackie's case, his own feeding frenzy entailed spreading bad energy and evil into every nook and crevice of Jefferson County.

With Mikey's antique telescope I could see what he was doing over there in the last fragments of light glowing on the horizon. As I stood, I heard him yell some kind of clipped command. Was he talking to someone? Yelling at someone, or worse? I picked up the fishing pole, left the bag of night crawlers to burrow into the dry dirt, and started on foot toward the truck. Of course I wasn't stupid enough to spy on Blackie. It just so happened that the truck was parked conveniently in his direction.

So I started walking toward the origin of the sound I'd heard. First just a few steps at a time, then running, then the fishing pole was clanging haphazardly against my legs and slowing me down. Blackie and the mystery form seemed an entire kingdom away still. I counted the seconds and reached three minutes. Yet he looked smaller, not larger. Darkness closed in on me. Now that Mary McCann had spoken to me from the grave, darkness had a whole new meaning. Tricks of the eyes and ears fooled me into thinking someone was behind me, a long-armed madman sticking his hands in front of my face every few seconds, jumping up and down in my periphery to con me into turning my head. So my eyes stayed fixed upon the two figures I saw now, both standing, about four feet apart. One was flailing his arms.

More conversation now. Still just truncated bits of conversation between what looked like Blackie, looming in his signature black cowboy hat, and something on the ground. A cow? Or maybe a dog? This made no sense at all, even for him. Blackie hated pets and said so all the time.

The other creature was talking now. Or yelling. Crying? Shrieking? The sound disappeared, then, as my ears searched for it along the silent plain. This alternating shrieking and silence, combined with the darkness, froze my head firmly in place—too scared to look either left or right, but equally terrified of standing still. The baseball diamond had been just like this. Still, quiet, no breeze, and neither hot nor cold. Almost like complete stasis in both atmospheres—the real and the esoteric. I could see Blackie's outline now, and he was talking, more like pontificating, the whole time I walked. I could see the other man lying on the ground now, moaning.

I realized what I was really watching, and it was too late for escape.

Parked only about two hundred paces from the crime scene, Nelda's clunky old truck would either be my death or salvation—only time would tell.

"Please," I heard the sullen man groan. "I don't know . . ." His voice spilled into another moan as Blackie's boot made contact with his innards. Most of the kicks, now, were laid into the stomach, groin, and chest, the exact parts his curled frame was trying to protect. Almost clinical in his actions, Blackie had stopped talking and concentrated on the precision of his assault. Closer now, I was a hundred paces from them but the dark kept me cloaked in inky silence. Besides that, Blackie Savage was enough of himself to notice external things. He was satisfying a primal hunger now, kicking, punching, and poking holes in the man's aura so that all his life essence spilled onto the cold ground.

The old man coughed and then couldn't stop coughing. I could tell he was spitting up blood now. Blackie didn't lean forward or make any gesture of acknowledgement. He stood tall and soldierlike, his black hat poking its hard edges into the sky.

"You wanna live, old man?" Blackie yelled.

No answer came through, except for the same medley of moans and coughs.

"You wanna live like a cockroach, old man? You wanna crawl around the greasy back alleys behind bars and pass out drunk on the ground in people's way, asking for money, asking for favors, and someone to save you from your own miserable cockroach life?"

I kept walking slowly and quietly, careful not to move my body any way that might betray my presence. I'd dropped the fishing pole a while back, as I thought it might reflect light from the slivered moon. It was just me now, in my dirty jeans, dirty sneakers, and short sleeved shirt, with nothing but Nelda's keys in my pocket.

The old man rolled toward Blackie and lifted his head a few inches off the ground.

"You wanna live like a cockroach?"

The man didn't move.

"I asked you a question." He was yelling now. "You want to live like a goddamned cockroach? Then you're gonna die like one too. And be despised and hated like one. Women hate bugs; they recoil at their presence and run and scream in fear. That's what you are now. Not a man, but a bug. You created this, living like you did: no job, no home, no money, sponging off people's favors. Just plain makes me sick, people like you. Shit. You wanna live like a goddamned cockroach? Then one of these days," Blackie stopped and spit on the ground, "you're gonna get squashed."

He took two steps back and seemed to wobble on one leg. I squinted and saw a bottle in his hand. He wasn't drinking from it, though. He'd confiscated it from the drunken man, and he held it out far from his body for God to see, like this alone would absolve him from the guilt of his forthcoming crime.

I could only hope God would refuse a man like Blackie Savage.

tHe burial happened quickly.

My pupils, having thoroughly adjusted to the darkness, allowed me to watch undetected from a distance of thirty feet, partially concealed by a shallow dip in the earth near clumps of scrub brush.

"Get up," Blackie kept yelling toward the end of the assault. With a few more gut-kicks, I saw something spring from the man's mouth—likely body fluid. Then after the final blow, he landed hard back down on the ground, as if his body knew it was the last time it would ever move.

After a few moments of silent vigil, Blackie vanished from the corpse for a good fifteen minutes. Of course in a state like North Dakota or Minnesota, a shovel would be something normally found in the trunk or wedged behind the driver's seat of a pickup. In southern Oklahoma, trunk items were likely gallons of water, bug-repellent, and a shotgun.

But Blackie Savage was always prepared. Mikey told me once that he kept enough provisions hidden in various parts of his truck to survive out on the prairie for ten days: water, food, clothing. I wasn't quite sure how a shovel fit into a survival kit, but we're not talking about normalcy, here.

I must've been staring with my mouth open because I kept tasting black gnats on my tongue. When it got too dark, Blackie angled the truck around to use its headlights to light the burial ground. Hat off, jacket off, sleeves rolled up to his elbows, even his body looked changed from its normal high-stepping lankiness. Hunched forward, wild-eyed, and constantly wiping sweat from his forehead with the back of his hand, he grew possessed by his all-consuming, ghoulish task.

Like I'd seen my father do several times before, Blackie approached ditch digging with clinical accuracy, paying attention to the angles and measurement compared with the size and dimensions of his subject. I inched forward toward the light, prostrate on my belly, and strategically waited for light wind to hide the dragging sound of my clothes against the cold ground. Blackie shoveled a long and fairly wide ditch, big enough, it seemed, for three large bodies rather than just one. A precaution, I supposed.

His form peeling up into the blue-gray sky took on a surreal visage. Even the wind died down for a while, augmenting the terror of his grunts and movements and shovelfuls of earth hitting the ground. Half expecting the headless horseman to gallop into the light with a jack-o-lantern on his head, I stayed quiet and still and tried not to focus on the shadows in my periphery.

My biggest problem, by far, was Nelda's truck. Equidistant between myself and the newly dug burial ground, it seemed all too miraculous that the lights from Blackie's pickup hadn't reflected against its worn, rusty surface. More than just a bloodhound for witnesses, he would see the truck any minute, pin it back to me, and start out on a hunting expedition. Unless he already knew I was there, in which case I might as well eviscerate myself and give the coyotes something to feast on during the night.

So I made the only sane decision possible—retreat.

Lying prostrate with my elbows digging into the earth, I pulled back inch by inch, lowering myself into the second ditch of my life, though this one was far more shallow than Lucy's Ditch up north. I had no earthly idea how I could get back to Grady or even to Jefferson County on foot, and if Blackie stayed out on the prairie 'til it got light out, he would surely see the truck then and come looking for me.

Everything I did was futile. Waiting him out, I realized suddenly, was hardly an option. I had one chance to throw him off track long enough to sprint to the trunk and get into safe territory. The deed was mostly done now—Blackie just hovered over the freshly dug mound like a Serengeti lion holding vigil over an antelope skeleton. While he was facing me, I grabbed hold of a mid-sized rock, large enough to fit comfortably in the pit of my palm, and used my best Whitey Ford pitch to send it soaring across the dry prairie. Blackie, as I had hoped, whipped his head behind him in response.

Now or never.

One chance.

I took off like a racecar toward the truck, holding my body weight as high above my feet as possible to hide the thudding of my frantic steps. Every step reinforced my urge to look back, but there simply wasn't time to see where his royal highness was looking or where his attention was, and if he was after me, and it didn't really matter. If he weren't after me now, he'd be after me eventually. I assumed, the way things were going lately, that the fates would conspire against me and make me trip and hit my head on some large stone or something. But my legs were like perfect, rubbery little liquid blobs, gliding silently across the prairie.

Then he heard me. It's not like he said anything, or yelled in my direction, but some part of me sensed his energy focused in my direction. I dropped down to the ground, pressed my face into the dirt, and pretended to be invisible.

"Who's out there?" Blackie said.

The sound of his voice on that dark plain, standing over the freshly dead, gave me a vomit impulse like never before in my life, like I saw, in one lightning-crack instant, all the bad things he could do to make me suffer. Too scared to pick up my head, I turned it half an inch and pulled it up over the dirt not more than an inch or two. He seemed very far away, and was only looking toward the tree where I'd been sleeping earlier in the afternoon rather than where I was now.

I wasn't wearing my watch and I couldn't tell by the sky how long we had 'til dawn. I couldn't even tell what day it was anymore, or where I lived and belonged, for that matter. I'd been dying to see Janet Lange, to hold her gently in my arms, for so many days now I couldn't keep track. And I wondered if Lewella had married Dr. Roman Laszlo by now or if Denny had killed him finally, like he'd been secretly plotting. I breathed in the smell of the earth and the dampness smelled of the clearest truth I had ever known before. Clearer than what you saw with your own eyes, and clearer still than what you could see looking into somebody else's. People don't matter to me anymore. All they do, all *we* do, is say what we don't mean and hide ourselves from the people who most want to know us. Right then, in that cold, empty place, I enveloped the clarity of the truth of the earth—the feel of cold dirt on my forehead and nose, the taste of it in my mouth, and I felt cleaner than ever before. Because that cold wasn't capable of the lies people tell each other. The dirt was plain, true, and solid, and didn't try to tell me that everything was gonna be okay and that I would live happily ever after. It told me that I was cast out by my own family, despised by my best friend, and now in danger of retribution from a man I'd just seen murder an old drunk. It's what I'd always loved about the flat prairie of Oklahoma—it didn't believe in fairy tales.

I waited him out. Starting with just small bits of time, I counted the seconds up to five minutes, then ten minutes, twenty, forty. I stayed there, buried and half dead, twigs sticking into my ribs to the point of drawing blood, as I could tell by the cold spot on my stomach, for what felt like ninety minutes waiting for Blackie to complete his sick vigil over the dead body and potential witness to his crime. I was sitting up when I watched the lights of his truck bounce up and down along the bumpy dirt road to the pavement half a mile away.

twenty-four

"Where you been, Jakie?"

"Don't be calling me that, Lewella. I'm not the same little runt you used to kick around when I was little." I shoved past her into my bedroom, pulled the rumpled duffel back from the bottom of my closet, and started throwing clothes in it. Pants. Socks. Stretched out old T-shirt and a light jacket.

Lewella was dressed in nice pants and a long shirt. From the corner of my eye I could see she had makeup on, too. I instinctively scanned the house for the interloper, Laszlo.

"You a man now, then?" she said.

Like Denny? I thought. And Daddy for that matter? But I held my tongue. After all, I was a witness to a murder and a fugitive now. One false move and I'd end up like the wino Blackie turned into prairie fertilizer.

"Must have something to do with that pretty girl who's been asking for you around here."

My pulse sped up at the sound of it, but I knew better than to succumb to Lewella's tricks. "What girl?"

"You know what girl, Jakie, don't you? Janet Lange. PJ's niece, Daddy said. Cutest little thing I ever seen." She came over to the bed, touching the clothes in the bag. "Where you going?"

"Just camping out with Mikey and Freddie and Jimmy Wilson for a few days. Freddie's got a tent we're gonna pitch in that field in his backyard." I turned to look at her before I ran out the back door. And I noticed then, for the first time, that I was looking at someone's mother. "You all healed up now then?"

"Pretty much back to normal, Doc says."

"Where's Faith?"

"Denny took her to town to have some tests done. Doc said I should rest and try not to go anywhere."

There was a lull in the conversation then, long enough for us both to think about Roman Laszlo and the influence he'd had on this family and, especially, on Lewella's heart and mind. I knew what was happening, and Lewella seemed to notice my knowing. It wasn't a threat to her, though. She was brazen in her love for him, uncaring of how Denny or the rest of us felt. Guess that's what love did to you sometimes.

"Got a lot of clothes here for just camping out."

Ignoring her, I lugged the duffel bag into the kitchen and loaded the side of it with fruit from the kitchen table and half a loaf of bread from the fridge. Lewella wasn't as much watching me as she was staring at my eyes. Did I look fiendish now? Is that what witnessing a murder did to a fifteen-year-old boy? My sister, the closest person to me, I supposed, saw things in me that I couldn't even see myself. With her arms crossed over her bosom, still swelled from childbirth, I couldn't tell whether she was my ally or enemy. I stopped moving after zipping the bag.

"You're not going camping. Are you?"

No sense hiding. I was a warrior now, and if I wasn't, it was time to start.

"Hear about Mrs. Sorensen?" Lewella said.

"The old lady in the back of the store?"

"Died. Last night. Bent down to pull a pie from inside the oven and never even stood up again. Just slumped over onto the floor."

Immune to death now, I had no response. Lewella moved closer to me, looming over me now with all seventy inches of her. I didn't pretend to understand her, or any woman, for that matter. Three inches from the back door, now, I weighed my options. I could run out before hearing whatever tirade she was planning, and risk having her tell Mama and Daddy that I'd run away. Or I could slow down and listen. *Warrior*, I kept telling myself.

"You in trouble, Jakie? Like real trouble?"

"Yeah," I said.

"Is it your fault?"

I shook my head, disgusted by the sound of it. I'd never been a victim of anything in my life and I hated to start now. But the cards had already been dealt.

"Wrong place at the wrong time, I guess." Lewella said.

"Wrong time, wrong life." I paused and felt a hot breeze sheer in through the screen door. Lewella was my ally then; I could feel the silent understanding growing between us. Two people trapped in different places, different ways—she with Denny, and me, well, that was a different story. Blackie Savage had a way of changing every known equation.

We stood there a good five minutes in silence—me weighed down by the bulging duffel bag, she pretending to scan the backyard for prowlers. "Wait a minute," she said and disappeared into her bedroom. She came out a second later holding something in her hand. "Take this." She shoved some folded bills into my shirt pocket and kissed my cheek. "And don't forget where home is."

When I asked her my next question, I spoke with my back to her to prevent her from seeing my inappropriately wet face. "What'll you tell everyone?"

"You know, you're camping out at Freddie's."

And there *was* a camp. A real camp with a big tent, a lantern, Charleston Chews, and Atomic Fireball wrappers dotting the ground with an array of empty cola bottles. I just wasn't part of it. Well, I thought, just give me time. If one thing could draw Mikey Savage out of a grudge, it was spy stuff: fishing rod microphones, cigarette lighter cameras. All I had to do was call him John Drake and the latest argument was forgotten. All I had to do was plant the bait and watch what happened next. But I had to do something else first.

I found Janet Lange sulking with her chin on her elbows on the front porch of her house on the edge of Grady. Her eyes widened at the sight of Nelda's truck, but there was a mistrustful scowl to her pink painted lips.

I bit my lip as I walked up to her, waiting for her to say something first.

Waiting, waiting . . .

"Hi." I had to break the tension.

"You find another girlfriend already?"

"Never."

"You haven't come around in a while. I spoke to your sister a few times and she said she hadn't seen you in days."

"So you thought I was dead?" I joked. Her face was like concrete. "I'm sorry. Something happened in, well—" Breathe, I thought, breathe. "I can't tell you about it but something happened that kept me away for a while."

"Where are you going now?" She was looking at the truck. The handles on the duffel bag stuck up over the edge of the window.

"Just camping out at Freddie's."

"With Mikey?" She stretched her long, tanned legs out in front of her after she said it, waiting for a reaction.

I gulped. "Yeah. He'll be there."

"I thought you two weren't talking."

In that moment and only in that moment, I wished I had been born female so I would know instinctively how to be coy, and to feign insouciance and casually, like Patrick McGoohan did as Secret Agent, put on a little show. Boys my age didn't know how to do this and it was questionable whether our gender ever really got it right.

"How do you know about that?" I asked.

"Marjorie Jeffers."

My stomach caved in like I'd just caught a medicine ball.

Janet was smiling now, and not in the friendly, cheery way she usually did, like that time she smiled at me as she unbuttoned her blouse in the truck outside her aunt's house. Not that way at all. "Carmella? Carmella Jeffers? Don't think I don't know, Jake, what went on in there!"

"Nothing went on. She was in the tree house with Mikey when I came up the stairs is all. I didn't see nothing."

The sight of a scowl on that beautiful, perfect face was more than I could bear, more than any man could have. I started to walk back toward the truck and bit down hard on my lower lip to keep my face from getting red.

"Wait." She ran up to me and had something in her hand. "Take this."

"What is it?" I asked. It was a polished bear chiseled out of some dark wood.

"A good luck charm."

"Where'd you get it?"

"Uncle PJ had it in his store," she said. "He gave it to me."

I fondled the bear, running my thumb over the smooth top surface. "Don't you want it? I mean, if it's from him."

Janet waved her delicate white hand through the air. "I never liked PJ. Don't tell my mother."

twenty-five

the hoot of an owl evidenced the onset of night—nearly one whole day since I saw what I shouldn't have and my life, unwittingly, changed forever. Then again, no more so than it had since one night in the baseball diamond from hell.

I was beyond just tired now. Sleep, last night, had been replaced by adrenaline pumping pure terror, which lasted eight painful hours. Since then, I had chomped down one of the bananas in my duffel bag that I grabbed from the kitchen table and some candy I kept in Nelda's truck. The casual, carefree life of a fifteen-year-old boy had changed overnight into malnutrition, insomnia, and murder.

After some consideration, I decided to tape my note to Mikey's bathroom mirror. This time of night, Mikey, Freddie, and Jimmy would be the only ones using it, as the twins and Mrs. Savage had already gone to bed. I'd kept the truck parked behind PJ's and walked to Mikey's from there. And, like the nomadic guise my life had recently taken on, I took the duffel bag. I recognized the shape of a woman walking toward me down the empty main drag of Grady. She was carrying a heavy bag and purposely adjusting her gait to reflect this. I tried to look sideways to make like I hadn't seen her, and then I saw her smile and set the bag down on the street. Here we go.

"Is that little Jakie Leeds?" she yelled from ten feet away.

"Not anymore, Mrs. Petit," I said, remembering her name only as the words exited my mouth.

The round, heavily painted face contracted, lips curling into a gentle frown. I remembered her from the post office—that gum-chewing-white-trash way of sorting mail and blowing the fresh nail polish on her fingers at the same time. She was close now. I could almost smell the mint from her chewing gum and the garlic it was covering up.

"My God!" She placed her palms on both cheeks. "Look at you, Jakie."

"It's Jake." I never liked her, so the way I said it I didn't have to be nice.

"You running away from home?" Her voice had a mocking, sing-songy twang to it, the kind a woman could use to torment a man to tears for not performing up to her expectations. As she loped up to me, I found myself wondering about her age. Not out of any sexual hunger, but more plain curiosity. I wondered how many of the men in Grady she'd slept with, how many boyfriends, husbands even.

"Just camping out," I replied, sticking with my same old story.

Rose Marie Petit licked her lips and looked up and down the street like she was about to do a striptease. My forehead sweated but I didn't move. Mrs. Petit came one inch closer, and this time I thought of her own husband and how he'd feel if he saw how she acted around the husbands of her girlfriends and around young, inexperienced boys. Her nostrils were like a rattler's tongue—appraising and absorbing the fear scent exuded from my pores. I had to get to Mikey's before dark, before all three of them passed out for the night, so Mikey would see my note and come out to Comanche Creek. I had things to do. I was on a mission. Mrs. Petit's face was close enough to touch.

"You know, Jakie, you're not such a little boy after all." She looked down at the crotch of my pants and I suddenly felt like a baby seal in the presence of a hungry polar bear. "You got a girlfriend? I heard you got one. All you boys got girlfriends, to practice on, I suppose, for when you graduate to women like me."

"I don't have no girlfriend, Mrs. Petit. And I better be going."

She frowned with her eyes and mouth. Even her nose seemed to change shape at the familiar sound of rejection. Two more steps, two more, now one more, and she slid her wobbly arms around my back and shoved her chest into mine. I kept thinking how clumsy she seemed, considering she'd probably done this with every man in

Jefferson County. A breeze blew her hair in front of her face as she carefully applied her lips to mine. First I just felt the bristle of the uncombed
strands, and then the gritty skin on her painted mouth. Her head was
tilted sideways and her hands, now, were gripping the back of my
head—pushing her mouth deeper into mine. In that one blind second
I tasted her mint gum, a hint of garlic, and the fifty years of baloney
sandwiches that showed on her hips. However grotesque this moment
felt, by the time I felt her warm tongue in my mouth, my crotch was on
fire. Nothing, in all my readings and mental preparation and late night
Mikey conversations, had prepared me for this type of female aggres-
sion. I couldn't breathe or move without making this gesture a blatant
sign of rejection and disgust, but that was what I felt and I had to get
out. Now. I'm on a mission, I said to myself as I gently unclenched her
hands from my body and headed west toward Mikey's house. When I
looked back, Mrs. Petit was still standing in that same amorous position, her heavy load on the ground beside her.

I hovered like a coiled rattler behind Mrs. Savage's big old Ford pickup,
waiting for the beers Mikey stole from Blackie's fridge in the basement
to take effect.

Laughter erupted in the tent set up under the tree house. When
I peeked my head out I could see the yellow glow of intersecting
flashlights and hear the fizz of beer bottles. I should have been in that
tent, not with Freddie and Jimmy but with Mikey, like old times, talking about Superman episodes and what girls we wanted to lay. But
things had irrevocably changed between us and now I had to resort to
drastic measures.

The note read:

> #1, 28
> " . . . with every move he makes,
> another change he takes
> odds are he won't live to see tomorrow."
> Signed, The Ubiquitous Mr. Lovegrove
> Behind the Stronghold—10:00 pm

I taped it to Mikey's bathroom mirror, then retreated to my perch behind the car and waited. It was dark now, and Freddie had already peed twice, though he preferred to do it in the backyard, marking his territory. Jimmy Wilson was a Navajo and the ones I had known just weren't subject to the same annoying urges as everyone else—bodily urges, human curiosity, nosiness, gossip. I heard the tent's zipper and knew it was Mikey by the heavy thud of his clumsy, sock-footed steps banging on the hard ground. He stayed in there a long time, longer than it took to read the note, scrutinize the contents, and take a leak. Did he pass out? I'd only heard the sound of four beer bottles being opened, and even Mikey wouldn't get drunk on just that.

The back door slapped against the hinges. I hid in the darkest part of the shadow surrounding Mrs. Savage's clunky Ford and waited.

He gave the universal whistle, but I stayed quiet. I'd left my directions on the note, after all, and there was nothing to discuss.

"Shit," I heard him say. Then he ran up the tree house steps and found his episode notebook from Secret Agent and scanned the pages for episode 28 from the first season. He wouldn't understand what this meant or how it related to me, but it was intriguing enough, I had no doubt, to get him on the road to the meeting place. I moved closer to the tent so I could hear the drama of his exit.

"I gotta go," he said, grabbing his sneakers.

Jimmy and Freddie looked up at him slowly. "Where?" Freddie said. "This was your idea. You're going out there?"

"I forgot I was supposed to do something tonight."

"Oh, yeah?" Freddie cackled. "Do something or some-*one*?"

"Shit. The only person he's gonna *do* is himself, under the quilt of his sleeping bag."

"Eat shit, both of you. I'm outta here. I'll be back later after you've drunk all the beers. You won't even know I'm gone."

"Hey," Freddie whispered. "What if your brother comes home? Won't he know we took his beers?"

"He he he." Mikey snickered all the way across the backyard, and in ten seconds Freddie and Jimmy took off like they'd never been there.

The street was partially lit up from the moon's glow and I knew

Mikey could see me a hundred feet ahead of him. But that was the rule. Once there was a meeting place, no talking 'til you got there. It's how spies did it. It's how Secret Agent did it, too.

My arm was killing me from dragging the duffel bag all the way there and back. I slung it onto the bed of Nelda's truck and sat on the flat rocks behind the Stronghold—our code for PJ's shop.

"Yo, Mogul?"

"Maxima?"

"Yeah," he replied. He couldn't see me yet but he knew about the flat rocks. "I'm still mad at you, you know. Whatever this is, it won't change that."

"Why? Because I stole a girl you never had in the first place?"

Silence.

"She never liked you, and you only liked her because she liked me. Admit it."

"Okay."

I was stunned at this sudden display of honesty. Maybe there was hope for Mikey yet. He sat beside me on the rocks and the smell of beer flooded the air.

"So what's the message, *Lovegrove*?"

twenty-six

"I have to show you something." I conveyed the urgency of the matter with the dead stare of dilated pupils. Mikey locked onto my frozen expression and I could almost feel the flutter of his heart against his ribcage. Poor thing. Right now, he was assuming the worst. I didn't have the heart to tell him it was even worse than that.

We drove in silence toward Comanche Creek. The atmosphere in the truck could be compared to Jesus's disciples at the Last Supper. Everything had already changed for me, and now, by sharing this curse with Mikey, it would be for both of us the end of everything as we had known it. If I were braver, perhaps, if I'd been born with a more commanding presence, I might have told Mrs. Petit to go home to her husband and then left the country. That way, Mikey could go on living with the false hope that someday, somehow, his brother Blackie might turn around and become some kind of human entity. But the dividing road at the border of Jefferson County marked the end of my speculation.

"We going fishing, Jake?"

The sound of Mikey's voice and the way he said my name evidenced his deepest fear, like he had to affirm it was me who was driving and not some dark stranger who had come to inhabit my body.

"Get out," I said, and walked around the truck. I was parked on the dirt road below the embankment that led to the flat prairie where I had fished yesterday afternoon and then watched the sky fall. "Over here."

"It's getting dark."

"Not too dark. We'll be fine."

Mikey wrinkled up his cheeks like he did when he needed more explanation. And he would be getting it soon enough. Stacks of dark clouds, preparing to dump rain on the prairie, cooled the air. The soft rain dampened my bare arms but I had no reaction to it now. I no longer felt any of the physical sensations I had before—hunger, hot, cold. I tromped across the dry scrub brush and Mikey lagged behind me. When I turned back, his face was the color of milk.

With a cluster of grain silos in the background, we climbed through a veil of wire fences arranged in rows two hundred yards from the dirt road. "Over here," I said, and ascended the embankment incline toward the tall trees and the fishing hole.

"This is what you've been doing for the past two days? Fishing? Jesus."

"You're gonna wish I was Jesus in a minute." I clamped my jaw tight.

"Why?"

"To deliver you from evil."

Mikey swallowed, scared less by my words and more by what he saw, and knew, of my face. "What evil?"

I nodded toward the dark mound of dirt in the clearing up ahead. And, afterward, I distanced myself from that prairie and concentrated on the soft watercolor landscape of the plains at dusk: vertical brushstrokes in ten shades of tan; the sky; a feather from a rain-spattered dove falling over them like a wet sheet from a clothesline. I imagined that clothesline now, a line separating one world from another, like my one dream of a normal life truncated by the intransigent truths of untimely death.

"Where?" Mikey whined and squinted his beady eyes.

"Goddamn it, there! There. See? Where I'm pointing?"

"All I see is dirt."

I nodded.

"A mound of evil dirt? That's what the Ubiquitous Mr. Lovegrove is trying to show me? Gimme a break."

"I don't want to get too close," I half-whispered.

He took a step toward me. "Why?"

"We're on Indian land."

Mike sighed and raised his chin to the sky. "There's not an Indian around for at least fifty miles. In fact, there's no one around for fifty miles."

I lowered myself to the ground and spread my legs out, fatigue working its fat fingers through my body. "He was buried face down. To Indians, that's bad."

Mikey's eyes widened.

"Keeps the spirit from leaving the body. Or that's what the Sioux say, anyway. Don't know about Choctaws."

"What are you talk . . . who?"

"Some old drunk."

"Dead?"

I tipped my head sideways. "Wish that was all of it." Now I was challenging Mikey to use what he knew of me, from our almost fifteen-year history, to discern the truth of my story.

"Somebody killed him?" he asked.

"Not just somebody. But yeah, someone killed him all right."

"Who was he? Did you know the man?" Mikey asked, characteristically changing course midway.

"The drunk, you mean? No. I might've seen him in Waurika that night I went there but I'm not sure."

Pause. "In Waurika the night you went to see Blackie? That's when you saw the drunk?"

I could almost see the spokes of his brain churning it all together. "Might have seen him. I was far away so I'm not sure." Then I waited to give him a chance to decide for himself.

A gust blew all my hair to the left side of my head. I had to bear all my body weight against it. Mikey hid his eyes from the dust. "You saying Blackie killed that drunk?"

I tried to answer but my mouth wouldn't open.

"Jakie? That what you telling me?" His voice had that shaky, squeaky quality.

"Yeah."

Three crows flew in a circle over our heads, cawed, slowed to a haunting pace, and then took off into the gray pulp of dusk. I had always believed in such premonitions from nature, in the way that animals seemed to instinctively know about the sins and secrets of man or, in this case, of one man.

I was waiting for Mikey's reaction to this news, prepared for the typical mannerisms of outrage, anger, disgust and, eventually, incredulity. But none of these things showed on his face now. Just a stray tear or two sliding down his cheek.

"Tell me all of it," he said finally. But I had no intention of reliving the whole scene. Living it once was enough. "Jake," Mikey pressed.

I stood. "Later. We need to go."

"Where?"

"Anywhere but here."

Mikey crossed his pudgy arms. "There's more, isn't there? The way I figure it, if you're gonna give someone bad news, you might as well spill it all out at once."

I saw something. Off in the distance and sort of in my periphery, I could have sworn I saw the headlights from a distant car. I started running back toward the truck.

"Jake! Where in the hell are you going?"

"We've got to get out of here. Now!"

"Why? Who's gonna see us? Is that it? Did you see this happen?"

"Of course I saw," I replied. Mikey was running behind me. "How do you think I knew about it?"

"Did Blackie see you? Is that why you're running?"

I stopped. "He might have. I can't say for sure."

"Jesus, Jake," Mikey whispered. "You know what that means."

"Yeah."

"You're dead."

I stared at him across the hood of the truck.

"What, you mean both of us? Blackie wouldn't kill me."

I laughed out loud. "Oh no? And why not?"

"I'm his brother, dummy. Normal people don't go around killing their own family."

I didn't bother responding.

"Fine then. What country do you want to move to?"

twenty-seven

"We'll stay at Nelda's a few days. I'll call my Ma from there and tell her, and you can call home and say you're staying up there this week to help me build a shed. Will your ma mind your being gone?"

"Hell no."

A song on the crackly radio made me think of Janet, made me wonder when I'd get to see her again, and if things would ever feel normal in my life.

"I found some things at Nelda's. They're in the glove box."

Mikey opened it and, naturally, everything fell out on the floor. He collected the handfuls of photographs and squinted to see the contents in the dark. "Where'd you find these?"

"A locked trunk in Nelda's basement. I went poking around there last weekend."

"They're just a bunch of babies. Did Nelda have other kids?"

I bit my lip before answering, wondering if now was the time to reveal what I'd been hiding in my heart all this time, or if Nelda's secret needed more time to germinate. "I don't think she had any kids. Not really." I didn't expect him to understand. Not yet.

"So who are all these? And why does she have them?"

I just shook my head. "All's I know so far is that Walter van Geller's at the center of the disappearance of two young women. When I went to see him alone that time, the day after we went together and scared the crap out of him, remember he told me all kinds of things? He said that when he lived on Denny's ranch, he and his wife had a cook named Althea, and Althea had an assistant named Mary. And then Nelda told me that Mary and Lillie Mechem were best friends. 'Thick as thieves' was how she put it, said they knew each other from the 4-H Club.

She said Lillie Mechem had a rich daddy who went to lots of business meetings, and so she got her uncle to drive her to the 4-H meetings."

"Van Geller was Lillie Mechem's uncle? There's too many coincidences in this story."

"I don't believe in coincidences. So that means everything here's gotta be related somehow. So not only was Van Geller Lillie's uncle, but the reward money her daddy set aside ended up in Van Geller's pocket. Remember I said he donated it to some Adventist Church in Ringling? It was *his* church."

"I never trusted that guy," Mikey said. "What about his connection to Mary?"

"I can't say for sure that he had one. Not conclusively, anyway. The way I see it, we start from the top and work down."

"Meaning what?"

I sighed. "Sherlock Holmes style. It's called inductive reasoning or retrograde analysis, where you start at the top with a truth, and then you work your way back down the ladder to reconstruct what events led you to that conclusion."

"So we know that Lillie Mechem disappeared from Ringling and Mary McCann was found dead in the baseball diamond. You think both of these things will lead back to Van Geller? He's just some cranky old man."

"He's a crooked old preacher, but he wasn't always. Mary disappeared ten years ago, and Lillie about five, I think."'

"Yeah. That guy's full of surprises," Mikey said, though he wasn't really paying attention. This was about the extent of complexity that his mind could handle. After a certain point, all his responses became automatic.

Full of something, I thought. "Then we saw him give that envelope to Nelda when we staked out his house."

"Did you find out what that was yet?"

"No, but we'll check it out when we get there tonight. I know where she probably put it, and if it's not there, I'll check her bank account. I went to his house the other night on my way back from Nelda's, just to see if there was any activity."

"And?"

"Nothing to report. He was out."

"Like out to lunch or skipped town?" Mikey said.

"Somewhere in between, I guess. I need to poke around Nelda's place to see what I can find to connect Mary to the Van Geller creep, or something to show us why Lillie Mechem disappeared."

"Girls disappear all the time," Mikey said absently.

I snapped my head at him. "That's your contribution to this investigation? Girls disappear? You've got to learn to—"

"Hey, don't tell me what to do. I'm four months older than you, don't forget. I ought to be the head of this investigation."

I rolled my eyes. "Fine. What are we gonna do now?"

Mikey stayed quiet, realizing he was out of his league. Then, out of nowhere, in a moment of unexpected lucidity, he said, "What did Van Geller do before he became a preacher?"

It was the smartest thing I'd ever heard him say.

We parked on the side of Main Street in the center of Enid and flipped through the baby pictures under the glow of two flashlights. It was dark enough that the truck wouldn't be seen, and far enough away from Blackie to restore some tranquility to my anxious heart. The pictures were of boys and girls, aged from about one to four from what I could tell, but no other common feature stood out for us, and neither did the implication of finding these artifacts in Nelda's basement. By the age of the photographs, the collection had to be at least ten years old. They were all stamped "Sand Bluff" on the back.

Mikey kept turning them over and looking surprised when he saw the indication.

"They all say that," I told him, to save him the trouble.

"How far is it from here?"

I shrugged. "An hour or two I guess. Out in Choctaw County."

"Now tell me what happened," Mikey said.

I shook my head.

"Jake? I need to hear it. I mean, did you see an old drunk stumbling around on the plains late at night or what?"

I set the pictures down on the seat of the truck. "Do you believe me or not? That's what it comes down to."

"I guess. I mean, if you're asking if I think Blackie's capable of doing it, yeah. Without so much as a flinch of his eye. But *if* he actually did it? That's something else."

"How reliable do you think I am?"

He looked at the floor. "Very."

"So I'm not likely to make up some cock and bull story just to get attention?"

"No."

"Well, I say he did it, and not just out of assumption either. I sat there and watched him for hours. First he interrogated the guy, then beat him to death with his fists and his steel-toed boots, and then buried him with a shovel in the dirt. What else is there to talk about?"

"Why?" Mikey said. "There has to be a reason."

I scrunched up my face. "For a sane person, maybe. For someone like that, they'd need to have a damn good reason for killing that became not a matter of choice but survival. Some secret, maybe, that threatened to rise up from the ground and expose a person's lies or deceit or weakness of character. But Blackie's not subject to the same rules as everybody else because he doesn't live in our world. You grew up with him. Hell, anyone who'd lock his own brother in the trunk of a car . . ." My voice trailed off into silence. "For grins, I mean. He did it for sport, to see how you'd react. None of the rules apply here."

He dropped it, finally, while I slowly made my way to Nelda's, completely unsure of what I might find. Was she having a tea party with her milkman ghost? Or was she talking to the spirits that haunted the plains behind her house? No, instead I found her smoking on the front steps, dressed in real clothes again, like a mother waiting up for her child to come home.

We parked by the curb and slowly, agonizingly, approached the porch.

"Too late to work on that shed, I reckon."

I swallowed the mound in my throat. "We'll start work again in the morning, but I was hoping we might stay here tonight, you know, to get an early start."

Nelda stood on her wobbly legs and shifted her eyes from Mikey to me. I would have given up comic books and Sherlock Holmes to know the nature of her scrutiny. She rubbed her chin and looked behind me at the truck. "That thing actually runs all right?"

"My Daddy and his friend looked at it. Replaced a few belts and hoses. They said it's got some leaky seals but nothing that'll keep it from running."

"Sure is loud, though," Mikey said, lapsing into his normal whine.

"You got one better that you can drive?"

"No ma'am."

"All right, then. There's two spare rooms down the end of the hall. You can stay in there and I'll make you breakfast in the morning. Hope you're not light sleepers. I'm up most of the night." She stepped down the brick walkway toward the street.

"Nelda?"

She didn't turn, but she stopped and cocked her head to the side.

"You going somewhere?"

"Don't worry about me. Looks like you got worse things to worry about if you show up here at eleven at night."

You don't know the half of it, I thought.

twenty-eight

$\mathbf{m}$ikey and I rummaged through Nelda's basement like two wolves searching for a rabbit in a woodpile. Hot, tired, bored, and fed up, even the radio was driving us crazy.

"Turn it off," Mikey said. "If I hear that Shirelles song one more time I'm gonna strangle someone."

"And The Four Freshmen."

He shot me a look. "No one plays them anymore."

"KTVI does."

He just sulked.

"How about Superman?" I ventured, knowing the subject was taboo. "Are you bored with him now too?"

"I don't know. He's not as omnipotent as I used to think."

I looked and laughed at the same time. "Omnipotent? Is that a word you typically use?"

"Come on, Jake. We're not talking about Jimmy Wilson. Superman's omnipotent, if anyone is."

"Not according to you," I reminded him.

"It's just the kryptonite thing's bothering me lately. I mean, if he's so strong and powerful, he shouldn't have any weaknesses."

"Everybody's got at least one," I said, anticipating his next question.

"Blackie?"

I stopped and considered this before answering. "I don't know about that, but I've thought of nothing else lately."

"Why?"

"Something to use against him. I mean, I'm not sure he knows I saw him, but if he even thinks I did, I'm as good as, you know. If I did see him, I represent a vulnerability, and guys like Blackie despise vulnerability."

Mikey nodded, trying to keep up with my logic. "What could you do, though?" he asked, stressing the word "you" as if I were no bigger than a carpenter ant.

"Try to buy my way out of his wrath. I have something he wants because I represent the potential for exposing his crime." I cocked my head, thinking as I spoke. "What if I offered a trade?"

The entire mass of Mikey's round face shriveled up. "For what?" His voice squeaked as he said this.

"I want access to the police reports on assaults on women the year Mary disappeared. I know the police precinct at the Waurika City Hall has them, because that's where he told me they were kept when I went to see him at No Name's that night."

Mikey set down the stack of books he'd picked up from the basement floor. "You're gonna, what, bargain with him? Are you serious?"

"Yeah."

"Idiot," this new Mikey replied now.

"I'm an idiot?" I stood tall and then quickly remembered how fast Mikey usually beat me in our play-wrestling matches.

"It's like giving a great white shark three good reasons why he shouldn't bite you. You can't reason with someone like him."

"Who said anything about reasoning?" I paused while the thought solidified in my mind. "We're talking about blackmail."

Mikey picked up the books again and pretended to sort them in stacks on the cellar floor. "*We're* not talking about anything, Jake. This is your deal. You were the one who had to start something up with Janet and get me all mad and cause that fight outside the tree house, then go off by yourself to the creek where we fish and see, you know." He stopped to clear his throat and coughed instead.

The old Mikey never would have said those things, or if he'd tried to say them, they would've gotten stuck in his throat and come out all wrong. We were like two Adams living in the Garden of Eden, and he ate the poisoned fruit first, opened his eyes, realized he was naked, and received instant intelligence. Or maybe he was Abel, just now learning of Cain's true nature and his plans of impending doom.

"So what do we do about Lillie?" he said.

"We don't know much about her is the problem. She disappeared from her home in Ringling, and her rich daddy offered a reward to anyone who had information that brought her back home. That never happened, and the money ended up you know where, in Van Geller's pocket. Like I said, not much. Ask me about Mary; that's a different story."

"What do you *actually* know about her?"

"She worked on Denny's ranch." Mikey's eyes shriveled to slits. "That's right, before it was Denny's, I mean. When Van Geller lived there he had a cook named Althea who's dead now. Her assistant was Mary."

"And now she's dead, too," he said, stating the obvious. "And she and Lillie knew each other from 4-H. . . ."

"And Lillie's uncle was Van Geller."

"Do we know that for sure?" he asked. "Or are you making assumptions?"

Assumptions. A very non-Mikey word. "I haven't asked him as much, if that's what you mean. It would be easy enough to find out, I guess. I was planning on talking to her daddy anyway." I heard the flap of Nelda's screen door in front. "Come on, she's gone for a walk."

"Where?" he asked, following me up the stairs.

We started with her desk. The little white envelope was gone, but I fumbled around and found her checkbook in the middle drawer.

"What're you looking for?"

"Stand lookout at the door. Give me a sign when you see her coming." He obeyed and sulked behind the living room curtains. I looked for a recent deposit, and found one dated one week ago for five hundred dollars. The scrawled writing to the left of the amount revealed two letters that had been crossed out.

"Could it have said VG?" Mikey asked, still breathing down my neck.

"Not VG. WG. Walter van Geller. And I don't know what it says."

"Check last month."

The old Mikey never would have suggested something so lucid. Sure enough, I flipped to the same date a month ago and found a deposit.

"Five hundred. Look!"

"Quiet," I hissed, listening for Nelda's shadowy steps. "He's keeping her quiet about something."

"About what, though?"

I considered this before offering an answer. I looked around her musty, cluttered living room that hadn't been cleaned or organized in what looked like twenty years. I focused on the cobwebs entwined in the array of exposed pipes near the ceiling and, as my mind wandered, my eyes landed on the one solid piece of evidence we had of Nelda's secret crime—photographs. Mikey watched as I examined them slowly, holding each one in front of my eyes.

"Those?" He flipped one of the pictures over and examined the same word written on each one.

I nodded. "I think the answer to a lot of our questions is in Sand Bluff."

Mikey smirked. "What, you mean go walking up and down the streets yelling Nelda's name to see who comes out running?"

"We don't have much to go on, but I'll find something. Just give me time." I looked toward the door. "I hear something. Check it out." Mikey returned to his place by the curtains and I perched precariously on the rickety steps leading to the basement.

"Nothing out there."

"Where is she?" I hissed. "Go outside and see if you see her. Stay on the porch and keep watch."

"Where are you going?" Old-Mikey answered in his panic voice.

I figured Nelda would walk as long as it took her to smoke two full cigarettes. So that left me with five, maybe ten minutes.

I tore down the hallway to the last room on the right. Nothing in the interior betrayed the look of a typical girl's room. Then again, Nelda wasn't the type to enshrine a room that belonged to a loved one. A more likely scenario was that she hadn't gone in there in ten years. Turning on the light would be too obvious, so I used my quick pupil-adjustment ploy from being locked in her basement to catch a glimpse of whatever I could.

> White dresser with gold trim, all the drawers empty
> Twin bed, with covers folded over—plain white sheet, pink blanket, blue quilt
> Rocking chair in corner by west window, empty plant stand beside it
> Tall, vertical chest of drawers, all empty

Mary McCann's bedroom closet was dark and cavernous, and large enough to stand in with the door completely closed. I turned on the light and hoped and prayed none of it seeped out into the darkness of the street. Nelda would be approaching the house now. The clock was ticking. I tried not to get distracted by Mikey's rustling the living room curtains. He was supposed to be waiting outside. So much for the emergence of new-Mikey.

At the back end of the closet was another tall chest of drawers that matched the one in the center of the room. This one was older, though, with chipped paint and dings on the corners. It was empty, like the other one. When I bent down, I saw that one of the drawers didn't close completely. I opened it and closed it again, having to nudge it from side to side to get it to come out at all. I shoved it back in with the weight of my body and felt it hit something hard. Nelda's coming, I kept thinking, imagining her sneaky footsteps and entourage of whispering demons. I kept at it, nudging the drawer, desperate for Mikey's signature whistle to cue me the hell out of there. I started pulling the drawer out, checking behind me for the necessary clearance. There was plenty of room for me to lay the drawer down on the floor behind me.

Mikey signaled. Sweat formed in droplets on the back of my neck and forehead. I could hear her coughing coming up the walkway, yet

I found myself buried elbow-deep in this mine of a closet, fingers rubbing against the dry wood in the back of the dresser. I pulled the dangling chain to turn off the light, and when I reached back down to the dresser, my fingers caught the smooth edge of something perched precariously on the drawer assembly. In one blind second Mikey signaled me again, the front screen flapped against the jamb, Nelda coughed and shuffled into the living room, and I yanked the object from the mouth of the dresser and closed the closet door behind me.

A second later I was standing calmly in the other bedroom across the hall.

"This where you said we can stay?" I asked. But Nelda's eyes were on Mary's bedroom. It was only then that I realized I hadn't put the drawer back in the dresser.

twenty-nine

Her knowledge of my crime showed in the deep crevices surrounding her contracted mouth. I had penetrated the fortress.

"You boys can lay down in here. There's sheets and blankets in the closet."

I could only see one closet from the hallway. I took half a step toward it and—

"I'll get it."

Aha, I thought, slamming my Sherlock Holmesian fist on an imaginary table. So you *are* hiding something. You *do* care about something after all, something more than just loneliness and how many cigarettes you can consume in an hour. The jig is up! Watson, get your coat and hat—we're going out!

After she settled us in the spare room, with Mikey in the bed and me on the floor, I could finally pull the object I'd snatched from the closet out from under the covers. There were no flashlights here but I had one in the truck.

"Where are you going?" Mikey said as I tiptoed down the creaky hall.

"Be right back."

But I wasn't. I lay on the front seat of the truck staring out the windshield at the twinkling night sky, wondering how I fit into nature's grand scheme. Mikey, waiting no more than five minutes, came out to investigate.

"What's that?"

"I found it lodged in the back of Mary's closet."

Mikey held the smoothly polished, carved wooden bear in his fat hands and ran his thumbs over the surface. "It's heavy."

"They call them spirit bears."

"Who?"

I shrugged. "Indians, I guess. I don't know which ones, either, before you ask me."

"What about it?" He searched the truck with his eyes, looking for evidence of my insanity. Maybe he was looking for an opium-clogged syringe, a rubber band, and my violin. Oh right, that was Holmes, not me. It was getting harder to separate myself from the Holmes I'd been reading about for ten years. What would he do in this situation? Who would he confront first? I felt as if I were hiking up the side of a mountain blindfolded. I slowly pulled the other artifact out from under the driver's seat.

"Two bears."

God help me, I thought. If I was really going to become Sherlock Holmes, I badly needed a replacement Watson, or at least a reasonable facsimile. "Yeah. Two," I moaned. "Janet gave me this one. I don't know why, but she wanted me to have it. Notice anything about them?" I asked before he had a chance to react.

"Where'd she get it?"

"I don't know. Turn them over."

He did, and held one up toward the streetlight outside the truck.

"Jesus. Gimme that. She's probably in the window watching us."

"Nelda? She's probably dead from collapsed lungs."

"Don't say that." I still wanted to believe that my search for Nelda's daughter was somehow, if only in an insignificant way, changing her life into a place she wanted to be in for once. The more Mikey and I scrutinized the bears, the closer we came to three solid facts: they looked the same, were not mass-market produced, and were made by the same artist. We went through a list of things we could do.

"Go through the phone directory," Mikey said, "track down all the wood carvers and, you know, whatever they're called . . ."

"Sculptors?"

"Yeah, sculptors, and find out if there's any around here that carve wooden bears."

"I guess I was thinking of a more subtle approach." I rolled my eyes and picked one of them up again. "Did you see this?" I asked, pointing. "Grab the flashlight out of the glove box." He handed it to me.

"Here." Mikey leaned over to examine the secret inscription—the outline of a heart with the letters "NF" below it.

"Someone's initials," I said.

"Whose?"

"Hell if I know." I grabbed the other bear and trained the flashlight beam on the bottom.

"Same inscription, but there's no heart on this one," Mikey said.

"I know. I want to try to find more of these pieces with the heart on them."

"You think they mean something important?"

"I think they're a love letter. Someone made this especially for Mary and put a heart on it. The one Janet had was probably sculpted by the same artist but has no connection to Mary."

We decided to split up, one of us in the secret basement room and the other in Mary's bedroom closet. Nelda's bedroom door was closed tight, but the light was still on. So I took Mary's closet and sent Mikey downstairs with explicit directions to look in the trunk in the secret room in the cellar. The basement noises started as soon as I got into the closet. Ignore him, I thought. I set the drawer back into the dresser, then checked behind it, on the floor, inside shoeboxes, and found nothing but folded old, musty blankets. The top shelf leaned twenty degrees to the right. Arms folded, I stood back a few inches to observe. Each end had about four shoeboxes stacked in two rows, and a larger box was on the left side. It had no top to it, and it wasn't taped.

In a second I had it on the floor of the closet, doing my best to obscure the sound of my movements. Then again, there was nothing stopping me from my quest, was there? Nelda knew why Mikey and I were there. We told her the first night we showed up. Why was I so afraid of being caught within the fortress walls? Maybe I didn't want to bring Nelda back to life at all. Maybe life, for someone like her, would be something I had never seen. This thought terrified me.

Miraculously, Mikey met me on schedule back at the truck. He was empty-handed and panting.

"What's with you?" I set five objects carefully on the front seat.

"Spider. Biggest one I've ever seen."

"Jesus. What kind of Watson are you?"

"Look, Holmes, you're a goddamned opium addict who bothers the neighbors with your gloomy violin playing." He got over it quick, though. "What's this?"

I smiled, rolled down the window, and smelled the cool night air. "More carvings. Another bear, an owl, snake, eagle." I turned my head toward the window again. "Smell that?"

"Rain?"

"Not that. Higher." I inhaled deeply. The twinkling sky had clouded over in the last half hour. Nelda's street was quiet and dark with the exception of one streetlight and a living room light in the house three doors down. The air felt static, heavy. I recognized it.

"Do you see anything?" Mikey said.

I didn't. The sky was a quiet, even texture of black silk. None of the telltale tornado signs showed in it, but I couldn't ignore the signature chemical smell that had preceded every one I had lived through so far.

We probed every inch of these new carved animals, and found the same "NF" initials on the bottom, as well as the same heart found on the bear from Mary's closet.

"How many people do you know in Grady who carve wooden animals?"

"None. Why?"

"No one I know—no one I've ever known—has ever carved animals like that."

"What's your point?" My eyelids were closing involuntarily. It was too late to be dealing with Mikey.

"There are lots of Indians who carve wood into animals. My Ma takes the twins to a craft fair in Norman every year and they always see stuff like that. Maybe it was an Indian."

"Giving them to Mary? I guess it's possible." I thought of the confrontation between Nelda and the Indian man in her backyard the other day. I told Mikey as much.

"You said that was an old man."

"No I didn't! You just weren't listening. Maybe Mary was in love with some Indian guy."

"What kind of Indian?" Mike asked.

"Sioux, maybe. Or Choctaw. He had long hair."

"All Indians have long hair."

I shook my head in disgust. "All TV Indians, maybe. You think there are Sioux in Sand Bluff?" I gestured toward the house. "The baby pictures. Remember? It was stamped on the back of each of them."

"Might be. Sand Bluff's in Choctaw County, so probably not Sioux, but I reckon they got Indians there. Maybe wood-carving Indians." Mikey checked the sky again and smelled the air. "You think there's a connection?"

I got out of the truck and lit one of the cigarettes I'd swiped from Nelda's canister. "Why yes, my dear Watson. Let's regard all the facts carefully."

Mikey slid over to the driver's side window and leaned his elbows out of the truck. He watched me with a mix of mild amusement and fatigue. "Mary McCann was found bludgeoned in the baseball diamond in Grady. No suspects."

"Right," I said in my best Holmesian monotone. I waved my hand to get him to continue.

"Mary's friend, Lillie Mechem, disappeared out of nowhere," he replied in his Watson voice. "Police investigation earned no suspects. Case unsolved."

"Correct. Those are the bare facts. Now the peripheral ones."

"Huh?"

"Watson, Watson. Read the dictionary once in a while, would you please? Peripheral. Tangential. Tell me the less important facts of the case."

"Case?" Mikey laughed. "You don't think you're really a detective now, do you?" The glare that showed in my eyes caused him to continue his train of thought. "Okay. Less important than one dead girl and one missing girl is the fact that Lillie's father donated the reward money to a phony minister, and that minister *could very well be* Lillie's uncle."

"And?"

Mikey lay his head down on his arms across the truck door. "And . . ." he moaned, "you know, he was all cagey when we went to his house and asked him about it."

I'd sucked down one cigarette and I was lighting another when I saw a light go off inside the house. "Now take the other road," I said, hoping he'd get my reference.

"You mean Nelda?"

I nodded.

"Mary's mother Nelda hasn't really left her house in five years. That's one."

I smiled and held up my index finger.

"She won't talk about Mary's disappearance. Number two. We saw her pick up something from Van Geller that we proved was a check for five hundred dollars, and it looks like he's been paying her off for some time. Three."

"Good, Watson, you're getting the picture all right! Now, the number four clue is the most significant so far, not because it points us to any definitive information . . ."

"Definitive?" Mikey said. "Gimme a break."

"Any definitive information, but for how it appears, on the surface, to be completely unrelated. And that's the clue of the baby pictures. I don't know what they mean, who the babies belong to, but—"

"But we found them in the dead girl's mother's basement, so it must have something to do with it."

"Might, not must. It might have something to do with it."

"What do you think?" Mikey asked, not to Holmes but to me, his old standby.

"I think going to Sand Bluff might lead us to where those pictures came from, and if we get there okay, we might be one step closer to learning what really happened in that baseball diamond and why."

Mikey closed his eyes as I stubbed out my third cigarette. "So how do we do it?"

"Proceed, my dear Watson. You mean 'how do we proceed,'" I corrected. I bared my teeth the way Holmes did in his greatest moments of arrogance.

"Whatever."

I sat down on the cool ground, watched a huddle of thick clouds float over our heads, and thought. "I guess we go to Sand Bluff and look in the telephone directory for an Indian with the initials 'N.F.'"

I hadn't been home in almost two days. They'd be frantic by now looking for me. Or maybe that's just a pretty story I told myself. Maybe they
weren't looking at all, and just believed my tall tale about camping
out. Lewella would be home taking care of the baby, Denny off somewhere pretending to work at his pretend job, Mama would be wringing
her hands, baking endless pies, and Daddy, well, who knows. Driving
around our ranch, mending fences, taking an inventory of the cattle, all
the things the ranch hands did but doing it himself gave him something
to do with his empty days. I wondered about the position of the scarf on
the hitching post.

Grady to Sand Bluff was about as dreary a drive as I could imagine.
We went north to Ringling and picked up Route 70, which was almost
a straight shot to Choctaw County. Then we took a bumpy, zigzagged
road north and crossed the Clear Boggy River and McGee Creek that fed
into Red River and marked the Oklahoma/Texas dividing line. Mikey
drummed his fingertips on the outside of the passenger door the whole trip
and sang along to Johnny Cash even when he didn't know the words.

There were no road signs, county signs or even markers on the hell-
ish road to Sand Bluff and, somehow, we ended up back on the freeway heading south on 271. After four hours of driving, we ended up in
Hugo. A shopkeeper at Midway Florist on East Jackson let us come in
the backroom. Her white plastic nametag read "Gladys Duncan" and
she had to be over a hundred years old.

"Y'all set a while and I'll bring in some lemonade." With some effort,
she stretched her mouth far enough to smile. Every inch of the store
smelled like fresh-cut flowers. Some were sweet, and others smelled
like grass.

"Ma'am," I said, and Mikey put on his panic face. "Do you have a phone directory for Sand Bluff?"

"Sand Bluff? Well no," she explained. "They don't have any phones out there."

I could tell Mikey and I were thinking the same thing. I excused myself and went out to the truck to get the only real piece of Mary Prairie I'd found so far.

"Ma'am," I said, panting, and holding out the spirit bear in my palm. "We're trying to find the artist who carved this. Does it look familiar?"

"Oh yes." She seemed certain about it. "We see these all the time. Reckon I just spotted one in a store down Hugo. You do know where Hugo is, don't you?"

"I thought we were in Hugo, ma'am," I said quietly.

"Heavens, I said Hugo and meant to say Durant. In the next county over. My daughter Francis lives there. It was my grandson's second birthday, God bless him, he's getting so bi—"

"Please, Mrs. Duncan," Mikey jumped in. "Do you know who carved this bear? We really need to find him. Here, look at the bottom. The initials say 'NF.' Anyone in Sand Bluff with those initials?"

Mikey's outburst put a strained look on the old woman's face. Her eyes got small and her mouth contracted, thinking, trying to remember where she was and what we'd been talking about. I could almost see the brain cells disintegrating by the minute—balling up and turning to fine powder.

"When I was a girl," she started, her head facing the window now, "we used to walk from Hugo west to Soper, and one time my oldest sister Eva, who was always misbehaving, wanted to walk into Sand Bluff on the dirt road. It was over twenty miles and so my brother walked with her part of the way. She collapsed before she got there and a cowboy found her and brought her back on horseback." Gladys Duncan looked up from her reverie. "She married that cowboy. It's her daughter who I went to see in Durant." Laughter. "They've got a little dairy now, and over a hundred Holsteins and Gurnseys. Now you boys go along to that little curio shop where

I saw those wooden bears. It's down the road a piece. Turn right at the feedlot."

The feedlot turned out to be in Durant where Mrs. Duncan's daughter lived. And sure enough, there were three curio shops on the same street that all sold versions of spirit bears. Some were carved out of polished stone and had shards of turquoise tied to their bellies with soft leather straps. Others were skeletal outlines of animals molded from tempered wrought iron. We were hungry, and the two restaurants in town only served lunch 'til 2 PM. It was 2:20. I stood at the big window of the last store, surveying the sinister sky that scared us in Enid last night.

"Jake!" I heard Mikey hiss behind me. He was waving me to the back of the store where he had found a small display of miniature carved animals. They were not the heavy, dark ironwood of the spirit bear I got from Janet or from Mary's closet, either. These were light wood and had a dull finish. "Look!" he almost screamed. I leaned down and saw a bulletin board with a pamphlet tacked to it with a picture of an Indian artist. It read, "Nash Farrell—Artistry in Nature. Wood carvings of animals, trees, and other beautiful inhabitants of Mother Earth." "Nash Farrell, 'NF.' What do you think, Jakie? Did we find him?"

I picked up a wooden bear and quickly scanned the biographical text on the artist. It listed a post office box in Boehler. It just so happened that Boehler was the next town over from Sand Bluff.

"Well done, Watson, well done." I picked up one of the bears. The tag on the bottom read two dollars and fifty cents. I brought it to the register.

"What are you doing? That's our hamburger money."

"We're gonna need this for a cover story. There's candy bars in the truck." What I didn't tell Mikey right then was that Nash Farrell, according to his photograph, was the same man who had argued with Nelda in her backyard. And in a gust of cold air, I felt Mary McCann's long arms around my body, as if she were once again rising up from the dead to communicate with me. This time, instead of screaming bloody murder, I felt she was glad to have me on her side.

We still had enough money for a hamburger, with the coins we had in our pockets. Then on the edge of Durant on our way back west, I told Mikey I wanted to stop at a pay phone. We found one in an abandoned gas station.

"Calling your mo-mmy?" Mikey joked. I ignored him, knowing Mikey could sap every ounce of my courage in a split second if I let him.

"No." I climbed out of the truck, walked quickly to the phone booth, and hoped he wouldn't follow me. I had reserved just enough coins in the bottom of my sneaker to make one long-distance call back to Ringling.

"Hello?" Walter van Geller's voice was slow and moaning, like I'd woken him up from a deep sleep.

"Mr. van Geller? This is Jacob Leeds." I no longer cared enough to change my name and hide myself from him. "I came to see you with my friend to ask you about those girls who disappeared."

Silence. Then I heard him breathing heavily.

"Are you there, Mr. van Geller?" I made myself sound annoyed, like I was just a kid who didn't know any better. "Hello?"

"Y—I'm here, what do you want, kid?"

"It's Jake."

"What do you want? I answered your questions already. You said, what was it now, that you were doing some research project for school? It's summer, though."

"Summer school, sir." I thought "sir" might get me somewhere. I sucked in a deep breath to steady my nerves and kept my eye on Mikey. "But that's not true."

"What's not? You're not in school?"

"No."

"What do you want, then?" he said after hesitating slightly.

"I know what you did." I was sure he could hear my heartbeat and the adrenaline sloshing through my veins.

Silence again. Time to play poker.

"I know you were Lillie Mechem's uncle, and I know you know where she is now. I'm not asking you to confirm or deny this because

I already know and I can prove it. I just want to come over and talk to you later today, you know, face to face."

"All right."

It seemed way too easy but I took it and ran. "I'm out in Durant now, so I'll see you in about three hours."

And I could never be certain what his last word was, maybe "yes," or "fine," because my auditory sense was diverted by Mikey's frozen face in the truck window—staring at a whirling funnel cloud heading right toward us.

thirty-one

tornado: a) a squall accompanying a storm in Africa, b) a violent destructive swirling wind accompanied by a funnel-shaped cloud that progresses in a narrow path over the land.

Over the land. Well that's not exactly what Mikey and me saw a hundred feet in front of us. Before any conscious thoughts formed in my head, I was screeching the truck out of the parking lot and onto the road.

"Shit, Jake! What the hell are you doing? Y-you're driving right—"

"Shut up, it's coming this way so I'm trying to get past it. Hold on . . ."

And in that precise moment, it wasn't the sensation of being lifted off the ground that was so alarming, but more the sound, or I should say the *howl*, that tore into my resolve. My left hip was five inches higher than my right, but I kept the accelerator rammed down as far as my foot would reach. A raucous *clunk* rooted us to the road again and I sped off toward the haunting stillness in the wake of the funnel.

"Look at that, sweet Jesus," Mikey said with his head angled back. But I didn't want to look. After Lucy's Ditch and Blackie's burial, I'd had enough brushes with death to last a lifetime.

"Where's it going? Still east?"

"Yeah, the funnel's thinning out. It split for a second but came back together." Mikey wiped his eyes and didn't seem to care that I saw him. "Guess we can breathe now."

We zoned out to the radio and the hot air blowing our hair around our faces. I don't think either of us could really believe all that had happened so far this summer—so much more than any normal teenaged boy dreams of happening. More than we wanted to happen. Nearly more than we could bear.

"What about Boehler?"

"We'd be there now if it weren't for the funnel cloud. Besides, we don't know he lives there for sure."

"What do you mean? You want him to knock on our door? Would that be proof enough?"

Mikey shook his head. I could tell he was getting sick of my blind faith in nothing but a dream. "It said it on the artist's blurb in the curio shop," he said softly. "You don't have to believe it, though."

"What do you believe?"

He laughed slightly. "About what?"

"You know." I didn't know, but I kept talking because the power of my thoughts in silence was too frightening to bear. "About Nash Farrell."

"I think a bear you found in Mary's closet has initials on the bottom."

"Not just in the closet but wedged between two drawers. Hidden, concealed. Why was she hiding it and who was she hiding it from? Nelda. Who else would go in her closet? Why would she be hiding something like that from her mother? It's not like it was a pack of pro-phylactics or love notes from her gym teacher."

Mikey had no reply to my argument.

"You think I'm jumping to conclusions? Fine. You can think what-ever you want. We'll do what my parents do. Agree to disagree."

"All I'm saying is," he paused, "I dunno."

"Are you coming with me tomorrow, then, or not? I mean to Boehler."

"What else do I have to do?"

The drive back home was more than just tense. Even though we had found where Nash lived, I still felt like I'd let Mikey down. I don't know why he expected so much more from me, but I hadn't measured up. I could read this truth all over his face. So I allowed my mind to drift to more terrifying possibilities. While driving, I daydreamed that Blackie showed up standing in the middle of the road with a shotgun pointed at my head. I swerved left, then quickly right, then my right bumper tailed into his lower half and he went spinning across the road.

Mikey was dozing, and I didn't feel like informing him of Blackie's latest ploy to interrupt my daydreams. I didn't know where he was at that moment, but I knew one thing for sure—he was looking for me.

"You stopping in Enid for anything?" Mikey was awake now.

"Ringling. That's our only stop on the way to Grady. You got something to do in Enid?"

"No." An edge to his voice. "You got something to do in Ringling?"

"You know what."

"Yeah. Harassing some old preacher, that's what."

That's it, I thought. I screeched the truck over to the shoulder and it skidded down a few feet on the embankment. Mikey's head hit the roof and mine hit the window jamb.

"What the fuck are you doing?" he blared in my ear. I hardly ever heard Mikey use language like that, mostly because he was too scared that if he started talking like that all the time, he'd slip around his mother and be grounded for a year.

"You tell *me*. Tell me! I mean it. You seem to know everything and you're convinced I'm barking up the wrong tree, so tell me how the fuck it is. Enlighten me."

He was rubbing his head, looking out the window. No funnel clouds in the area. As a matter of fact, it seemed suspiciously calm, even more so than usual.

"Got nothing to say now?" I sighed. "Loser."

Mikey changed positions so he could look me straight in the eye. Boys my age didn't do this much, not unless they wanted to get accused of all kinds of things. My hands were sweating and there wasn't a single sound outside the truck. The quiet scared me.

"I'm afraid, Jakie."

I lowered my head and felt like doing something, but I hadn't a clue what it was. I knew Mama or Lewella would know just what to say and do in a situation like this. Women were born automatically versed in how to handle delicate situations—smoothing things over, handling awkward moments and tense emotions with a palm on the shoulder or iced tea poured in a tall glass.

"You think I'm not? I'm scared all the time now. I can't sleep, I can't eat, I went camping overnight in that goddamned field and now I have no life. Someone took it from me and I'm just a kid. I want my freedom and my family back. How long's it been since we played baseball and went down to the creek, not Comanche but the 'old' one, and just sat there drinking Blackie's beers and playing Secret Agent? Maybe we've outgrown that stuff now, I don't know. But I don't think I'm supposed to have this pressure right now in my life. I don't know anything about people, really, or about how the world works. I don't even know enough to know what I *don't* know. I'm just taking every day on instinct." The Blackie-panic set in my bones again. "I don't know what else to do. I went out to that creek to fish one day and now your brother's planning to put my head on a stake because of what he thinks I saw. Talk about the poison fruit on your family tree." Mikey didn't laugh. "And that was just being at the right place at the wrong time. But Mary's something different. I know what I'm doing."

"How could you when there's no proof of anything?"

"Because I feel it. That's how I know. And because there's this thought that I can't get out of my head."

Mikey was waiting to hear it, but the truth was that I hadn't formulated anything yet.

"I know her," I said finally and lurched the truck back into gear.

I don't think he really knew what I was talking about for a long time. As we chugged closer to Ringling, I felt his tension growing by the second. He sat there, with that indelible Mikey-expression, full of awe and wonder, but something longing, too, like a prowling coyote searching for food and companionship, for a place in which to belong. Blackie, on the other hand, was the hungry bear of the family in an endless search for prey. Then something seemed to flash through Mikey's brain because he snapped his head in my direction.

"You found something," he said, as a statement rather than a question.

"Yeah."

He sighed with impatience. Coyotes aren't impatient creatures, so maybe I'd have to attribute him to something else. I reached into the pocket of my T-shirt and pulled out the photograph I'd kept close to my heart since I first found it in Nelda's basement. It had been unfolded and refolded so many times, the hair surrounding the face looked frayed and yellow. Still, I unfolded it properly and held it out to him. I watched him peripherally and even with my eyes on the road I could tell he was sucked into the haunting image. From my best estimation, she would have been fourteen years old when it was taken.

"That's her, isn't it?"

"Yeah."

Mikey turned and looked at me now, as if staring at the side of my head might steal my attention from the road.

"What?" I said finally.

"Notice anything special about her?"

"Aside from how she's dead and . . ."

"Not that. Look at her, Jake."

Yeah, I was looking, all right. "Lewella?"

"More than that," Mikey said. "She looks like *you*."

tHIRty-two

It was high time I went home to connect, or reconnect, with my family and the ties I had to real, living people. I had absolutely none of the requisite qualifications for chasing the dead, whatever they were. And now, where I least wanted to be, I was standing outside Van Geller's door with my mind on other things and other people. I'd never noticed what a nice door it was, too—tall and white, freshly painted.

Freshly painted.

In another time and space, I might have asked myself why the door was just painted when it was chipping off the rest of his house, but this cycle of running circles and standing still was tiring me.

When I knocked, dots of white paint stuck to the tips of my knuckles. I knocked again, three times, but nobody answered. I felt a light wind blow against the back of my neck, and recognized this sign as the same wind that blew the night Blackie Savage delivered one of his victims into the endless dark. Wondering now, just wondering, I saw Mikey wondering too. He slowly stepped out of the truck.

"So?" he said.

"No one home."

"He didn't answer?"

I knew what he was asking me. I think my stomach knew before the realization traveled upward to my brain. And in that instant, with Mikey standing on the front lawn and me still on the porch, we became transformed into Maxima and Brainiac, instinctively knowing what to do and unafraid of the action necessary to effect change.

"I'll take the back," Mikey said, holding an invisible revolver in his right hand. I looked in the narrow windows outlining Van Geller's front door, and remembered him that first day we met—screen door clamped open and sweating lemonade glasses making watermarks on his antique coffee table.

The ground was flat around the old man's house. Sure, the front door and porch trim had been painted, but it didn't change the twenty-degree slant to his roof or the carpet of matted brown grass surrounding the house. The topography of his street, all of Ringling and even Oklahoma, for that matter, was flat, so Mikey got around to the back of the house in no time. I could see him back there from the front window when I squinted my eyes. That was when I wished I'd never started looking for Van Geller. The glasses gave it away first—large, black, pointy things that never looked quite right on the old man's face, lying upside down on his kitchen floor. I had a feeling that fact would never matter again to Van Geller, but I wouldn't let myself decide for sure 'til I got a good look for myself.

I tried the knob on the front door—locked.

But then I took a step back, really looked at it, and remembered something. The human memory is just like this—a jaded, devilish trickster, letting through one or two isolated facts and not formulating the necessary thought sometimes until years later, its sole purpose being nothing more than to confound, confuse, and irritate.

I ran around the back to grab Mikey.

"What?"

"C'mere. Round front."

He followed me, reluctantly peeling his face from the back window.

"What do you think?" I pointed to the corner of the doorjamb. Mikey bit his lip, and though he hated any kind of a mental challenge, he smiled when he caught my drift. "Door's hanging crooked on the hinges."

"Yeah. Remember—"

"The cabin," he interrupted, speaking of the little shed his mother rented once near Waurika Lake for the only family vacation I was ever invited to attend. "Where we found all the dead fish under the house . . ."

"But that little out building, how'd we break into it that time?"

His round, bleary eyes blinked as he remembered. "Lifted it up."

"From the bottom?"

"I reckon that's better than from the top. Some cheap piece of ply-wood garbage, too, that never hung right on the hinges. I had splin-ters wedged so far down my thumb they came out my elbow. I lifted it up and you pushed it in and tripped the lock." He laughed. "Then we busted the lock off with a hammer and got into the . . ." Mikey stopped mid-sentence and glanced quickly at Van Geller's front door. "You wanna break in *here*?"

I pointed at the eyeglasses lying haphazardly on the floor and didn't say another word.

"Shit, Jakie, you think he—"

"Grab the bottom and I'll push," I said.

"You—but—this ain't some old junkster door. Might even be solid."

"It's not; it's hollow. I could tell when I knocked."

Mikey crossed his arms in defiance and drew in two deep breaths of quiet deliberation. "You think it'll work?"

I stood back from the door and examined Mikey's round, meaty face. "Try. That's all I'm asking. Okay?"

"What about neighbors?" It was a valid concern. "It's still light out."

"Unless you want me to flatten you right here . . ."

"I'll get my brother after you if you do," he said, nine simple words that immediately changed the tenor of our argument. I didn't have to remind him that his brother was already after me, and probably would be for the rest of my life. I nodded soberly toward the house.

Mikey crouched down on all fours. "Not much clearance down here."

"Room enough for your fingers, I guess."

"Barely," he grumbled, and managed to lift the door up a few inches. I jiggled it from the top and shoved hard against the fresh, white paint.

"You get it?" he asked.

"Do you see me in his goddamned house yet? Again. This time lift up and then pull it toward you."

He lifted, higher this time, and yanked it toward himself full throttle. I heard a blast of wind tumble through the leaves of the willow tree towering over us. We both heard something click in the lock mechanism, but when I shoved my weight against it, nothing moved. Sweat beads dripped from Mikey's face onto Van Geller's faded welcome mat. With his pathetic, scared rabbit face, he looked up at me and pointed into the house.

"What?" I looked and pressed my face against the glass.

The glasses were gone.

Had the old man picked them up himself, or had his killer done it to cover his bloody tracks?

"What's going on in there?" Mikey said.

Scanning from room to room, nothing looked necessarily out of order, except for a dark spot on the living-room carpet, lit up by the sun in the backyard.

He put his hand on my shoulder. "You know. I can tell. Is he dead in there or what?"

I rang the doorbell again, and this time heard a thump in a far corner of the house.

"What do you think you're doing?"

"See if someone answers," I replied meekly, not really understanding anything about anything at this point. I felt myself fade into a kind of bubble, where there were no emotions or second-guessing or self-doubt. I rang that bell again and again, sweat pouring off my chin and not even caring enough to wipe it off with my sleeve. Somehow, I was ringing it to send a beacon or alarm to whatever superheroes were tapped into the doings, or wrongdoings, of our humble scratch of panhandle slim.

God help us, I thought, now banging on the door with both fists. Mikey was behind me, trying to hold my arms, scared of arousing suspicion among the neighbors, or maybe because he was used to doing the right thing all the time. But for me, in my family, wrong was right and right was something for TV stars and sheriffs. Slowly, in the fat, humid air and the tall willows weeping behind us and with Mikey silently begging me to come to my senses, I started to understand things one at a time.

"Is he dead, Jakie?" came the small, panicked voice of my lifelong friend. I motioned for him to try the door-pulling scam once more. So he crouched low and stuffed his fingers under it again, and this time he yanked it up so hard I thought it might spring right off the hinges.

"Try it now," he said with strained vocal chords. I sort of fell into the room and then the foyer of the old man's house, Mikey panting like an overweight basset hound behind me. He keyed into my crazed expression now, studying me. I knew what I looked like and knew what Mikey would see in my eyes—something had changed and was still changing. We were both looking at the floor where the glasses had been not five minutes ago—wondering.

"You think he's okay?" he asked me.

"I know he's not."

"You mean—"

"Yeah Mikey, dead. Dead. That's why there's blood on the carpet. What the hell do you think?" I pointed but he'd already seen it.

As usual, the quiet scared me more than the notion of more dead bodies. And still, I could not yet reconcile why I had been chosen to proctor the space between dead and alive, heaven and earth. I could hear the soft, summer wind blowing outside and a car motor somewhere down the street. But I'd come here for a reason, so the silence no longer mattered. There was work to do.

And, once again, I found myself magically at the center of a Greek tragedy. Mikey and I were leaning over the old man's bashed-in head when the first knock came at the door. The door's open, I thought, looking back at the root of all my trouble—cops. Okay, well, we've established already, I suppose, the ugly truth that Blackie Savage is as much a typical cop as I am Superman. Even so, things were bad this morning. But I hadn't really known the meaning of bad until right then.

"Get up, boy."

There was only one inside the house. Five or six other coppers circled the house like a starving murder of crows.

"Now!"

I could tell if this guy had kids it was only so he'd have little things to boss around. Only five-nine or so, much shorter than Daddy, even Denny, but what he lacked in height he compensated for in mental stature. A drill sergeant in the Army? Navy admiral? They were all grown from the same poisoned tree as far as I was concerned, just with different names. Boss-ers. Do this, do that, and not tomorrow or later but right fucking now. Any second, the uniformed man would grab me by the hair and jerk me up like a puppet. Mikey tried to suppress the tears in his eyes and I just sat there in quiet vigil over a man I never had the chance to figure out. I know it was sacrilegious to scold the dead, but what good would he do anybody in this state? What about all my questions? If not him, then who would give me the answers I needed?

"What's your name?" the admiral said.

"I didn't kill him," I said coldly.

The scary admiral leaned in close, so close I could smell the sweat beading on his forehead. Our noses were almost touching. "That's your name, then?"

the worst part was that they hauled us off in separate cars. I had seen this tactic used on cop shows on television, and at the picture shows, I guess because cops thought they'd get different answers to their questions from everyone involved. And probably true, too—if adversity of the murder variety couldn't break down human defenses, nothing could.

There was no telling what Mikey might say under duress. In other words, if I threw him under the bus, I'd lose my best friend forever and risk even further wrath from his brother. But the only alternative was turning myself in.

Before I had a chance to decide, I found myself in a small, windowless, gray room with a concrete floor. Somehow this single, isolated feature augmented the gravity of my present situation. The admiral barged through the door, looked back and answered someone's question, then looked at me and exited. This happened three times before he sat down across from me at the round table.

"Any questions?"

"More than you could answer, I'll bet." This snappy tone simply erupted from my mouth without any preparation.

The admiral lowered his eyes, brushed his sweating palm over the top of his neatly cropped buzz cut, and slid his glasses up to the bridge of his nose. I knew his understated behavior was an attempt at inspiring fear, but he wasn't scaring me.

"When do I get my phone call?"

"Who you gonna call, your Daddy?"

"What if I was?"

"We've already called him. He's on his way down here now."

Good Lord. I needed him right now like a gunshot wound to the belly. Him driving out to the Ringling police station this time of night, after he'd had his usual three or four shots of hooch, they might even smell liquor on his breath and keep him here overnight. Wouldn't Mama be surprised, waking up tomorrow to pick us both up from jail? I might as well kill myself right now. But there were no visible, potential weapons anywhere in the room. Guess that was the point.

"Got nothing to say about that, do you?"

"No sir."

"Don't like your Daddy much?"

I tried to imagine what kind of trap he was wriggling me into, and decided only the truth could save me now, if anything could. "Not much to like, I reckon."

The admiral centered himself squarely up to the table and pressed his back against the chair. He was a smoker. I recognized the deep lines in his face on each side of his mouth—just like Mama's. I bet he would have liked one right now.

"That man dead?" I asked.

"That man? Like you don't know who he is?"

"I know *what* he is."

Admiral shook his head. "What he was."

So Walter Van Geller, ordained minister, high school teacher, operator of what I suspected to be an illegal adoption agency, and not to mention the only man remotely qualified to answer all the questions in my head, was shot and killed in his own house. If there really was a Superman, I needed him now more than ever. But I had a feeling Mikey needed him even more.

Admiral sat up even straighter now, pulled a small notebook out of his shirt pocket, and unhooked the pen from the top coil.

"Why not just tell me one thing—whether there's any hope of you answering my questions tonight. Because if there's not, I'd just as soon toss you downstairs for the night and get home to my wife's fried chicken."

This statement made me like him a little more, maybe because he was using a particular tactic on me rather than just barking out his answers and trying to scare the bejeezes out of me. It made me, in a way, important enough to be thought of and considered a real suspect. "I don't know nothing." The man lowered his head. "Sir."

"How's about how you got in that house?"

I looked away with my look of feigned disinterest, and rested my chin on my palm. This made him madder. "Front door was open. He always left it that way."

"You know this about him?" Admiral was talking soft now, almost whispering. "But you just finished telling me that you knew nothing. That's something, boy. Details, when it comes to murder, are more than just something—they're all we have. I want you to try to understand something here—that man's dead. He ain't never gonna breathe again, or make himself coffee and biscuits for breakfast, or fill up his car with gasoline or brush his teeth before bed. He's on his way to the morgue right now where he'll lay on a metal slab with a bunch of other bodies waiting for an autopsy by the medical examiner, and after that, I suspect, he'll be buried in the ground with the rest of the dead. You see what I'm getting at?"

"Not really." And I'd probably seen more dead bodies lately than he had.

"See, the problem is this—we came upon a crime scene, that's what we call the resting place of a dead body, and you know who was the first person I seen there?" He stuck his index finger out toward me now. "You, boy. You the one I seen leaning over the body, with a spot of blood on your hand."

The interrogation closet was like a tomb—no air coming either in or out, and I was more than just hot. My heart wouldn't stop racing up and down my ribcage and I had the oddest sensation of heavy bricks pressing down on the tops of my shoulders. "I'm—"

"Now, supposing you were gonna tell me you just came in and found him that way." I tried to interrupt him, but he put his long finger up again. There was a piece of black lint stuck to the edge of his nail. "I hope you would carefully consider every word you told me in this room before you just blurted out the first thing that come to your mind. And the reason for this is that we got a murder to solve now, and you're the closest thing we got to a suspect."

"W-what about Mikey?" I hated how I stuttered sometimes under pressure. It was the opposite impression of how I wanted Admiral to see me. I wanted to be a worthy adversary for him, someone, a suspect, to tell his wife about over a dinner of fried chicken and mashed potatoes with gravy. But to him, I knew I was just some little runt in the wrong place at the wrong time. His demon eyes were planning my arrest and conviction right then.

"He's with another officer."

"He don't know nothin' so it don't matter what you ask him," I said, lapsing into the rebellious street language that Mikey and Freddie and me practiced in the tree house.

Now the Admiral scratched his head. "Now," his finger wagging, "I thought I saw him helping you break into that house less than an hour ago."

I swallowed hard.

"We watched you break in, boy. No sense lying to me now. We know how you got in and what you did when you got there. What we don't know—"

"I didn't do nothing when I got in there but check to see if he was breathing!" I slapped my palm on the grainy table. Admiral's eyes were curious now. "We saw his glasses through the windows on each side of the door."

"Eyeglasses?"

"On the floor, that's right. Just where they shouldn't have been. So I showed them to Mikey, but when I turned my head away for one second, the glasses were gone."

He was pretending to take down my account in his empty notebook. "So you thought, what, 'I know I'm not no police officer but I think I'll break into this house and see what I can find out'?"

I took a breath and considered how to respond further. "I guess when I saw the glasses, we thought he was . . ."

"You said I and we. Which is it?"

"Huh?"

"You said 'when I' and then 'we thought.' Did your friend see the glasses or not? You just told me that you saw them, but when you brought your friend to look at them, they were gone." Admiral put up his palms and gave a mock shrug, another nervy tactic the police use to psyche out teenaged boys. I wasn't falling for anything now. "Let me just check my notes here," he said and started flipping, "but I could've sworn, right, here it is. You said," he was reading now.

"Mikey never saw the glasses." I thought I'd save him the trouble of reading back my words. "I saw them, and when Mikey came to the window, they were gone."

"What does that tell us?"

"I thought, when I saw them lying on the floor, that the old man got in a scrape with someone and now he was dead, but when I saw the glasses gone ten seconds later, I knew he was either still alive, or the killer was in there with him."

"Interesting theory," the man said and unbuttoned the top button of his uniform shirt. "But what made you suspect death in the first place? Are you used to so much household order that you automatically assume someone has died if you see something on the floor?"

Grown-ups and their trick questions. They must have sat up nights, communicating through some secret network, and giving each other tips on how to outsmart teenagers. Assholes. It was a smart question—I'd give him that, even if it were crafty. He wanted crafty—I'd give him crafty. "I saw something on the carpet."

"What was that?"

"I wasn't sure at the time, but now I know it was a spot of blood about a foot from where the body was," I said, anticipating his next round.

"And from that tiny little window by his front door, you could crane your neck far enough to see the living-room carpet?"

"Yes sir."

He wrote feverishly in his notebook now, looked up at me, and then wrote some more.

"Can I go now?"

A half smile cracked across his lips.

"And what about my phone call?"

The admiral knocked on the door to the interrogation room. "Fergus? You there?"

A red-faced man opened the door a crack.

"Would you be so kind as to bring this boy downstairs for me?"

thirty-four

Downstairs. Hmmm.

Before I actually moved off the interrogation chair, I envisioned those dark catacombs in the Roman Colosseum where they kept prisoners before they fed them to the lions. Then I wondered if "downstairs" meant a cozy, carpeted room with soft lighting and an old woman reading in a rocking chair with the scent of oatmeal cookies in the air.

Fat chance.

The red-faced cop had a round body that barely fit within the confines of his uniform. And his eyes bulged out, the way Mama told me about thyroid patients. The way he said, "Come with me, okay?" told me that he was kind, perhaps too kind to be part of the unfriendly order of which Blackie Savage was a member. I followed him down a tight staircase and saw a comfortable, yellow light spilling over a scratched wooden floor. Too nice to be a jail, I thought, and I was right. It wasn't the jail. Not hardly. Red, my transition proctor between interrogation and incarceration, took a heavy set of keys off his belt and unlocked a steel, echoey door.

"Down there," he said, pointing down the hallway.

I couldn't make my legs move. I even tried talking and opened my mouth but no sound came out. Was this it for me? Would Mikey and me be in neighboring cells where we'd play clandestine games of chess with two boards and a mirror? It was so dark I couldn't even see a foot in front of me, but the kind voice of my new friend Red convinced me otherwise.

"Just go on in there and your eyes'll adjust in no time at all."

"Aren't you gonna lock me in?" I asked, like a five-year-old asking to be tucked in at bedtime. But I was never going to be five again, and this was the farthest thing I'd ever seen from the bedtimes of my normal life. And yet, a distant part of my consciousness assured me that Mary had sent me to this awful, barren place with these awful people, because it contained an answer to her puzzle. Her life was the puzzle, and all the people who affected her life, and subsequent death, were pawns in this confounding chess game of murder and lies. All right, Mary, I said to myself. You put me here because you must know that I can survive in this cell for one night. But no more than that, okay? I stayed out in that God-awful baseball diamond long enough for you to scream and for me to go completely insane, and now I'm afraid there's not much left of the little nerve I had before. I'm trusting you now, so don't let me down. One night in jail in return for hell in a baseball diamond. Okay? Is it a deal? Are you listening now, Mary McCann? And if you are, can you listen again sometime?

It was after hours, so none of the lights came on once I got into the cell. I shuffled in a tentative, terrified dance across the concrete floor—eight feet long and seven feet wide. Seemed like kenneled dogs had bigger cages than this. My friend Red was nowhere in sight, despite his many promises. So it was just me here alone in jail.

Alone in jail.

The entire cellblock wasn't more than about three hundred square feet and divided into a corridor of four or five cells. None of them were occupied, I quickly discovered. So where was Mikey? Did this tiny police precinct have more than one set of jail cells? Or was he sent home? I thought the likelihood of him crying, literally, was very high. But unless sympathy for pathetic souls weighed into a place like Ringling, he was shit out of luck.

I thought of Daddy, and of Mama, and if he'd bring her with him when he came to pick me up, and the idea of his not coming at all crossed my mind more than once. He definitely had the vindictive streak of an entire lineage of Leeds blood, which didn't do much to improve his already bitter outlook. What would he do first, I asked myself. Remove his belt from his pants and whip me right then and

194

there in the middle of my cell? Or maybe just torture me with his special breed of silent treatment that he'd perfected over the past fifty years?

Sleeping was out of the question, so I fumbled my way to a cot with a stinky mattress on top and tucked myself in the corner with my knees up to my chest. This position would protect my vital organs in case I got attacked in the middle of the night, and also kept me awake and my defenses up. This strategy meant, though, that when I woke up I saw Blackie's head peering into my cell.

thirty-five

He stared at me, all curled up and fetal on the mattress, for a good five minutes. I didn't speak either. After all, what was there to say to someone like him?

There were two windows covered by steel grates up high near the ceiling. They spilled in blocks of sunlight that lit a path from the block door to my cell at the end of the row. There was something about the sight of thick metal bars, both on the door to my cell and on the windows, even on the back of the security door leading to the precinct, that shot me back ten years into the past in my grandfather's basement. Grandpa Leeds, father to my daddy and to all four of his brothers, and one sister Agnes who died as an infant, was about as hard a man as I ever remember meeting. Even harder than Blackie Savage, in some ways. Blackie at least knew how to relax when you got four or five beers in him—the tie loosened, and sometimes I'd seen him with his shirt untucked and one cigarette in his mouth and another behind his ear. He seemed to celebrate an innate sense of freedom in knowing he was the toughest man around and could, therefore, do whatever he pleased to whomever he pleased, anytime he wanted. I guess something like that could give the weakest man confidence, or enough to at least fake his way through life.

But Grandpa Leeds had even more than that. He had money.

I remembered, glancing at that divided wall of steel pillars, being in Grandpa's basement. He kept his bottles of moonshine stashed down there, and not in the special room where he made it, either. Lewella and me would find them buried under piles of clothes in Weaver's laundry area, and inside drawers and cupboards under the staircase. I'd been staying with them on an overnighter, like I did in the summers sometimes when it got too hot to sleep. Grandpa Leeds screeched into the driveway after midnight, crashed into the hitching post out front, and stumbled out drunk. Weaver found him lying in the dirt out front and ran inside to call an ambulance.

She must have screamed on her way inside, because the commotion woke me. When I ran outside, I saw him move his arm and try to get up.

"He ain't dead," I told her, and she proceeded to correct my English before adjusting her story to the emergency operator. And after she went out after him, I called Daddy and told him Grandpa was sick and to come over. It felt like a hundred degrees after midnight, and all I had on was my blue bathing suit when Daddy screeched the truck into the drive five minutes later.

"Where is he?" he hollered in a thick voice. I told him Weaver took Grandpa in the living room and he stormed in without even looking at me. "Stay out here Jakie, you hear me?" And then he changed his mind and looked back mid-step. "Get back to your room and you stay there a while. Okay? Just stay, and go back to sleep."

Well, sleep was the last thing on my mind. It wasn't so rare for drama to unfold before my very eyes, but to a five-year-old boy in the middle of the night, it was better than the Creature Double Feature at the Norman picture show.

Grandpa and Weaver allowed me to call the east spare bedroom my own when I stayed over; Lewella got the west room, which got way hotter in the afternoons, but she had lost the coin toss.

And it just so happened that the east bedroom had a vent inside the closet, where if you put your ear to it, you could hear everything going on in the rest of the house. At first, this discovery made me feel like Columbus when he landed in what he thought was India. Then, like most things in my life so far, it wasn't at all what I thought.

Weaver stayed at the sink pretending to wash already clean dishes and Daddy stood over Grandpa, who was sprawled prostrate on the couch. And at first it was just a chain of talking and mumbling, with occasional moans as Grandpa tried to move around. Then the word "drunk" cracked out of the silence, followed by a plate breaking on the kitchen floor.

"See what you done?" I heard Grandpa say.

"What I done? You're the one too drunk to stand on your two feet."

"Don't you raise your lip to me, boy. Hear me now? You just remember who done raised you and made a place for you in the world."

There was a short pause before Daddy talked again. My heartbeat bonked in and out of my chest so loud I was sure Weaver could hear it through the door. Then he said, "What happened, Pa?" By now, I was out of the closet and crouched behind the door to the dining room. From a split in the wooden door, I could see half of the living room and hallway. "Where you been all night?"

"That's none of your concern, Gordon." He said it formally, like how he talked to the other ranchers and businessmen with whom he wheeled and dealed.

"It is when my five-year-old son calls me up in the middle of the night and says that Grandpa's passed out drunk and he's scared to stay there. Now I wanna know what's going on."

Then it sounded like someone was crying, but it wasn't coming from the kitchen. I carefully changed positions to see through the hole in the door hinge—more risk of being seen but I didn't care anymore who saw me. I was as much a part of this as they were, or that's what I decided when I was five anyway.

"It's all gone to hell, Gordy," Grandpa said. Then he rolled onto his back and seemed to wipe his eyes with the back of his hand. I'd never seen a grown man cry before then, and it made me want to cry myself.

Weaver appeared like a quiet soldier in the doorway. "Wood?" she said in a small voice. My grandfather's name was Woodrow; most people called him Woody. Weaver just called him Wood for short.

"The VAC deal fell through. All gone." Grandpa waved his hands in the air and wound his body up to a sitting position. "All that work, all those years of dealing and negotiating, and placating and ass kissing, ah . . . signing papers, lawyers, you know how it works."

"Afraid I don't, Dad. I'm not part of that same circle. Never was before, likely I never will be. I'm just a plain old rancher."

But Grandpa wasn't listening to Daddy, and neither was Weaver. I could see she was crying too. She probably wanted to go over to Grandpa to sit with him or do whatever it is grandmothers do to comfort other people. Daddy was pacing now in front of the couch winding his hands into fists and letting them go. He had his scared face on. Really scared.

"What can I do, Dad? Do you have enough saved up to pay your mortgage? Lorina and I got some stashed away in the—"

"You and Lorina. Yoouuuuuuu and Loriiiiiiiiiina," he sang in pure Broadway fashion. "That's what got me into this mess in the first place."

"What's that?"

"You know just what I'm talking about and don't pretend like you don't." Grandpa's anger gave him newfound strength. He stood and walked to the fireplace, where he drummed his fingers on the polished oak mantel. I watched as a villainous expression took hold of his face, which affected more than just his lips but also his eyes and cheeks. Even his hair fell differently over his temples. "How old would it be now?"

Daddy looked confused. "Would what be?"

"Don't you remember? After all, it was your seed, Gordy. You loved that little woman of yours so desperately that you knocked her up three times in five years. Kept her busy for a spell, didn't you?"

Daddy was looking back and forth from the carpet to Weaver. "Please." His hands were shaking.

"Or, wait a second, that's right now, the second one had somebody else involved, didn't it? Now what was that name again . . . lemme see, I think it was—"

"Stop it!" Daddy's shrill voice cut through all other noises and kept even the dust mites still for over a minute. "Enough! You hear me? That's enough about all that . . . misery. I know what happened and I know how disappointed you were. And there was nothing I could do but . . . what I did!" His voice rose with his last two words, and his face had turned a frightening shade of red. Daddy turned on Woody just then and came within a few feet of his face. "So tell me now, would you please, what my mistake, my entire life's one unforgivable indiscretion, could possibly have to do with one of your dirty deals falling all to hell?"

"They're moral people, Gordy, from the Bible Belt for God's sake. Columbia, South Carolina, and Arkansas, most of them. You know, Jesus worshippers, churchgoers, people who believe that the integrity of a businessman's entire family and lineage is what governs their impressions of him as an honest man."

"And because of me you're deemed dishonest?"

Grandpa groaned and leaned his head on the fireplace mantel.

"Answer me, damn it!"

"Gordon," Weaver begged from the kitchen.

Grandpa spun around toward her and pointed his finger into the kitchen. "This is between me and the boy, Mama. Go in there where you belong."

I watched Daddy's face as Grandpa shunned Weaver. He wanted to say something on her behalf, I could tell. His lower lip quivered and he sort of leaned out toward where Weaver was standing, but I guess he thought there was enough trouble spinning around the room already and didn't want to make it worse.

"Pa? You trying to tell me something?"

"They know, is all. Don't know how they know, but they know you and Lorina, you know, had some trouble and got yourselves, well, married to cover it all up."

I tried to keep track of all the details I was hearing. I wish I could have written them down for later perusal, but I was only five and didn't know better.

"And they're holding that against you? Using it to throw away the whole deal?" Daddy's head hung down like it might fall off his neck. "That just don't make no sense. No sense at all. What happened is between Lorina and me and no one else."

"Oh yes it is, all right, between you and Lorina and someone else. Isn't it? It's that someone else that's spoiling this whole thing now. Not you, as you had very little to do with any of it from what I recall. But that . . . wife," he winced when he said the word, "of yours and . . ."

Grandpa went to the bar and poured himself a shot glass of whiskey. At that time in my childhood, I saw him do that ten, sometimes twenty times in one night before he staggered upstairs to bed.

"Can't keep a handle on your own wife. What's that say about how you conduct yourself with everything else?"

"May I at least point out that Lorina was not my wife when this happened?"

"No!" Grandpa poured shot number two and swallowed it whole. "She was, what, two months from being your wife, and you should've known better, shouldn't you? If that's the kind of woman she was, a man's supposed to figure that out before he marries her. Isn't he? That's the way it used to be done. In my day there was none of—"

"Don't give me that crap, Pa, please. You think you grew up in Bethlehem, for God's sake? In Galilee? There was just as much philandering and hanky-panky and adultery back then as there is now. It's just that it's more out in the open now."

But Grandpa Woody wasn't listening anymore. He seemed far away, like he was there in the living room but his thoughts were on other people, other worries, and the bleak future that beheld him, beheld all of us. Daddy caught me walking down the hallway when he came to fetch me from the spare bedroom. At first, it was like he didn't notice anything out of the ordinary, and then the realization of my witnessing the ugly words and ugly scene flashed across his panicked face. "Get your things; we're leaving," was all he said to me that night, and all he said to any of us for many nights after.

I never knew what Grandpa's strange words meant back then, but ten years later, crouched on the mattress of my first jail cell, staring into Blackie Savage's diabolical brown eyes, I realized that my mother had, one way or another, given birth to three children.

thirty-six

"You're not Daddy," I said.

Blackie lowered his head. "Ain't as dumb as you look then."

"You can't kill me in jail. I don't know much, but least I know that."

"You know, Jake, you're the only kid your age who's ever surprised me."

I took a few beats to size up the situation. "Where's your gun?"

Blackie standing there in uniform, I knew the answer already. But he slid his right hand down to his holster and winked.

I glanced up again at the steel grates on the upper window, then slowly stood in the middle of my cell. "What do you want with me?" I fixed my face all tight when I said it so he'd know I was serious.

"Break you outta here, that's what." He pulled a set of keys from his front pocket and unlocked my cell. "Let's go."

"And then what? You stuff me in the trunk of some car and push it into a lake, or how about tying some concrete weights to my hands and feet and flinging me off a bridge? That what guys like you do with kids like me?"

It was awkward between us then, more so than ever before. The cell door was open six inches and Blackie was standing in the opened crack, with me still in the center of the cell. Everything stopped for a second—the ventilation system, the eep of morning crickets, the wind, thoughts, hope. I could feel the tiny hairs on my neck rubbing against my shirt. He took a step closer now into the cell, arms crossed over his bulging chest, and bent his head down toward me in preparation of a whisper. I wanted no part of any secret conversations with Blackie and I would have preferred to rot in jail 'til I was eighty than be sprung loose and in his custody. And where was Mikey? Was he springing him too, or did he even spend the night here? The only person I knew I could trust, wholeheartedly, one hundred percent, was myself. Even that worried me now.

"You were there. You know it, I know it. Not much else to talk about, I guess, except I'm the only get-out-of-jail-free card you got. Take it or leave it."

Well, it didn't take me long to examine my options. Get out of jail and have Blackie torture me, or enjoy the slow and painful demise of all my mental and emotional faculties within the confines of a concrete closet. If I was out, there was always at least a small chance for escape. My assets, few as they were, included the ability to run fast, a stronger escape mechanism than most, and I was at least sure I could outsmart Blackie when he had a few beers in him.

I followed him out of the cell and studied his crooked gait as we walked down the hallway and up the stairs to the main part of the jail. Not that I was interested in why Blackie walked crookedly, but I couldn't help being curious. He acknowledged my accidental crime, noted the gravity of this realization, and seemed to move past it. Ten minutes later, I found myself sitting beside him in a police car en route to hell.

At the Ringling-Grady border, I finally spoke.

"Where's Mikey at?"

The corner of Blackie's mouth twitched when I said Mikey's name. "You think the brother of a law enforcement officer would ever spend a night in jail? He's home, probably crapped out on the couch in front of the TV, or cowering on the corner of his bed. That's what he does, you know. Cowers." Blackie gave me a quick glance, then tore his gaze back to the road. "I've got no tolerance for that."

"So I've seen," I said without even thinking.

Blackie screeched the police car into the dirt on the shoulder of Route 32. We were facing east, so the bright morning sun was blinding my vision. But even without it, I couldn't look at him. He slowly turned off the engine, whipped his head toward me, and leaned it back against the seat. "You're a liability now. You know what that means?"

"Why not just kill me right here, then?"

Blackie laughed, but not from within his dark, wolfish self. It was another part of him that laughed now—like we were old friends kicking back in some dingy bar pounding back brewskies one after the other—like I'd said something funny, like I was his equal. "I don't scare you no more," he said with a sideways smirk. "For someone like me born without brains or good looks, no woman, uneducated, scarin' people's all I got."

"Who said that?" I asked. "Anyone not scared of you, Blackie, has got serious reality problems."

"And you don't?"

"I've had a little too much reality lately, if you know what I mean."

He lit a cigarette and gazed out the window while he took the first few drags. "What do you intend to do about it?"

"You mean if you decide not to kill me?"

"Right."

I swallowed. "Well, I guess we got some negotiating to do."

Blackie's eyes widened, like he was half-interested in what I had to say and half-astounded by my gall in saying it. "Don't see as you got much to barter with."

"How about the promise of my silence?"

"That's implicit enough, I reckon."

I watched him now as I formed my next sentence, knowing somehow that it might be the most important one I'd ever uttered in my life. I looked at him while he leaned on the door, glaring at something behind me through the dirty passenger-side window. I mentally formulated my toughest badass voice and knew that the delivery would mean more than the actual words.

"In return," I began, "you've got to find someone for me. Someone I need to talk to."

"A girl?"

"A man."

"Find him yourself."

I shook my head. "Only a cop's got the resources to really find anybody. I've got the Yellow Pages but that's it."

He ignited the engine and started back down the road. And after twenty silent minutes, he turned into Hooper Circle. When Daddy stepped onto the porch, I saw all fifteen years of my life flash before me. Blackie's demonic face showed a toothy grin.

"Home sweet home," he said.

"Drop dead."

thirty-seven

Blackie and me sat on one side of the kitchen table, Mama sobbed in the corner, Daddy rocked in his power chair, and the gluey silence between us was augmented by the screams of Lewella's spoiled offspring. Enough to drive any normal man insane, to our family it was just fodder for another dreary day.

"Did you do it?" Daddy asked finally—a delayed reaction to Blackie's description of events.

"Do what?"

Daddy slapped his large palm on the tabletop. Mama shot up in her chair like a jack-in-the-box, then the tears started again.

"We think we've got a suspect in mind," Blackie stepped in. And to this day I've never been sure why his secret save-the-day quality crops up at times.

Daddy chewed on the inside of his bottom lip, like he did when his conscience tried to control his evil words. "Got yourselves some kind of witness?"

Blackie nodded. "Old woman across the street saw a car, turns out. Big, black, shiny Chevy with white-walled tires. Said it parked in the drive, one man went into the house and came out again five minutes later." He removed a wrinkled foil of Red Man tobacco and piled a furled pinch in the side of his mouth. "Found out this morning," he started, then stuck his long finger in his mouth to redistribute the tobacco load. "That's when I sprung Jakie loose."

"Your brother involved in this too?" Daddy asked him.

"We went there together," I said.

"Why? Why'd you go there in the first place is what I can't understand."

"Just to talk to hi—"

"About . . . what? What would you possibly have to talk to a Ringling preacher about, Jake?"

Mama sat forward now and wiped her eyes. "I'd like to hear this myself." I lifted my gaze to Mama's pink, swollen face and suddenly imagined the Comanche Creek drunk lying on a metal slab with a sheet being pulled over his head. I saw the ice blue blanket on my bed, the white sheets the Ku Klux Klan wear when they burn crosses in front of black households, and zipped-up body bags from the newsreels on Korea we saw at the picture show before the daily feature. And in the time it takes to swish a fly out of your potato salad, the beginning of a thought crystallized in the pit of my brain—that what I was seeing was the grandest of all cover-ups.

tHiRty-eiGHt

When I started toward the door after Blackie got up, Daddy swung his good ear toward me. "You're not going anywhere," he sniped.

"I just want to have a little talk with Jake, Gordon, if it's all right with you."

Mama nodded affirmatively at Blackie, being the lifelong groupie of law enforcement that she was. Daddy skulked into the bedroom and slammed the door.

From the porch, I stood a while watching Blackie's crooked spine and bowed legs negotiate the dry brush leading to the hitching post. The scarf wasn't even there anymore. I couldn't recall the last time I'd seen it. Blackie leaned against the post and crossed his arms. It was morning, still, but it felt like night. The open sky, eighty percent blue with patches of impending gray, seemed too evolved for this time of day, like it had already made its decision about my fate without waiting to weigh the day's actions.

"Guess you're not gonna kill me, then."

"What makes you think that?"

"You sat down with my parents, that's why. If you were gonna off their only son, I would think someone like you might want to avoid family contact."

Blackie's face stretched out as he adjusted the tobacco in his cheek. "Someone like me? What's that mean exactly? You think a cop's got no feelings or longings for decency?"

"A cop? Never said that."

"So it's personal. Just me then. You think I don't got feelings?

"Yeah. That's what I think."

He kicked the dirt under his boots. "Don't much care what you or anybody thinks. Let's you and me get some things straight. I don't got all day to stand around like this."

Upon hearing this, my throat suddenly rose up and nearly blocked the passage of air to my lungs. I couldn't swallow; my lips were coarse-grit sandpaper. He's gonna kill me, he's gonna kill me, I couldn't help thinking. Right here in front of my own house.

"Let's take us a little drive." He leaned down to look straight in my eyes and nodded toward the truck. "Get in."

As I opened the passenger-side door, I heard three sounds: a door inside the house slamming, a voice raised in grief, and the sound of glass clanking against itself, like when Denny, already drunk, rummaged around the liquor cabinet for a fill up. Even if I was about to meet death, I was glad I was leaving.

We drove for nearly twenty miles before I recognized the route. Blackie was taking me to Comanche Creek. And despite my burning desire to fill the silence with useless chatter, I kept quiet and bravely awaited the inevitable. Blackie stopped at a gas station outside of Waurika and came out with a tall paper bag of God knows what. He had a gun and his victim was sitting idly in his truck. What else was needed to complete the assignment of an assassin?

I started to wonder what people would feel when they learned of my death. Mikey—well, I'd come back to him. I started with Denny Simms, my sister's half-retarded fiancé who impregnated my sister and then left her to be informally claimed by a rich, continental doctor. He would mourn my loss because I was the only person on earth who accepted him for the loser he truly was.

Lewella. When we were kids, we made great partners when all of Hooper Circle got together to play hide-and-seek in pairs. And sometimes, if I caught her being mean to me for no good reason and threatened to tell our parents, she would arrange a conciliatory meeting between myself and one of her older girlfriends, one of whom, Glenda Dearden, taught me how to kiss like a high school boy. I was only eight.

Janet might wonder what our lives could have been like if I had lived. She might sit up nights, for the first few weeks after I was gone, thinking about the night we spent laying down on the seat of Nelda's truck, with my hands half on her raw flesh and half tangled in the soft folds of her clothes. She might, in my absence, even look at Mikey differently. What if I was some sort of karmic catalyst, meant to propel the two of them together and they would one day grow up and solve the world's greatest dilemmas? Janet and Mikey. I could only hope that the image of that wouldn't haunt me in the afterlife.

Mama's face would start to change. It would happen slowly, to people like Daddy and Lewella who saw her every day. They would wake up and see her every morning and not really understand that she was disappearing from the face of the earth, speck by agonizing speck. They wouldn't notice this change because they were too close. But one day, she would drive up to the post office carrying a batch of Christmas cards to her extended kin, and Mr. McGhilley, not having seen her for a couple of months, would look up, smile, sell her stamps, and barely recognize the thriving, smiling, pretty wife she had been before her son was killed by that rogue Waurika cop.

Skipping entirely over Daddy, I went back to Mikey. I traveled, in my mind, back to the day we first played together. Being nearly the same age, we couldn't have been more than three, maybe younger, but I could still recall the cold, wet chill in the air from the November rain, and that torn yellow raincoat Mikey was wearing—it probably had belonged to Blackie years before that. He stood there in the center of Hooper Circle while his mother parked the truck by our hitching post. He was so small compared to that truck; the top of his head barely touched the undercarriage. And I remember noticing the sad, lonely look in his eyes. I felt a pressure in my face behind my nose now, as I thought of that Mikey. I wanted to remember something else, some happier, rebellious, teenage-boy type of memory, like Carmella Jeffers in the tree house, or smoking Blackie's cigars 'til we threw up behind the shed, or drinking Blackie's beers and refilling the cans with water just to see if he'd take one from the fridge and try to drink it. But it was no use. Sad, three-year-old Mikey would burn in my memory for the rest of my existence.

We were at Comanche Creek, a short distance from where I had parked Nelda's truck on the second night that changed my life. Blackie glanced at me quickly and opened the paper bag on the seat between us. He fumbled inside and from the sound of the items, his weapon of choice was not in there.

"Get out," he said. He was pointing at the mound of dirt covering up the old drunk's body. *Good Lord Blackie*, I thought. *You're gonna bury me right next to him? Even for you . . .*

I just shook my head and resigned myself to the fact that Blackie was going to do whatever he wanted because he had me by the britches. I was scared to death of him, at this moment and for every moment I had known him. He started walking toward the mound and didn't even look back to make sure I was following him. That cold confidence made me even more scared of my own fate. With his back toward me, I quickly scanned the area and examined my options. This didn't take long, as there were no options. It was open and flat, and the only thing I could do was jump in his truck, try to hot-wire the engine, and take off. But what about tonight? What about tomorrow, and the next day and every day after that? Was I going to run from him for the rest of my life?

No.

So I followed him, stepping directly in his footsteps and obeying my directions like a soldier to a drill sergeant. He stopped when he got to the top of the little berm and stared out at the expanse. I wondered, then, if he had grandiose dreams of his reckless, criminal nature, and envisioned the entire prairie filled with topsoil mounds covering the bodies of his luckless victims. Did Blackie Savage dream of ruling the world someday, or of killing all its inhabitants one by one? Funny, that in my list of survivors, I hadn't considered Blackie's reaction to my death. It was at least possible that he'd feel bad about it. But regret? Forget it. There was no way a man like him felt regret for anything in his life, except being born without brains or good looks.

He crumpled the paper bag against his chest. "Come and sit down, Jakie."

Hail Mary, full of grace . . .

"Let's start our negotiation."

Blackie reached into the tall bag and pulled out the last thing I ever imagined—a notebook and two pens. I gulped, and when I wiped my palms on my pants, they immediately felt muddy. I tried to remember the last time I'd bathed or at least put on clean clothes. I would have done anything, right then, for a home-cooked breakfast and a heap of chilly clothes fresh off the clothesline.

"Go ahead and start."

There I was, sitting on top of a rocky berm with Blackie by my side, a notebook and two pens on his lap, and our faces aimed away from the sun high up in the clouds. "Start?" I asked, careful not to sound too surly.

"Negotiating, of course. That's what we're doing here. You tell me what you're gonna do for me, and I'll think of something I can do for you in return."

"You mean instead of shooting me in the back of the head?"

Blackie laughed like he'd been caught sneaking out some girl's bedroom. "I ain't gonna shoot you, Jake. That'd be too obvious. Too many people know you. Besides, it'd break my little brother's heart. You're the only good he's ever had in his life. Without you, well who knows." Another chuckle. "He could end up like me."

"Lemme get this straight," I began, a little less conscious of my delivery now that death seemed a bit father away from me. "You're gonna sit here, in the shadow of the man you killed in cold blood, and offer to do me . . . what . . . favors in return for my silence?" I stood and started pacing in front of him. "Do you think I'm a complete idiot? Just shoot me now and be done with it. Better than toying with my ass for the next two hours."

"Ain't gonna shoot you. I already said that."

I looked down at the notebook in his lap. "What's that for?"

"Let's just talk first. You start now. Say what you're gonna do."

I was growing more irritated every second now and took on a guise of self-possession I would only have been capable of in the face of impending death. "Blackie, you couldn't get me to tell anybody about what you done for all the money in Oklahoma, for all the Bibles in Alabama, and for all the comic books ever printed."

"So you're putting it behind you?"

"It's already there," I lied, in my resigned, sullen voice.

He cleared his throat. "Then as a symbol of our agreement, what do you want from me?"

He was serious. I didn't think so at first and still secretly envisioned a .32 caliber revolver in the paper bag, even bigger than the one on his belt. But instead I was negotiating with a hardened killer. He wanted something, and I'd give him something.

"Find me Nash Farrell."

thirty-NINe

"Who?"

"Never mind who and why I want him. But I need to find an Indian artist named Nash Farrell."

"Where?"

"Out near Sand Bluff."

"He Choctaw?"

"Choctaw, Sioux, maybe Chickasaw, I'm not sure. Does it matter?"

Blackie looked out in front of us. "Lots of Choctaws in Sand Bluff."

"Well, just think of what horrific memory I'm agreeing to forget in return for your trouble."

"What kind of artist?"

"A woodcarver." I saw Blackie's mind working the puzzle. "And no, I don't know if he lives alone or where he buys groceries or what kind of beer he likes to drink. I can look in the phone directory but—"

"Sand Bluff's got no phone directory," he said. "Anything else?"

"Sure, how about stealing me all the money from the vault in City Hall? Don't pretend like this isn't some sadistic exercise for the sole purpose of your amusement. Did you ask these ridiculous questions to the drunk the other night, before you bludgeoned him with the end of a shovel, that is?" I glared right at him, and I no longer cared about consequences. This morning, right then, I was either going to live to see beyond Comanche Creek or be cemented down into its communal grave and there was nothing I could do about it.

"You got one last chance to answer."

I cocked my head to the side and scanned through my childhood list of wants and desires. Baseball cards, more baseball cards, tickets to baseball games, meeting Mickey Mantle. "I need access to all the police reports filed in Grady ten years ago."

He looked dumbfounded, like a hungry wolf that comes upon a clearing and finds ten dead rabbits. "Grady police reports for one year?"

"Nineteen fifty-one."

"I can guarantee they won't be many. Place like Grady, well, you know, you live there. Might be ten the whole year."

"Shouldn't be too hard then."

He recorded another note in the notebook, then tore out two clean sheets of paper. He handed me one and a pen. "Write down the arrangement we just worked out."

"Why should I?"

He didn't answer for a long time. I listened to the wind howl over our heads and wondered what Mary would be thinking about all this, about how I'd taken on her quest and how far off the track I'd gotten myself. "Because we're both men, and this is a gentleman's agreement."

"Call it what it is, Blackie." He glared at me. "A silence contract. That's it, isn't it? You're gonna do two favors for me in exchange for me not telling the authorities, well, any *other* authorities, what you done. You want me to sign m—"

"No names, for God's sake! Don't sign it or put either of our names on it. Just write, I don't know, 'I' or something. I'm not signing any confession and letting you walk back into town if that's what you're thinking. I'm a mite smarter than that, I reckon."

Even the roar of his angry voice couldn't scare me now. In only the span of a few minutes, I had changed from a soldier terrified of looming death to a brave colonel having reached the opposite front unscathed. I looked into Blackie's demonic eyes now, crumpled up my sheet of paper, and threw it in his lap before walking back toward the truck. A minute later, he followed with the two sheets of paper smoothed out in front of him.

"You keep this now, and when I deliver my end of things, we'll exchange them and shake on it. This is what grown men do," he explained in his paternal voice.

"Really? This is what grown men do when one of them sees the other kill an innocent person?" He didn't respond. "You ever killed anyone else?" My heart raced at the possibilities.

"No."

"Never?"

forty

That night, and for the three nights after that, I dreamt about Indians. I was in the barn, don't forget, my room overtaken by a seven-pound swaddling prone to screaming fits at 3 AM. I hadn't been home, really, in days. And in those few days, I seemed to be watching the very fabric of my nuclear family disintegrate before my eyes. Lewella had taken to going out on dates with Dr. Roman Laszlo, while Denny brushed all the hair off the horses' backs. Mama took frequent naps in the afternoons, and now kept a bottle of Valium in her medicine cabinet. Her eyes always looked red and puffy, and our house, which had smelled of apple pie since the day I was born, smelled empty and cold like stale cigar smoke. She and Daddy hardly said a word to each other, and every day she slipped closer to depression and fringe madness.

Daddy had been vomiting blood. I heard him in the bathroom when Blackie dropped me off, and every night before dinner we'd stand outside the locked bathroom door to the sound of retching in the toilet.

"Everything's fine," Mama said, that night and every night, and Lewella and me knew that meant something was terribly wrong.

I found myself hiding in the barn a lot. I hadn't talked to Mikey since we were each yanked from Van Geller's living room. I knew he was okay, because people like Mikey couldn't survive when things weren't okay. He had someone protecting him. Maybe Blackie did it, or maybe Mary was protecting him, and maybe she did it selfishly so he could continue helping me. I didn't feel like going out and being with anyone; I was almost in a self-imposed imprisonment for my crime. It seemed the right thing to do and no one questioned my being around the house all day. Every time I saw Daddy over those next few days, he was holding his stomach, and the retching increased to two, sometimes three times a day.

I heard the baby screaming after dinner that night. When she finally calmed down, Lewella called me from the porch.

"You out there, Jakie?"

"It's Jake."

She pulled open the heavy barn doors and, in her long white night-gown, she looked a little bit like a china doll. Her face was pretty, round and small, and her hair looked too long for the rest of her. She came over to my encampment in the back of the barn and pointed at the oil lamp.

"Better watch out for that. Burn down this whole spread if you're not careful."

"I know. I'm just reading a while."

She sat down on the end of my bed and shivered. "Getting too cold for you to sleep out here much longer. Mind sharing the room with Faith? She's not crying as much as before."

"Does it matter what I think?" Since the experience of conquering the Blackie virus, I'd taken to an honest, brutal style of speech. "I mean, there's nowhere else to sleep but the barn and my old room." She raised a brow. "Unless of course you're moving out."

"Why'd you think that?"

"You're not sick no more."

"You want to go riding with me tomorrow? I'll saddle the horses after breakfast."

I sat up and laid my Sherlock Holmes book beside me. "I want you to tell me what you're trying not to. Where's Denny?"

She shook her head. "Den's a lost soul, Jakie—you seemed to know that long before anyone else. The fact is . . . I just don't love him anymore."

The wind blew one of the barn doors closed in a hard slap. We both jumped out of our skins, half expecting to see Denny carrying a pitch-fork. "Go inside; it's getting cold out here."

She stood, but lingered near my bed, watching me, waiting for something.

"The fact is that you never loved him, Lew. Did you?"

She half snorted and half laughed, a gesture that quickly turned into tears.

⊰ ⊱

"It's not mine to give, Mikey."

"Course it is."

"I'm borrowing it, that's—"

"What the hell does Nelda need a truck for? She never leaves her damn house."

I'm working on that, I thought. "What do you need it for, anyway? This about Janet again?"

Mikey stared at the dirt. "No. Carmella."

"Jeffers? What are you doing with her?" And the fact that I laughed slightly as I said it betrayed my true impression that Mikey would never really make it with any woman. He caught the sad implication.

"Nothing yet," he chuckled. "She was over here last night for a little while, and let me kiss her on the mouth."

"How much you have to pay her?"

"Not a damn penny! She just let me. For, you know, I don't know."

"I don't know either, but don't trust any girl who gives it away for nothing or charges too much."

"Who would you have me date? A goddamn nun?"

"What kind of nun would have you?"

"Loser."

I jabbed him in the arm. "Eat shit."

"Hey! I almost spent a night in jail because of you. You'd better be nice."

"Because of me? Who broke into that house with me? Who pulled the damn door up so I could jimmy it open? Harvey the rabbit?"

Mikey, or the "old" Mikey anyway, wasn't that adept at snappy comebacks and that day was no exception. I could feel the unresolved tension between us, mostly due to his misplaced anger at me for getting him arrested and for my guilt and a hundred other emotions about

Van Geller's loss. It's not that I liked him at all, or that I even trusted him, but the fact that he was now gone forever felt like another hole in the pit of my heart. Mary was the first, Nelda was sort of in that category even though she was on the fence between life and death, Van Geller, even Denny in a way was dead now. And I couldn't help but acknowledge myself as the unifying link between all of these disparate wandering souls.

Without formally ending our conversation, I left Mikey to his Carmella fantasies and got back into the truck. An unexpected object stopped me: an envelope, white, sealed, with my name spelled incorrectly on the out-side—"JAK" in block letters. And who else could possibly get the spell-ing of "Jake" wrong but that social mutant, Blackie Savage?

> Come by the Waurika precinct for those police reports. You can't take them with you but just look at them there.

And down below the oddly scrawled text was a name and address:

Nash Farrell
Wood Carver/Sculptor
Hi Lon's—edge of Sand Bluff

"What's that?" Mikey said, startling me from behind.

I sucked in air. "You better cut that out."

"What are you, a horse? Gonna kick me?" He tore the sheet of paper from my hands and ran off toward the tree house, jumping.

"I don't care; I've already memorized it."

"Hi Lon's? What's that?" He walked back slowly toward me and the truck with his sad-dog face. "Whatcha doing, Jakie? Off chasing more ghosts?"

"He was her boyfriend. Mary's."

"He's a ghost just the same." Mikey crumpled the paper and tossed it on the ground. "Don't you see? He's connected to the girl that's ruined our lives since I sent you out to that goddamned place. It's my fault, I know that now."

New Mikey.

"Shit, go on without me then. Just don't forget I'm older than you!"

Old Mikey.

"I'm driving out to Sand Bluff," I said. "Come with me if you want."

He stood awkwardly, sizing me up. I mean, Mikey wasn't capable of anything *but* awkwardness, but right now it was a different variety, like he was reaching some inner epiphany about me, about himself and his place in our teeny tiny world. He was squinting when I looked up, and then he picked up the crumpled paper. *Here it comes.*

"Blackie got this for you?"

I looked at him briefly.

"You said you'd tell on him?"

I laughed now, not at the irony of his words, but at the irony of the weight of our conversation and how little I cared about any of it now. Prairie hauntings, not so long ago, used to be the worst of all my problems. Ah the days of it.

I saw Janet walking up to us in a scandalously short white skirt and a bright pink shirt with no sleeves. Mikey's eyes nearly bulged out of his head when he saw her. I knew enough to keep my face tight but felt all the same emotions he did. My mouth was dry when I tried to talk.

She was glaring at Mikey, tacitly asking him to leave us alone, but he wouldn't budge.

"Hi," I said finally.

She smiled back at me. "I've been—"

"We saw a dead guy and went to jail," Mikey blurted. I could have strangled him with my bare hands then, and I nearly did. Instead, I shoved him down on the ground in a raw impulse and grabbed Janet's hand and pulled her into the truck.

"I'm sorry," I said to her, trying to convince myself not to run Nelda's tires over Mikey's lumpy body.

"What's going on with you, Jake? Is that true, what he said?"

"No. Don't believe anything he tells you."

She was leaning against the inside door now, and had Mikey not been panting on the ground below us, I surely would have kissed her. She had on bright lipstick to match her shirt and looked as close to any piece of candy as I'd ever seen. But her face was tightened into a scowl. I could tell only the truth would satisfy her now and she was getting tired of my absence.

"You got any other boys taking you out lately?"

"You mean since you're never around anymore?"

I nodded.

"No, Jake, but I'm not gonna wait forever. What about the dead body?"

I glanced down at Mikey, who lumbered himself up to a stand with the melodrama of a Shakespearean actor. And he wasn't walking away.

"Yeah, we saw a dead guy. We found him after he was already dead though."

"Did you go to jail?" she asked, and I could tell the entire subject was as alien to her as if we'd been talking about astrophysics.

"No," I lied, and the moment the word left my lips I gave Mikey a fat lip with just my eyes. He turned, finally, and went toward the tree house. Back at the truck I put my arms on Janet's shoulders and leaned my forehead against hers. I could tell she wanted me to kiss her but instead I whispered something. "I missed you."

"Where've you been, Jake? Have you found what you've been looking for?"

"I don't think I ever will."

She unclenched herself from me and started up the hill again, but then turned back and took a few steps toward me again. "Someone was at PJ's looking for you."

"When was this?"

"Yesterday, I guess. PJ said some Indian cop was asking for you."

forty-one

Since I'd never even been to Choctaw County, with the exception of our bungled attempt a week ago, I had no idea where to look for a bar called Hi Lon's. It sounded like an Indian bar—the Indians gave all their stuff the weirdest names. They named their horses things like "Low Stander" and "Apple Eyes," and their schools were often called just "School," or maybe "Young School" and "Medium School." Roosevelt High School had taught me how the white man tried to take away their land and was then surprised when they fought back. And I had no trouble understanding why the Indians, in general, didn't want any part of our civilization. Hell, I was starting to feel that way myself, even though I'd never really been a part of anything. I never once felt that Grady was any kind of community, in any real sense. Communities were places like Mayberry—places on TV—little American microcosms with storefront downtowns lined with American flags on each side of a three-block area. These communities had schools with mean princi-pals, active PTAs, and were the kinds of towns where everyone, every single member of every family, attended the football games in the fall. There was a town fair every summer, and every old lady baked apple pies and the old men huddled together, making clouds of pipe smoke and complaining about decisions by the city council. I had never been to a town like this, but I knew they were there, smoldering in our coun-try, somewhere.

It was a sad feeling driving across the straight road. In all those hours, in the pit of my solitude—and don't get me wrong, I'd never shied away from solitude in my life—I had never felt emptier in my life. Maybe looking out into that hollow prairie on each side of the road didn't help matters. And if rural Oklahoma wasn't empty, nothing was. But my emptiness went deeper than that. Normally, when I had felt emotion in my life, it was a strong feeling. Jubilation, triumph, fear, pleasure—these were, for the most part, big emotions, with a palpable buzz in the center of my palms and a corresponding flutter in the pulp of my chest.

That day it was a quiet resignation that haunted me all the way down the freeway. I wasn't bored with my life and I don't think I had ever really felt depressed. It was like I knew what my life was becoming. I knew I couldn't stop it and didn't really care. My life and sanity, and probably my friendship with Mikey and whatever it was now between Janet and me, depended on finding the truth about Mary's killer. I had to know, worse than ever, how she died, at whose hand, and why. I had a mission and knew what I was going to do next. But the dark feeling in my chest reminded me that I'd better not get too cocky about it.

The reservation.

I could tell I'd ventured onto one when I stopped seeing houses and trucks parked on the street. Far off in the distance, some low-lying hills tricked the eyes. From maybe two hundred feet away, the land was a tangled ribbon all wrapped over itself, looped on one side and braided on another. But as I got closer, it was just the same, dumb old flat road again with little berms on each side.

A small town came into view when I turned right at a sign that read "Store." The Indians I had known weren't accustomed to using too much language at one time. Store, I thought. Okay. If there's a trading post, maybe there's a bar called Hi Lon's. The sound of that name made me laugh every time.

Indians everywhere. There were clusters of them now, which oddly reminded me how far from home I was. Mostly old women and men stood outside a big metal Quonset hut, waiting for a door to open. I wondered how my own culture would behave at a time like this— checking their watches every five seconds, pacing back and forth, sighing, grimacing at the supreme inconvenience of having to wait. Indians seemed just more patient than any of my own people.

I slowed to the edge of the dirt road and looked up hopefully at the huddles of tan, wrinkled skin and made eye contact with a lanky old man. He had long hair and a wise pair of eyes that sized me up from the doorway. The man nodded at me and smiled. I didn't know if I should get out of the truck and walk up to him or if the presence of a young white boy might cause undue curiosity. I stayed fixed in the truck and the man approached. His walk was labored. He had been hurt in the leg, and not so long ago. Anyone associated with ranching would recognize this as a symptom of horse-stomping. I'd recognize that gait anywhere.

"Halito, chim achukma?" the man said to me. I didn't speak any Indian but instinct told me what it meant. I said it back and the man's smile seemed to appreciate my lame gesture of respect.

"I'm looking for a bar."

"Little young." The man peered into the truck as he said it, like he expected a sawed-off shotgun on the front seat.

"I ain't no outlaw, mister. I'm looking for someone, and heard I might find him at Hi Lon's."

"Hi Low," he corrected. "Not Hi Lon."

Blackie, that half wit. I'm surprised he got the "Hi" part of it right. "How do I get there?"

"Up Sand Bluff."

"Isn't this Sand Bluff?"

The man shook his head slowly. It made me wonder about him. "This here's Bluff. Sand Bluff's up the hill 'nother fifteen miles."

Fifteen miles. I pictured the rocky, pot-holed dirt road tearing out the undercarriage of Nelda's truck, but it turned out to be a smooth enough ride after about two hundred yards of nightmare bumps and thank you ma'ams.

A sign read "Hi Low" with an arrow pointing south. I turned and found a sad settlement of slapped-together plywood houses, some with no doors, one without a roof, and then a bigger building that probably served as a community center, hospital, and church all at once. At the end of the block I saw trucks parked straight up and down. Only the white man would create diagonal parking spaces.

I parked at the end of a short row of trucks, most of them dirty white, and thought about John Wayne as I walked through the front door. "Hey Pilgrim," he would say in that surly voice, with boots, spurs, cockeyed hat, and his gun belt sagging way below his waist, and then saddle up to the bar and order beers "all around." Mikey never understood how I could idolize cowboys and Sherlock Holmes at the same time. I guess I didn't either, except for the commonality that they were both, in a way, the superheroes. I thought about Red Ryder, who represented the only part of the newspaper a boy my age read on Sundays. He and Little Beaver, well, they were superheroes too—warriors and pacifists all in the same comic strip. Mikey had been asking for a Red Ryder BB gun all his life, and I never had the heart to tell him Daddy had bought me one a long time ago. I never took it out of the basement storage.

Even with fifteen men drinking beers at tables, and a few loners at the bar, it was oddly quiet. Hi Low's, I thought, glancing around. Mostly I was checking to see how many people were watching me, checking my age, wondering about a white boy on a reservation. I must have bored them pretty quickly, because no one looked for more than a second.

"Get you something?" a longhaired young man said from behind the bar.

"Coke, please." I'd seen this done on TV and at the picture shows. You go into a bar wanting information and make like you just went there to drink and ruminate about your problems. I stayed silent as long as I possibly could, about thirty seconds. "I'm looking for some-one named Nash."

"Why you looking here?"

It was an honest question and, yet, I had no idea how to answer.

forty-two

Several answers came to mind. *My murderous cop-friend found you and told me where you were.* Or I could tell him about the argument I witnessed between Nelda and him. Then there was always the truth, but I'd avoided it this long and I could surely do it a while longer. Besides, what would I actually say anyway? *Since you were Mary's boyfriend, maybe you could tell me how she died and what you were doing on the night it happened.*

Yeah, right.

So I did the only sane thing I could think of. I left the bar, went out to the truck, and returned with the only artifact I owned to connect me with Mary McCann.

No one was behind the bar now. I squeezed out the back entrance and saw him leaning against the railing. He stubbed out his cigarette after he saw me.

"You're him, ain't you?"

"Who?"

Games. Not what I expected from him. "Did you make this?" I said, holding the wooden bear in my palm.

Nash Farrell's face was calm and smooth, with gentle lines grooving his forehead and the edges of his eyes. He must have been almost forty, which would have made him far too old for Mary McCann. Watching him there, long and lean with his dark hair tied back, I could almost see them together—see what she might have seen in someone like him. On the surface, to people who thought they knew her, she might have been dating a Choctaw man just for the shock value it would bring to a place like Grady. I'd never met her before but even I knew differently.

Mary was a searcher. She didn't like the easy answers to hard

226

questions and refused to believe only the pretty things about human nature. She wanted the truth, ugly as it could be sometimes, ugly as it was in the end for her. Ugly as ugly truths ultimately had to be.

Without answering my query, he took hold of the bear, stared intently at it, and I knew immediately that his hands had crafted the work of art. "Drove a long way to find me." Now he looked up. "Why?"

Now it was up to me. Games or no games?

"Who'd you carve that bear for, Nash?"

"Seems like you know already."

I didn't avert my gaze and I knew, somehow, that this was some kind of psychological cue between men. Looking away from him now would reinforce his opinion of me as just some kid with an overactive imagination. And my penetrating stare right back into his dark eyes would be, well, something else.

An old man walked to the back of the building from the alley and leaned against the wall while he lit a cigarette. He wasn't too far away but I still had to squint to make him out. He looked just like the man I talked to in Bluff.

Had he followed me here, or was I just one of those people who thought all Indians looked alike?

"Why don't you just tell me what you want to know."

"You'll tell me anything?" I asked.

He laughed slightly. "Least I'll know what this is all about."

"Not what, Nash. Who. And don't pretend like you don't know."

He sighed and kicked a soft patch of dirt under his sneaker.

"Okay, I'll tell you myself then. You carved this bear for Mary McCann and put a secret love letter on the bottom so no one would find out she was in love with an Indian."

"That it?"

"Hell, I'm just getting started."

The man swallowed and crossed his arms. "Her mother send you?"

Nelda. Another loose end. "Not directly."

"Who then?"

227

Now I was the one who laughed, and not at all like a nervous fifteen-year-old kid. It was the sardonic laugh at an unanswerable question. "You wouldn't believe me if I told you."

"The old man? Van Geller? Leave it to him to send some kid on one of his missions. How's he doing anyway?"

"Dead."

Nash Farrell's dark eyes doubled in size. "How did—when?"

"Does it matter?"

The old smoking man had disappeared from his spot at the end of the building, and now a ruckus of burning rubber could be heard out front. It reminded me that I was in Sand Bluff, four hours from Grady, and it was already getting dark. The one thing about this odyssey so far was that I never knew what to expect around each corner.

And I had no idea of the surprise waiting for me next.

forty-three

I must have proved my salt to Nash Farrell, because he brought me into a secluded back room with a bottle of whiskey and two glasses. I shook my head but he made me drink one shot.

"One for each of us. Like a peace pipe, so there'll be no lies between us."

"There've been lies already, I reckon."

Nash Farrell shook his head and lowered it before swigging the liquid back into his throat.

I'd drunk plenty of illicit alcohol before, but only with kids my own age. This was whiskey and I was with a grown man old enough to be my father. I obliged and Nash smiled when I coughed up the fire in my throat.

"I hope you didn't come all the way here to find her," Nash said. His words seemed looser now, and he put his feet up on the chair between us.

"Mary? It's not a matter of where she is. I need to know who put her there."

His eyes widened again, like he was really seeing me for the first time. "What's your name?"

"Jake."

"Jake what?"

"Don't matter. To you it's just Jake. You and I got nothing in common but this wooden bear and a story you're gonna tell me about a dead girl. I ain't leaving 'til I get that story, Nash." My heart was pounding in my chest from this newfound speaking ability. I'd always had it around kids my own age, but I clammed up like a trap-door around adults. And I'm not saying Nash Farrell didn't scare me.

He was plenty scary, tall as he was, and the quiet, restrained way about him scared me even more.

After a moment of digesting my words, Nash Farrell poured himself another shot of whiskey and, after swigging it back like the first one, picked up the telephone on the desk.

"She there?" I heard him say. He waited a few minutes, tapped his fingers on the wood, and kept from looking at me. "Tell her to come on over here. I'm in the back," he said and hung up.

The back room of the Hi Low bar in Sand Bluff was furnished with two old sofas, each with torn fabric on the faded plaid cushions, a clunky, mahogany desk with two of the drawers missing, and a rickety end table. There were ashtrays on every surface. Nash lit a cigarette and offered me one. I nodded, feeling the sudden urge for reinforcement of some kind. We were waiting for someone, and I found myself terrified of who that person was.

"You didn't answer any of my questions yet."

Nash nodded toward the doorway. "In a minute, all your questions will be answered."

I bit my nails and tried to smooth the dirty creases out of my pants, like I was about to meet God, or worse. We waited there an awfully long time, and I started drifting off from the whiskey effects. I could hear Nash fidgeting beside me, and music from the bar pounded through the thin walls. And then my eyes popped open suddenly and landed on a young woman standing half in the room. She had the lightest shade of blonde hair I'd ever seen, and light green eyes like some kind of lizard. I kept looking from her to Nash and back, wondering what possible connection they could have.

"Hi," I said.

That's when the tears started.

Nash jerked out of his chair and stood frozen by the door, watching her and waiting. The girl had her hand on her mouth and didn't take her eyes off of me.

I had no idea what was going on but distinctly felt the sensation of being left out of an elaborate joke. So I reverted to the manners Mama, Woody, and Weaver had taught me. "I'm Jake," I said. Nash's eyes were wild, and there I was, sitting in a weird little back room, half drunk and completely bewildered. "I'm from Grady," I added.

The girl shook herself from grief and angrily dragged her palm over her wet eyes. "You can't be him," she said and ran off.

"Lillie!" Nash shouted. "Wait!"

forty-four

from the pictures, Mary was about five foot eight and had a wide frame without looking either fat or stocky. She looked Indian from far away, but the close-ups revealed dark hair, light skin, and freckles on the bridge of her nose. There were so many Irish families in Oklahoma at that time. For a while, Hooper Circle was referred to as "Mack Circle" because everyone's name was Mc-something. I assumed that Enid was the same way, but it was likely Mary was spawned somewhere else. She didn't resemble Nelda in the least—not in bone structure or coloring, and from what little I had gathered from various sources, not in personality either. Nelda's whole manner was zipped and restrained, like she'd been scolded one too many times by Catholic school nuns. I had no idea where she came from, but I knew her just the same.

Nash Farrell sat on a flowered couch with one arm around Lillie Mechem. I didn't know whose house it was, but I could only assume they lived there together. He was too old for her, just like he'd been too old for Mary once. I sat across from them in a squeaky leather chair and let my eyes continue to drift over the photos on the coffee table.

We had driven the three-mile stretch from the Hi Low to this strange house in silence, all of us crammed in the front of an old yellow pickup, and I hadn't said one word so far. I could've asked a lot of things, so many things. But I was sure my voice would betray the emotions quaking just beneath the surface. Mary, Nash, Lillie, Nelda, and Van Geller in every possible combination. I'd collected a large, unkempt pile of photographs with my hands and flipped through them quickly, but one of them stopped me. I couldn't stop the tears from leaving my eyes; the tighter I used my face muscles, the worse it got. My whole head felt on fire. I saw Nash nod to Lillie, who was sitting away from him on the edge of the couch. The close-up shot of Mary alone instilled a fear in the marrow of my bones that I never could shake. Not even undeniable proof of what I suspected could have absolved me from the terror of that moment, the realization of something so wrong and so large, and the anticipation of what would inevitably come as a result.

"Could I please have something to drink?" I said directly to Lillie in my meek little boy voice. She bit her lip and went to the kitchen and opened a soda can. I watched as she took ice from the freezer and decided I had about ten seconds left to ask my question. Nash, suspecting as much, leaned forward carefully.

"Did you kill her?"

He shook his head, stared down at one of the pictures, and looked like he might cry. I wasn't surprised at how Mary, even in the afterlife, could inspire real tears from the unlikeliest of sources. And in the few frozen seconds while Lillie Mechem fumbled around in the kitchen, I could see the cold truth about Nash Farrell, how he still loved Mary.

"When did you two start up?" I asked. And this was yet another question with no answer. After spending time with Nelda, I was getting used to such things.

"We don't know what happened," Lillie said and slammed the soda glass on the table in front of me. I grabbed it.

"I would think you'd be a little nicer to someone whose best friend's brother was a cop."

Lillie's round face contracted. She was standing over me but I wasn't afraid of her. "I already told you. We don't—"

"Nothing to tell, boy. Time for you to drive home to Grady." Nash stood at the door waiting for me. And right there, in front of both of them, I slid the close-up photograph of Mary into my back pocket. I would have excised a finger to leave with the whole bunch of them, and I was surely entitled, but I had already learned that life, with the big things anyway, didn't play according to the rules of man.

The three-mile drive took over an hour. Nash offered me a cigarette and I accepted, causing another accidental camaraderie with him. Now would be the time. His face was primed for it.

"What was she scared of?" I said, deciding that would be the best opening question.

"I already told you I don't know who—"

"I don't mean who, but what. Like was she afraid of spiders and bugs like most girls or was she a tomboy?"

"Definitely a tomboy." He smiled a little and didn't hide it. "She wasn't scared of nothing. She'd go walking at night in the darkest parts of town that had no streetlights. She jumped trains and slept on the ground without a tent, and drove Nelda crazy with all her pet rattlesnakes."

"I saw pictures of dogs in Nelda's basement. She must've loved animals."

Nash peered at me. "*You're* the one building her shed? That's how you got to the old man, I guess."

"Got to him? I sure as hell didn't have nothing to do with that. I found him on his living-room floor." As much as I protested, though, I couldn't help feeling flattered that Nash Farrell thought I could've killed a man like Van Geller. Were shavings of Blackie seeping into my being? The thought of it made me want to jump in a vat of chemicals.

"You knew enough to go there, though."

We were smoking in his truck with the windows down. I waited 'til a tractor-trailer tore past us before answering. Gave me time to think. "The only thing to know about Walter van Geller is that he wasn't no preacher and he had a lot to hide."

I gave Nash a moment to pretend he hadn't heard me. He fidgeted in the seat and angled his head up to look into the darkening sky.

"What was Mary looking for?"

Without moving his head, he made eye contact. "What do you mean?"

"That's why she died," I said. "Like me, she was searching for some truth. I want to know what it was."

"How should I know?" he said flatly.

"Right before she died, what kinds of things—"

Nash sighed and shook his head. "She went crazy. Don't you know that?"

I didn't. "Of course. But why? Was she always crazy?"

"No. Not until she started badgering Nelda about, you know, things Nelda couldn't tell her."

Her birthright.

Nash took out his crumpled Marlboro pack. "Why'd you want to know so bad anyway?"

"She was my sister."

forty-five

"Thought you'd died or something," Nelda said, looking at me with her droopy eyes.

I went in and asked for a beer before I'd even said hello. Without looking up, she went to the refrigerator and brought me back one. And I sat there, sprawled on her couch, for at least an hour before I opened my eyes. I was awake the whole time, but words and thoughts were beyond my reach.

It's like I hadn't even realized it before the words came out of my mouth. And when I said it, Nash looked at me like he'd known this all along, like it was yesterday's news.

Nelda knew there was something terribly wrong with me, but it wasn't her style to ask probing questions. That was my job, I guess. So she hovered gently around the living room, organizing stacks of magazines, turning on lamps, dusting things. We were communicating without really talking and it seemed best that way. She knew that I knew something, and though I'd never say the words in a million years, I couldn't hide any longer from myself, or Nelda, even Blackie. All the energy I'd spent searching for and then concealing the truth flew out the window when I told Nash the truth about my mission.

It made perfect sense, the more I thought about it. Her love of animals, just like Mama and Lewella. Her rebellious wild side, like me and Daddy. I could only guess that she was my half-sister, the other "kin" that I remembered Grandpa Woody and Daddy talking about that fateful night. The dead giveaway, though, was her haunted eyes—same as those in my own head, just like Lewella's, and her light skin, too. Even Mikey, not realizing what he was saying at the time, said she looked like me in that picture we found in her bedroom. My Godforsaken half-sister, Mary McCann, was searching for the truth of her birthright, and someone silenced her to keep buried the most scandalous of all of Grady's lies. And now, I feared more than anything, it had to be me to dig it all up.

I called Mama before I left Nelda's the next morning, and told her I'd be staying with Mikey that night. She didn't have much to say, except that Lewella and the baby were moving out pretty soon and starting to get things ready. Oddly, she didn't ask where I was or where I had been. There was an inverse relationship, it seemed, between the life making its way back into Nelda's bones and the very same qualities dripping out of Mama day by day.

"I shouldn't be telling you anything."

"What did I do?" Mikey whined.

I ignored him and climbed the tree house stairs. He followed me and when he reached the top step, I dragged him inside and tossed him on the grungy mattress opposite me. "Did Blackie leave anything for me?"

Pause. Then, "Some big envelope, I think. He made me store it under my mattress."

"Go get it." He could tell by my eyes that I wasn't fooling around. Ten seconds later he handed me the envelope.

The tree house was cold, as it was barely summer anymore. Now was the time of year when the mornings and nights were cold, but the warm afternoons hung on forever. I shivered as I opened the clasp and pulled out a thin stack of papers. Mikey's face showed more than curiosity. He was going to bust a lung if I didn't tell him something.

"It's nothing."

"Cut the crap, Jake." His words were soft, almost whispered. When I looked up, I saw the new Mikey. Well, that was different, wasn't it? The new Mikey could clearly be trusted with this kind of information. Old-Mikey, never.

"These are all the police reports of all the crimes committed in Grady in nineteen fifty-one."

"The year Mary was murdered."

I hated hearing the words "Mary" and "murdered" in the same sentence. Better get used to it, as the forthcoming truths, some deep part of me instinctively knew, were going to be even worse than what I'd already learned.

"Here." I shoved half the pile in his hands. "Start looking."

"For what? And what the hell do you and Blackie have going? I thought he was trying to kill you a week ago."

I looked up at him with a stern face, and looked down again. Maybe he got it, maybe he didn't. I now had bigger problems than Blackie.

"Breaking and entering," Mikey narrated, fumbling through the papers. "Wow! Looky here—old Farthing broke into the . . ." He started laughing, "Post office?" Mikey laughing uncontrollably now, I snatched the papers from him with a deathly stare.

"You want me to look myself?"

He took the pages back and read aloud. "Fine, party pooper. Auto theft . . ." He looked up at me. "And mind you, I still don't know what I'm looking—"

"Just read, damn it!"

"Okay, okay, ah, another breaking and entering, cattle rustling, theft of pigs, domestic disturbance, disturbing the peace . . ."

I sighed and started looking through my stack. Same things, mostly. B and E, auto theft . . .

"Obstruction of justice—"

"What's that?" I said. "I mean, who was involved?"

"Tartolla. They don't live in Grady no more. Pig farmers I think. Refused to . . ." he was reading, "give the police information about a theft."

I found another grand theft auto in my stack.

"Here's one—looks like someone changed the locks on the post office and they couldn't open the doors. Ha! That'd be a good gag."

I found myself glancing out the tree house door every few seconds, maybe scanning for Blackie, maybe Mrs. Savage, who surely blamed me for Mikey's arrest, if she even knew of the incident.

"Assault and—"

"Assault and what?"

Mikey scratched his head and read on a little further. "Just assault, looks—"

I ripped the page from his hands, scanning, searching for a familiar name or even someone who might be connected to that familiar name. "Grandville. Who's that?"

"I don't know anyone like that. Maybe they're not from Grady."

I read further. "Yeah, they're from Fleetwood."

"Close enough," Mikey said. We heard a vehicle driving down Mikey's gravel driveway and my eyes froze.

"Blackie?" I asked.

Mikey peeked out the vertical split in the wood slats we called the "treekhole," for tree house peekhole, and shook his head. "I don't know who it is, but it's not his truck."

I caught my breath for a moment and suddenly felt as if I hadn't eaten a good meal in a week; maybe it had been longer than that.

"Another assault, right here in Grad—"

I grabbed the paper and quickly scanned for that familiar name I'd been searching for, then I folded the sheet and stuffed it so far into my back pocket I was sure it had grafted onto my skin. Some old woman got out of a pickup carrying a pie, which I saw as I scurried down the steps.

"Jake," Mikey hissed. "Where in the hell are you going?"

I made a straight line to Nelda's truck, got in, and started the engine. Without looking up, I started to back out of the drive. Mikey tore open the passenger-side door and plunked down on the seat.

I stopped the truck and, for the second time that day, held back a waft of tears.

"What the hell's wrong with you?" My lifelong best friend bored holes through my skull with his staring, and I sensed real concern from him now rather than his usual sordid mix of anger and curiosity. "Something scared you up there. Tell me. Come on, Jakie. It's me. Tell me!"

It was already late August, and I'd been running, literally, all summer long. And by now, more than just my legs were tiring. I permitted a few tears to cloud my vision and didn't even wipe them away. Mikey'd seen this display before, once or twice in the fifteen years we'd known each other, and thankfully he didn't utter a peep of acknowledgment. I slowly withdrew the paper crammed in my pocket and unfolded it. Staring straight ahead, I passed it to him. I kept my eyes on the license plate of the old woman's truck, as I was parked diagonally behind her. When I looked at Mikey, his face was white.

"What's this mean, Jakie?"

"It's my Daddy."

"Arrested?" I could hear the panic in his voice. Although he hadn't put anything together yet, I knew a part of him sensed the gravity of what it all would mean to us, to Grady, and to the way our lives had been all this time. We were free-roaming teenagers, living in a hick town that we owned outright and could do nearly anything in. Everyone knew us and we knew everyone, and no one had any secrets. That was the beauty of Grady and of every middle-American small town during the simplicity of 1961. By then, everyone had mostly healed from the trauma of the Korean War and things had settled into a comfortable routine. There were the small mercantile shops scattered around Jefferson County, and the rest of its inhabitants were busy operating small-time farms and ranches, just barely scraping by on enough of a living to feed their families three times a day. It was enough to just live in a small, intimate place and be a part of something slightly larger.

And yet the single piece of paper in Mikey's hand proved the seed of a lineage of poison infecting the very heart of Grady. It would affect all of us eventually, and mostly me.

"What's going on, Jake?"

I was still staring at the license plate and couldn't have torn my eyes from it if Mikey's head were on fire. The scuffed up, dirty white plate was a small piece of glue holding me together.

"That assault was on Mary," I said in an icy voice. Mikey didn't move or breathe for a long time. The windows were partially rolled down and made the sound of the howling winds whine even louder. The elm trees hanging over the tree house were bent down sideways from its force. The sky was foreboding. I no longer recognized my own life.

forty-six

Without talking, I drove to the Stronghold. A little rocked-in dugout behind PJ's Auto Body Shop, it was in a central location in Grady and where Mikey and me had all of our most serious talks. PJ must have left early because only the nighttime light was on outside the shop. It was seven o'clock and I wasn't even hungry.

I parked in the usual place under the lightning-charred oak tree. Mikey got out first, and before closing the door, I watched the fated police report on the front seat being blown by the wind. It was so windy, the report could easily blow clear out one of the windows and end up who knows where. Part of me didn't care who saw it now. I had seen it, so had Mikey.

I picked it up anyway and put it back in my pocket. The secret had been hidden this long—it could stay hidden a little longer.

Mikey dug in the dirt for our emergency stash of cigarettes and alcohol. I had lit two from the pack in my pocket and passed him one. We hunkered down against the dirt walls of the trench and watched the sinister sky taunt us with its swirling patterns.

"I don't understand it," Mikey said finally.

"I know," I replied, as a sad an inadequate symbol of bewilderment. The wind blew a sheet of dirt into my face. I coughed and spit it out as best as I could.

"How'd your Daddy even know her? I mean, did he go after her or something?"

I hadn't had time to make sense of the chronology yet, so I just talked my way through it, hoping I'd find the truth in there somewhere. "She went after him. Mary went to him with some information, I don't know what, maybe a question, and as good as I can figure, he either didn't know the answer or didn't want to admit to her that he did."

"What question? I mean, what would she want to know from him? No offense, Jakie, but your Daddy's just some broken-down farmer."

He was a mite worse than that. Ironic, though, to hear these words from Mikey. "She was adopted by Nelda when she was a baby, you know, through Van Geller's shady little backroom adoption ring. I think, when Mary got old enough to ask Nelda about where she came from, and was old enough to start insisting on knowing the truth, she took matters into her own hands."

Mikey had stubbed out the cigarette and held another one, unlit, between his fingers. I watched the realization spread across his round face and settle into tight creases around his mouth and nose. He barely looked like himself right then. I'd felt like someone else for so long, I couldn't remember anything else.

"So Mary went looking for, you know—"

"Her birthright," I said, completing his sentence.

"From your Daddy."

"Right."

"What gave her the idea of it, though? I mean, Enid's a long way from Grady."

"She worked in Grady, remember? Van Geller told me that. Van Geller owned Denny's ranch before the Simms bought it. His family had a cook named Althea, who died, and Althea's assistant was Mary. That was right in Grady. So if Mary started wondering about her real parents, she'd have had plenty of time and opportunity to scope out the folks in Grady."

Mikey lit the cigarette and took two long drags before speaking again. "You think maybe Van Geller, knowing the truth of where she came from, purposely set her up in a job on his ranch because it was in Grady, so maybe she could be near her own kin even if she didn't know it?"

I shrugged. "No telling what went on in his mind. But she got the idea in her head, I don't know how yet, that Daddy might have been her father. I think she might have gone to the house once or twice asking questions, bothering Mama, maybe threatening to bring it all out in the open."

Mikey stood up quickly and walked around the small dugout. His face showed a lifetime of fear in it. "Mary Prairie was your sister."

"Half-sister, but yeah, looks that way."

"Why'd you think that? Half-sister?"

"Mama had three babies. One of them she had before she and Daddy got married. I heard about it once when I was real little. I was staying at Woody and Weaver's. It was the night the oil deal fell through once and for all. Woody got real drunk and started smashing things and talking crazy, so I called Daddy from the bedroom and he came over." My face was cold, I realized, from tears drying on my cheeks and eyes. "Some terrible words were said. I never saw Weaver look so scared, not by what was coming out, but by how Grandpa was talking to Daddy. Saying things about Mama and how she was a bad choice for a wife, and how he just sat by and let it all happen and how the oil deal collapsed because of Daddy's soft morals."

He knelt down in front of me and leaned in close. "You think your Daddy mighta killed her? You think he could do that?"

"I don't think killing's beyond anyone, and not just 'cause I seen Blackie do it, neither. Anyone could kill if they had a good enough reason. To save their own life, the life of their kin, or even better, to keep a secret buried in the earth up to its eyeballs." I couldn't look at Mikey right then. The fear on his face scared the daylights out of me. "Someone else was Mary's father."

"Not your Daddy?"

I shrugged, or nodded, I wasn't even sure of my own reactions. Everything felt surreal, like I was stuck inside someone else's body, some alien mind with an empty, hard heart. At some point, the sky had clouded over.

"I think it was PJ."

forty-seven

Mikey slumped back down on the hard dirt. "PJ."

"I've got no proof; just a feeling I've always had when I saw them together. Like they'd been in prison together or were privy to the same sick scandal that bound them together in hateful partnership. I seen it last time I was there, matter of fact."

He was barely listening. He took one of the police reports out of his pocket and held it up in the air.

"More bad news?" I said.

"Missing person's report."

"Yeah. For Mary, filed by Nelda, betcha."

He slowly shook his head. "It's for Lillie." There was a question in his voice. I thought it too.

"Lillie disappeared five years later, though—in 1956. What's the year on it?" I asked.

"Nineteen fifty-one. Like the rest."

I hadn't even told him the best part yet. Thinking aloud again, I said, "So she ran away before she disappeared."

"Ran away, why would you think that? Don't you think someone took her? Maybe killed her? Like Mary?"

"No." It was starting to rain. Miserable night to end a miserable day. "She's alive," I said.

Mikey's face turned white. "Lillie?"

"Lillie's alive. I saw her yesterday."

Doc Laszlo had kept himself strategically scarce over the past few weeks, while Lewella was deciding to move herself and the baby in with him. I'd been so absent from everything lately, I had no idea how they'd ousted Denny from the picture and from Lewella's life and heart. Sure, he was the world's biggest idiot, but I knew my sister, and knew some part of her would always love him, even if it were out of pity. And Laszlo, well, we all saw the immediate effect of his presence on her. I didn't know yet if I trusted him, but I knew he wanted her. That want reminded me of Janet. I was only fifteen but I knew that type of desire already. Maybe Janet had another boyfriend by now, but this possibility failed to quell the howling in my bones. Maybe I would never have Janet Lange the way any man has a woman. And maybe I'd never live to see the sun come up tomorrow. And while my family was hanging together by tape and threads, I still felt a distant hope that we'd all be okay. Maybe a long time from now.

I found her moving boxes of clothes out onto the porch when I got there. I brought them from the porch to the hitching post and decided, later on that night, that I'd go looking for the red scarf. I was sure Daddy had burned or buried it, but it was a family tradition and was worth the effort to find it. Lew and I didn't say much to each other.

"Thanks," she mumbled, avoiding my eyes.

Mama was watching me from the kitchen window. The redness in her eyes told me how she felt about losing her daughter and granddaughter at the same time. I wanted, right then, to be Superman, to have been born superhuman, able to fly, able to save not only the day but also humankind from its own destruction. On a small scale, though, I would have been happy to just save the women in my life—Mama, Lewella, Janet, Nelda, and of course, Mary. I thought I'd never get used to the phrase "my sister Mary" as she was long dead and buried, only my half-sister, and even that had yet to be proven.

"You going far?" I asked Lewella. She stopped in her tracks, and set the box down at her feet on the front porch.

"No. Hastings is all. Still in the same county. You can visit us on your way up to Enid."

"I won't be going there much once school starts. That was just a . . . I don't know," I let my voice trail off.

"Summer job?"

"Diversion, maybe."

Lewella was standing under the porch light and a dozen moths flew around the bare bulb. She looked beautiful to me, her hair long and

combed, her cotton dress cinched tight around her waist and a rosy
glow in her cheeks. "Look at you," she said.

"Can't imagine what I look like right now."

"You're all grown up, looks like. When'd that happen, exactly?"

I wanted to laugh, or cry. They both seemed to come from the same
place lately.

"Happens when you're not looking, I guess. Like everything you
really want."

She opened the screen door, flushed by the awkwardness between
us. "You gonna look after Mama now?"

"I'll try." And when I looked through the kitchen window again,
the light was off.

I slept in the barn that night. The baby cried at midnight. Daddy got out
of bed and smoked three cigars on the front porch, and then got in the
truck and drove off. I felt it was some tacit cue for us to have the talk I
would have done anything to avoid. When he came back and it sounded
like he was coming out to the barn, I did my fake snoring routine.

All three girls were asleep when Daddy went out drinking whiskey
from a bottle wrapped in a paper bag. Walking through the darkened
house, the sideboard on the west wall of the living room attracted my
attention. I went to it, tiptoeing over the creaking floorboards, and jerked
open the bottom drawer, the one that always stuck. I dug my hands
through the folded papers and old photographs and half expected to
find the red scarf crammed in a corner of the drawer, full of burn holes,
dirt, and debris. Restlessness itched beneath my skin. I was looking for
something, wandering around the house in the dark. I guess on some
level I needed proof, something tangible that I could hold out in front
of my Daddy and say, "Yes, you did this—here's how I can prove it."
So far I'd found nothing but a wooden bear, the reappearance of Lillie
Mechem, a murdered preacher, and my half-sister's boyfriend.

From the half-moon's glow filtering in from the kitchen window, I
saw a note tacked on the pegboard by the refrigerator. It was for me—a
phone call.

From Nash Farrell.

forty-eight

I found a note pinned to the seatback in Nelda's truck. The words "To Maximus, From Brainiac—Lex is on your trail," were scratched on the back of a paper shopping sack. The only difference between Lex Luthor and Blackie Savage was that Lex was smart. With more important things on my mind, I could forget about Blackie for the next few hours, or maybe the rest of my life.

Route 89 was the darkest patch of road in all of southern Oklahoma. On the way out of town, I took a shortcut around the Wilsons' farm that led to the old baseball diamond. I didn't get out, as no sane person walked in that field after dark. I just parked and listened to the crickets and the wind fanning through the coarse reeds. My eyes could only make out some wildflowers peeking over the wire fence, but my inner eye felt her there.

Mary Prairie. Mary Prairie, I chanted to myself. She wasn't bound up or bleeding or crying tonight. In a silver flash, I thought I saw her walking. The flow of her long black hair moving with her languorous steps, the half-moon's stingy glow lighting up just a speck of her pale flesh. She was there in that field now, and she was walking. Mary. My sister.

God help me—I'm still seeing ghosts.

Finally I reached Route 70 and started toward Sand Bluff. The radio was tuned in crystal clear and both windows were rolled down. The cool air felt good inside my lungs. I took it in and remembered the beginning of the summer, when Lewella was happy to be pregnant and was making wedding plans with Denny Simms, the father of her child, and Mama smiled as she pulled her daily pies from the oven. Mikey and me played cards and Superman trivia and stayed up late

247

in the tree house with Jimmy and Freddie. I felt like a teenager back then. It was only two months ago, this carefree, wide-eyed Jake. Now he was gone forever. In a way, we all were.

I saw headlights in my rearview mirror. My stomach clenched even before I decided it was that infectious virus, Blackie Savage. He tailed me from a healthy distance and stayed there. Blackie was curious. But he wouldn't wait forever.

Even in the dark I remembered the way to Nash's house. Even before I knocked on the door, Lillie Mechem was on the front porch. She had to be the only blonde on the reservation. I wondered how long she'd been there and how it was that they came to accept her. She and Mary shared the same sad smile. I had a feeling they shared more than that.

"Come on in. Nash has something for you."

"More wooden animals?" I said.

I followed her through the house and found Nash smoking on the back porch.

"It's late," he said, looking at Lillie.

"You're not in bed, neither," I replied. "What did you want to show me?"

"What you're looking for."

I sat tentatively on a metal chair beside him and just waited. It was a trick, along with some other Indian customs, I'd learned from Jimmy Wilson's Indian grandmother. I knew nothing of the Choctaw culture, but had to believe there were commonalities between each nation. I sat there silently while Nash finished his cigarette. He sipped from a beer, looked at it, and then seemed to realize he should offer me something. "What do you most want?" he said, finally breaking the silence.

"You a genie or something?"

"Might be."

"To know how Mary died, of course. And by whose hand and why."

"You know that already, don't you? How else would you have found your way here?"

I looked intently at Nash Farrell, at the side of his head and the gentle, impish smirk lurking under his skin.

"She was looking for her parents," I said. "I think Van Geller got her a job on his farm in Grady so she'd be close to her own kin, though she didn't know it at the time."

"So that's the why. What about how?" Nash grinned like some demonic game show host, asking what he thought I wouldn't answer.

"Bludgeoned, I reckon. Maybe with a shovel or a hoe—something real hard. She was bleeding bad and from several places when I saw her." My throat constricted and I started coughing and couldn't stop. My tears were from an inability to breathe, nothing more.

"Who?" he said, onto the next question.

"I know who. You know who. Let's go ahead and skip over that one."

"All right," Nash said calmly. "So what do you need?"

"Proof of what I think happened. I found a police report with a familiar name on it. That mean something to you?"

"You need proof," Nash said, standing and stretching his legs. He tossed an envelope onto my lap and went back in the house. "Good luck," he said.

The envelope contained two birth certificates. One read "Child: Mary McCann. Parents: Nelda McCann and Jerome Wilder," the last one a made-up name, I was sure, since Nelda never married. "Born August 11, 1934." That would have made her seventeen when she died.

Birth certificate #2: Child: unnamed. Parents: Lorina and Paul Joseph Lange." Mama and PJ.

forty-NINE

Blackie was sitting on the hood of my truck when I came out. Nash stayed on the back porch brooding, but Lillie followed me out front. The light was off now but I was sure Blackie saw her.

"Hi," I said in my careless voice. I tried to pretend I was seeing Mikey instead of his evil brother, but my eyes and body betrayed me when I saw Blackie holding a branding iron.

"Get in," he said. I just stood there, staring at his tool of human destruction. "You drive."

It was a smart idea, really. That way, after he tortured me to death, the "real police" wouldn't find my truck abandoned on the side of the road. Blackie would either drive it to the police salvage yard or plough it into a lake. Hi Blackie, good-bye Jake.

He had me drive all the way down Route 89 past Grady to the Texas border, to a dark, abandoned police shooting range the Waurika PD used to use. After I stopped the truck, Blackie opened the passenger side door but didn't get out. "You got it with you?" he asked. And I couldn't help but laugh at the frayed strands of Blackie's logic.

"You mean that stupid silence contract? Why would I sign it anyway?" I had no idea where my cockiness was coming from, but I could no sooner control it as I could control what he was about to do.

"You got one chance, Jake," was the last thing Blackie said to me that night.

First, he grabbed me by the arm and dragged me far out to the two-hundred-and-fifty-yard mark on the range. That same mocking sky bore down on me—cloudless but with no stars. I knew what it was saying.

There was a pit dug out on the edge of the shooting lane with embers spitting up into the air. Blackie tied me down on the ground with long, steel stakes and I didn't even try to get away. Everything in my life, I felt, had led me down this path and some part of me felt like Mary wouldn't let me die. Not like this—alone in a dark, empty place, like she had.

I was tied at my wrists and ankles and Blackie was getting his branding iron to just the right temperature. I saw flames spit up. He stuck the end of the iron down into the reddish glow and held it there a long time. He knew I was watching. The watching was part of his game.

Something occurred to me then—where Mary had been buried. And I wondered how I could come so far with this investigation and never think of it until now. Maybe she was buried in Grady, in that terrible place, or had she been set ceremoniously in the earth with a proper burial surrounded by weeping kin? Did Blackie know where she was? Was I about to join her?

I could almost feel the heat of the iron from ten feet away. And that was because it was just next to my skin.

The ceremony opened with one of his signature beatings. He'd always worn steel-toed boots, which he used for the kicking part. My eyes were on the branding iron, growing hotter every second, and Blackie's first kick told me all I needed to know about my fate. If he'd chosen my shoulder to kick first, I might have felt a tinge of hope, but instead he applied the first three kicks to my kidneys, and after that, my upper back and my lungs. There was no doubt he intended to kill me now—maybe with the iron, maybe just with the beating, but either way, I would not be waking up in Grady the next morning. From a film we saw in school one time, I remembered that keeping your body loose and relaxed when you fall down stairs keeps you from breaking all your bones. So I tried to stay loose in spite of the sharp pains now in my upper and lower back. Like a practiced predator, he knew enough to pause between kicks to catch his breath and pace himself for endurance. He walked around me slowly, out of breath, and stopped in front of me. The next assault was on my stomach, as he was trying to puncture all my organs. My breathing was gurgling, so fluid had no doubt begun to fill my lungs, and the abdominal kicks climbed a few inches higher to my rib cage. The ribs protected the heart and . . . well, analysis was futile.

He crouched down, peered at me, and checked my breathing. He straddled me and sat on my sunken chest, which made it impossible to breathe.

"What'd you see that night, Jakie?"

He hadn't used the branding iron yet and needed an excuse.

"I'm not asking you again!"

"I watched you kill an old drunk and bury him on the prairie." I barely got the words out before the second round of kicks started, these on my head and face. I smelled blood before I even saw it. It was about nine o'clock at night. Coyotes would probably gnaw at me, along with buzzards, wild dogs, and bobcats. By morning, I'd be a carcass that no one would even recognize as having been human. And Blackie, well, he'd never been human his whole life, so no one would wonder about him.

fifty

Death, disguised as a sinister star, blinked back at me from a black tapestry. Now it slid down from the sky and shape-shifted into an African lion. To death, I was a half-dead gazelle begging for an attack. Then it was the star again.

Blink.

Every time it blinked, I drew a centimeter of air through my deformed nose and mashed esophagus. It made a gurgling sound. And even though I'd never felt closer to the other side, I felt more determined than ever. I dragged in another agonizing scoop of air.

Blink. Blink.

One by one my faculties returned—I heard the wind dragging through miles of scrub brush on the prairie, I tasted blood on my face, and I was terrified of opening my eyes.

Blink. Blink. Blink.

Death was working harder. The knowledge of my emergence into light, instead of darkness, did not sit well. It was losing control. The star, blinking frantically, was a vacuum salesman ringing your doorbell fifty times on a Sunday morning. It won't work, I told it. Besides, if Blackie wanted me dead, he would have shot me through the forehead with his pistol. He wanted me to live and remember.

The stakes were hammered far enough into the earth that all my body weight, wagging back and forth, only loosened them a little. I had to take breaks every three or four seconds, and I lay panting and sweating for ten minutes. At this rate, I might be home by Christmas.

Blackie had cruelly parked Nelda's truck ten feet from my burial spot. Close enough for me to see and plan my escape, and too far to actually get to it while bound to the earth. When I flipped my head quickly left and right, I breathed that chemical, bloody smell again. And in that stupor of charred flesh, nervous exhaustion, internal bleeding, and dehydration, my epiphany was this: Blackie had just recreated my sister's murder . . . in me.

An hour later, estimated by the change in temperature, I got the first stake up. The other three came shortly after. I stood weakly, like a newborn calf balancing on spindly legs. Breathe, I told myself. I'd passed out after the iron seared my skin for the first time. That one was on my right hip. The others, I realized just now, were on my back, my chest, and shoulder. Someone like Blackie should never be allowed around farm equipment. It was bad enough he was allowed to carry a gun. Pulling open the truck door, I laughed and recalled talk, a few years back, about electing Blackie sheriff of Jefferson County.

Even driving down the dark road, I wasn't completely all back and wondered if I ever would be again. My right leg was numb and the insides of my body burned and ached from the impact of steel-toed boots. How does the body heal from something like this? How does the mind? If Mary had lived through her assault, would she be one of those street girls now, living in abandoned factory buildings, wearing the same clothes every day and mumbling to herself? Then an even worse thought came to me. If my body didn't properly heal from the iron scars, would Janet ever let me come near her again? I tried not to think about that part, and quickly redirected my memory to the arousal of her lying beneath me on the truck seat.

If I could go back in time, I wondered if I would sacrifice the truths I'd learned about Mary to complete my carnal transaction with Janet Lange. It all reduced to two opposing forces—pleasure and pain. Pleasure had a scintillating, almost electric charge to it, but like electricity, it was fleeting, shallow, and burned out quickly. Pain, on the other hand, dug its claws deep into the bone and was often accompanied by truth and enlightenment. My frazzled brain, incapable of big questions now, resorted to Superman trivia. Clark Kent, Lois Lane, soaring over skyscrapers . . .

fifty-one

"Jacob!!" Mama shrieked and tore out the kitchen door. She must have seen me slump over on the seat after the truck bowled over the hitching post. For an instant, I heard only the clogging of her steps on the porch stairs. She screamed for my Daddy. "Gordon? Gor-don?"

My mother never weighed more than about one hundred and twenty pounds ever in her life, but she flung open the truck door and whisked me off the seat like I was a silk scarf. Consciousness faded in and out—in when my head hit the pillow on Lewella's bed, which was closest to the front door, and then out again shortly after. When my eyes opened next, Roman Laszlo stared down at me from the top of his long nose. I heard mumbling, and then Mama slowly peeled off my clothes. After my shirt came off, the crying started, and turned to sobs when they saw the rest of me—my bruised, bloody limbs and the charred indentations from the branding iron.

Laszlo leaned in close. He had on fancy clothes and smelled of Camel cigarettes and Old Spice. "Who did this to you?"

I rolled over.

But Laszlo rolled me back toward him and kept his rigid hands on my shoulders. "Jake, who-did-this?"

Mama, unhappy with Laszlo's effect upon my resolve, took matters into her own hands. "You've got exactly five seconds to tell us what we want."

I didn't know what would happen after the five seconds had expired, but knew enough to fear Mama's wrath. "What if I said it was Daddy?"

Mama and Laszlo blinked silently, exchanged glances, and moved closer. "Don't be silly," she replied. "Your daddy was here all day and all night."

"I didn't say he did it. Just what if."

Ah. In two seconds, I'd caused complete bewilderment and a temporary breakdown in one hundred years of prairie logic. Yes, that's right, I thought. There are gray areas, and unanswerable questions and tricks of the mind and heart. I was happy, if for only one fleeting second of happiness, to be putting my knowledge of Sherlock Holmes to good use. Nearly every story I've ever read showed Holmes at the end playing such a game to trap someone into a confession. Or even, if not the decided villain, such a question posed with just the right type of execution could cast doubt on the most solid witness.

Daddy. A possible assailant. I had planted the seed.

Laszlo asked Mama to help him with the salve. They started with an oatmeal poultice that dripped all over the bedsheets, and after a while replaced it with a thick salve that reeked of sulfur.

Next time my eyes opened, the sun was bleeding yellow rays onto the floor. I had slept on my stomach, as the worst burns were on my lower back and side. I saw shoes. Big, clunky, thick-soled shoes.

Daddy.

I watched his right foot move toward the bed and in a blind reflex I rolled toward the wall and toppled onto the hard floor. Mama ran in from the kitchen, staring.

"I don't know," Daddy said to her expression.

"Did you touch him?" She was using her shriek-voice, the one Daddy tried to avoid at all costs.

"He's my own son, for God's sake."

Mama put me back on the bed and sat beside me, cupping my face in her hands. Her head was turned slightly in Daddy's direction, but the angle of it threatened violence if he did anything but retreat. Ah, the magic of doubt. Thank you, Holmes. I liked spending those few isolated minutes with Mama, having her check my wounds, the glassiness of my eyes, and my body temperature. She poured water in a tall glass and gently asked me to drink from it rather than forcing it down my throat. There was a kind of solidarity between Mama and me, on that one isolated morning. Even without talking, we both seemed to understand that our little family was on the very brink of all-out war, and nothing would stop it other than an all-out miracle. Mama believed in miracles, but I didn't. Mama believed in everything that held even the slightest, most remote possibility: superstitions, aliens from other worlds, secret government conspiracies. Daddy, on the other hand, believed in the power that whiskey could have over people's behavior and he intended to live and breathe that very truth for the rest of his life. He also believed wholeheartedly in the power of a man's word. Honesty. It made me sick to think about it.

"What happened, Jake?" Mama whispered these words in my ear, but enunciated them in a way that I knew was serious. "You've got to tell me now."

I looked around the room, then at Mama's wrinkled face.

"He's gone," she said.

"Daddy?"

She nodded. "And Doc Laszlo's coming by tonight to check on you."

"I'll be gone by then," I said.

"Gone? Don't be ridiculous." She studied my face. "You can't go anywhere." Then she laughed nervously.

I didn't answer.

"Did Blackie do this to you?" She shook my shoulders 'til I looked at her. "Jake. Jake! You tell me right now and—"

"What, you'll send Daddy over to Waurika to have a little talk with him? You can't talk to people like him about reasonable behavior. Besides," I paused and sipped water from the tall glass, "Daddy'd never go on my behalf."

"Oh yes he would. If I asked him he would."

Well, maybe the history and precedence of this family dictated that certain truth over the years, but everything was different now. I sat up on the side of the bed and saw Daddy backing Nelda's truck away from the crooked hitching post. Ignoring Mama's attempts at restraint, I stood on the wooden floor in just my underwear and walked through the kitchen to the front porch.

Though his head was bent down, Daddy watched me through the top of his head. He pretended to be fixing the hitching post. I pushed the screen door open, then leaned against the house, panting from over-exertion. My legs were still wobbly, and every two seconds I thought of steel-toed boots.

"You never knew her Mama, did you?" That was my first question, my first foray into this strange new world of prairie truths. The prairie lies had been easy enough to learn—all you had to do was lie once and the rest snowballed, then pretty soon you couldn't tell the difference between what was real or what was made up. "Her real Mama, well, naturally you knew her, *know* her."

"Go back in the house, Jake. You're not well," Daddy said without looking at me.

"I might not look well, but I've never felt so clear about what this world really is and why I'm in it."

He looked at my eyes just then, and seemed to understand, in a quick instant, the gravity of my words.

"You never knew who adopted her."

"Jake." It was Daddy's last warning, my last chance out.

"Or if you had, you never would have let me take a job with her up in Enid." I was gambling now, standing a little straighter, regaining use of my body and mind. "After all, a boy like me might find any-thing there." I couldn't hear her, but I felt Mama's presence vibrating behind me. I pictured her standing in the living room, wringing her hands, watching me and feeling the threads of her suppressed, phony life rip apart forever.

He had stopped moving now and stared back in disbelief.

"You know, mementos, baby pictures, toys, or birth certificates. No telling."

"What are you trying to say, Jake? Stop playing games."

"Come back in the house," Mama murmured from behind me. Anything to get me to stop talking.

"I've been telling lies to you, to everyone, all summer long. And you two, well hell, you've been lying for the past twenty-five years." Mama let the porch door slam when she came out. "Did you think I wouldn't ever find out? That no one would, just because you kept it all quiet?"

I could tell they did, thought, and hoped. But I wasn't lying anymore and I felt beyond the point of ever having to lie again. I was no longer scared of my own words. Hell, after a branding iron, I'd never be scared of anything anymore.

This is what I thought to myself, until I saw the sheriff's truck wheel around the front of the house.

fifty-two

a stranger in these parts, serving in any capacity as law enforcement, carried the gossip value of an extra-terrestrial. Sheriff Wiley Deane exited his shiny county truck and squinted to assess our family's version of madness.

When I launched the speech of my life, all of us reverted to one of the other realities that existed beside us, below us, and within us simultaneously. I no longer recognized my own family. I felt like a misplaced, unclothed entity hidden in a bubble on a front porch in Middle America. I was a stranger to Hooper Circle and Roosevelt High School, and to the hills and streets in Grady. My new kin were the memories of near death and a history of bleeding sounds inflicted on the Oklahoma plains.

Sheriff Deane let out a half-hearted chuckle and approached Daddy. "Howdy." He was looking at my wounds.

Daddy turned quickly on his heels and shook the man's hand.

"You know, if I'm catching y'all at a bad time . . ."

Mama, with just her eyes, pleaded with Daddy. Their nonverbal communication had always been well practiced. It was likely the only good between them.

"No sir, Sheriff," Daddy said. "What can we do for you?" Daddy walked him up to the porch, and Mama pulled a chair out. "Jake, go on inside and get dressed."

Sheriff Deane stood about six feet tall, maybe taller, and had a protruding belly that sagged over his belt and holster.

"Our son was attacked last night, Sheriff," Mama explained. Sheriff Deane's clean-shaven baby face studied me through the screen door, trying to put the scene together in his head.

"You know who did it, son? You must be Jake."

"Yessir."

"Yessir what?"

I shot Mama a panicked look. "Yessir, Sheriff."

Sheriff Deane shook his head. "I mean, never mind. So you know who did this to you then?"

A murder of crows circled eerily overhead, following their silent vigil in perfect formation. Except this time, they weren't celebrating death necessarily, but the single death that unified all of our tangled lives. "Yessir."

"Mind telling me who it was?"

Through the metal porch screen, Daddy and me read each other like loyal adversaries. He was clenching his fists behind Sheriff Deane, and I stood gawking at them, hands at my sides, with my thin, underdeveloped body covered with burn marks and bruises. Daddy was looking at my scars, but mostly studied my face. "Do you really know?" he seemed to be asking me, "and, if you do, do you really understand anything?"

Mama led me back to the bedroom and told Sheriff Deane I needed to rest.

I heard their conversation through the open window in Lewella's old bedroom. Sheriff Deane took out a cigar. "What brings you here today?" Mama asked with her best Saturday smile.

Sheriff Deane told them that the Waurika Police had more questions for me regarding the death of Walter van Geller. Mama jumped to my defense and said that Blackie told them they had a suspect.

"You see, that suspect sort of disappeared, Ma'am, but—"

Mama jumped in. "But that's got nothing to do with our son, Sheriff. If Waurika's got evidence that ties your missing suspect to that crime, the fact that he's gone at the moment doesn't change a thing. Except to make your job harder maybe."

It was one of her best talents—stabbing the truth into an embarrassing question, then using a bit of sugar to soften her logic. I don't know what else she told him but I heard Sheriff Wiley Deane's truck screech out of Hooper Circle a minute later. She came in the bedroom and turned on the lamp on the nightstand.

"What did Blackie tell you about that other man who was arrested?"

I tried to roll toward her but pain throbbed from every part of my body. "There were two, I heard. He owed them money or something."

"And you don't know any more about it than that?"

Mama's eyes blinked and darted in wild patterns, like Nelda's did when she was talking to ghosts.

"I saw him."

She put her hand on my wounded shoulder. "I didn't think you had anything to do with it. But you've seen too much of everything lately, and it's my fault. I guess I've been so overtaken by Lew's baby and then her moving in with her, well, doctor." Her face was puffy like it had been for the last few weeks. Red and puffy. It made me wonder if she'd been drinking again, by herself, like she had a long time ago. "I think you're all grown up now, and I wasn't even there to see it."

Mama hung her head down and let her forehead touch the clean white bedsheets.

"Jake, you've got to tell me what you know about that old man who died."

"He was killed, Mama, you can say it. Murdered. Hell, they shot him in the head Al Capone style."

"What did you want with him?" She looked up now, pleading. "Why were you there? If you had nothing to do with it, how did you happen to go there on the same day that it happened? If you don't tell it to me, you might have to tell it to the police and they could put you in jail."

"I'd be safer there than anywhere else right now."

"Jake."

I looked at Daddy's shadow skulking across the wall in the kitchen. I saw the outline of a bottle in his right hand. For some reason, I pictured him cracking that bottle over Mama's skull. My eyes had seen too much violence lately. Now I was projecting what wasn't really there.

Wasn't I?

"Let the boy rest," Daddy said, and I knew it was the tone of his voice that caused Mama to stand up and slam the bedroom door closed. Ten seconds later, Daddy left and slammed the front door behind him.

"We've got to stick together, Jake," she said from the doorway and came to sit near me on the floor. It was the first time I'd ever seen her relaxed and casual, nearly intimate, us sharing secrets, and she with her housedress riding up her tanned, bare shins. "We're all that's left of this family, you know. Now you be a good boy and tell me about that old man."

I sat up and sipped some water. "How about telling me some things first."

Mama leaned back on the floor against the wall. I could tell a part of her wanted desperately to talk about this, and have someone else bear part of the weight of her secret. But with the big things in life, it always took her a while to get started.

I propped up my pillow and folded my arms. "Like starting with PJ."

And something drastic happened to her face when I mentioned PJ's name. All of a sudden, the rocklike façade powdered off her face and neck, and some old, ancient part of her sat up and breathed for the first time. I knew about secrets. I knew about doing and saying and thinking things so bad and so reckless that you had to literally bury them in the darkest brain-sediment to be sure they wouldn't rise up and taunt you when you least expected it. My asking about PJ was the same as handing Mama an invisible shovel and holding a gun to her head. The door was closed. Daddy was outside getting drunk by himself. Lewella had moved in with Laszlo the interloper. It was just the two of us, now, holed up in a stuffy bedroom during an Indian summer. It was time for the telling.

fifty-THRee

"He knew even before I told him," Mama said with a smooth, steel voice. "Your Daddy. He knew I was pregnant almost before I was, and he knew it wasn't his."

PJ.

"Gordy and PJ were like you and Mikey growing up. More than just friends, they sort of lived the same life. The same childhood, same adolescence, same friends. Like brothers." Mama took a deep breath and went to the opened window and sat under it. I think we both knew that Daddy was lurking outside somewhere, waiting for us both, the two sinners, revealing our hefty secrets in a confidence he was not privy to. "When I met your father, I think I met PJ the same day. We were thrown together, the three of us, day, night, and everything in between. And it wasn't 'til after your father and I got engaged that PJ and me realized we'd had feelings for each other all along. Your Daddy saw me first and, according to the rules of men, PJ would remain a quiet shadow. But it was like I never had a say in the matter. So I allowed myself one night with the person I truly loved and never planned to think about that night, consciously, for the rest of my life. But he knew. Your Daddy knew what, and who, and even knew the sensible solution after it all came out."

She was becoming that young, teenaged girl again while I was watching. Sitting cross-legged on the hard floor with her skirt all twisted up between her legs, this was not the woman who gave birth to me.

"Who killed her?" I said as my opening question.

My teenaged mother snapped her head up and caught my gaze.

"I think all of you were involved in it. Mary knew you were her kin,

264

and she wanted the truth and neither you nor Daddy would give it to her. Why? Would it have been such a scandal?"

She was crying again. "You'll never know how much."

"But to who? It all happened when you were young. No one would care anymore. Most of those people had moved out of Grady by then anyway."

"Most."

She was trying to tell me something, but before my foggy brain could process what it was, the bedroom door flung open. Daddy was standing behind it holding his shotgun.

"Gordon, what in the hell are you doing?"

"Come out here," he said to her, staring at me the whole time.

Instinct drove me off the bed and into the closet where, hiding more than anything else, I put on fresh clothes, socks, and boots. I usually wore sneakers; most boys my age did, and kept the boots for special occasions. I had no idea why I reached specifically for them on the back ledge of the closet. Before I came out, the bedroom door slammed shut as hard as it had opened.

I heard Daddy's low, whispering voice, the kind he used when their bedroom door was closed late at night, and some kind of muffled noise of distress from Mama. Through the keyhole I saw Daddy's shoulder locked under Mama's arm and his lips pressed into her ear. Two fat tears slid down the left side of her face, which was growing red. He must have whacked her while I was in the closet. Goddamn him. The inside part of me wasn't going to let him hurt her, either emotionally or physically, but Blackie had seen to my physical limitations expertly.

He'd wrapped both arms around her body, the gun gripped tightly in his right hand. Knowing I was just behind the door, Daddy kept his voice muffled. I heard "the boy, the boy," a few times in growing intensity.

"No, Gordon, it wasn't that," Mama pleaded. She tried to wriggle out from under his arms. "Let—me—Gor—" A screech came from her voice at the end of Daddy's name.

"All right," Daddy shouted, and tossed her toward the kitchen table. My knees were shaking so hard I could barely stand. Mama,

Daddy, the alcohol in Daddy's glass, and the gun in his hand. I couldn't help wondering if I was the one who had caused everything, every last detail leading to the breakdown of my family.

By the time I heard the unmistakable groan of Woody's truck engine, the hitting had already started. He dragged her into the bedroom, closed and locked the door. At first I just heard the clank of a bottle hitting the edge of a glass, then the impact of skin on skin, my mother's scream, and her body bouncing down on the copper bedsprings. Unsure of what to do, I stood behind the door, behind the keyhole, waiting, watching, and biting the fleshy edge of my hand. Woody came through the screen and almost tore it off the hinges. He clomped in heavy boots through the kitchen, then stopped and looked at Lewella's closed door.

Mama whimpered and Daddy screamed something at her. That's when Woody yanked open their bedroom door.

"Woody, what are you doing here? This is none of your concern."

And before it went any further, I left the bedroom and flew out the front door. Pacing on the front porch still gave me too close a proximity to the violence within, so I stood in the dirt, looking out at the pasture. I saw a light-colored shirt and the bounce of curly hair coming over the hill. Aware of her entrance, I kept my gaze on the house, at the nexus of three tormented lives and the sins of circumstance, resulting in three adults and two shotguns in one bedroom. Janet put a hand on my back.

"Jake?"

She came around me and looked at my face, then at my body.

"I know," I said. "I'm a sight."

Her hand covered her mouth. "My God, what happened?" she said finally.

She leaned in close and kissed me. I put my hands on her shoulders and turned her around, with my back facing the house. Some part of me had to at least try to shield her from whatever might be happening or about to happen in there.

"What's—"

Her voice was interrupted by a chorus of shouting. Woody's voice penetrated the loudest, and seemed to silence the other two for the moment. "My parents are in there. With my grandfather."

She must have seen something in my face, because her entire body seemed to shrivel. She backed away from me and stayed there in the middle of the shadowed street.

The voices inside erupted one more time, a door slammed, and I could tell Mama was getting dragged back into the bedroom. I started up the stairs, then, with no prior knowledge of how to break up a gunfight.

"Jake!" Janet followed me. "Please, I beg you, don't go in there."

I gazed down at her smooth, pretty face, at the way the porch bulb lit up her cheeks, and knew I was not destined for such things in my life—for such gentility, beauty, and purity. I could have corrupted Janet Lange if I wanted to—she loved me enough to allow me to have her over and over. But Janet was pure, and I would rather experience charms of the flesh with someone else if it meant keeping her beautiful face the way it looked that night, right then, on my eerie front porch.

Walking through the screen door, I stood in the kitchen. More conversation erupted, and then crying, another impact of fist to skin, and then high, guttural shrieks. I put my hand on the bedroom doorknob and as I was about to turn the handle, a shot went off in the room. I jumped back. Janet ran in the house, crying. And when I opened the bedroom door and saw Mama lying on the bed and Daddy standing over Woody's slumped body, I knew that Woody, to his crooked, Bible Belt cohorts, had more to lose than anyone if Mama's indiscretion had been leaked out and the family name disgraced. Mary McCann. Woody Leeds. Jesus.

fifty-four

Our family had no funeral for Woody. Grandma Weaver didn't leave her house for three days and refused to eat or drink anything. Mama told me in private that she believed Weaver was relieved to have him gone, and that he had roughed her up more than once, and not just in the beginning of their marriage.

I'd been avoiding Daddy like an infectious disease, and the only real reason I stayed there was to protect Mama from whatever retribution he might inflict upon her in response to Woody's death.

But there was none. Not that day, nor the day after. Daddy left that night, after answering a load of questions by Sheriff Deane, and didn't come back for two whole days and nights. Mama used cooking as a defense against grief and cooked the best batch of peach pies, brown potatoes, and coffee bars I'd ever tasted. We made an art form, Mama and me, out of not talking. Lewella came on the third day and sat and cried with Mama at the kitchen table over a pot of extra strong coffee, and Doc Laszlo rocked the baby on the front porch. I heard he was going to adopt her after Lewella and he got married. Time and space were stagnant that night, thick blocks hanging in the muted sky. I no longer knew what to think about any of them.

Daddy was smoking on the porch the next morning when I came outside to get the newspaper. We eyeballed each other like two jackals—circling slowly, both aware of their power over the other and of what they had to lose if they succumbed to its whimsy. For a long while he watched me but didn't speak. I had a feeling this might be the last time we ever spoke, so I waited, too. Mama's rocking chair on the porch was so old and splintered; no one ever sat there anymore. But today was special. It felt like my first day of freedom from my family's history of enslaving secrets.

"Start school this week, don't you?"

I blinked and looked at the hitching post. I wondered when he had had time to fix it over the past few days, but sure enough it stood up tall and erect just like it always had. "I'm going up to Enid for a while."

"A little far, don't you think?"

"Nelda needs me. And God knows you and I need each other like two bullet holes in the head." There was no argument about it.

Later that day, I waited 'til Mama went out shopping for groceries before I moved my belongings from the horse barn and the closet of my former bedroom. I found the old, familiar red scarf tied to the top rung of the hitching post as I carried my small suitcase and duffel bag down the porch steps. I wasn't sure what he meant by hanging it up there again. Maybe to mock everything that happened, maybe just as a symbol of change, but I knew someone who needed it more than him.

fifty-five

"There's so much I want to tell you," I said aloud in the darkness of the baseball diamond. The wind was up, as well as a crisp coolness native to fall. Wind, Grandma Weaver used to tell me, meant change. I held the red scarf up in the air. "And this," I said to my dead sister Mary, "means hope."

I laid the scarf on the ground at the bottom of my blanket, and put a rock on one part of it to keep it from blowing away. But that's how hope is, isn't it? Fleeting, oscillating energy that keeps us tied to the future when every grain of our consciousness feels stuck in the sediment of past. Hope is an impish reminder of who we could be.

I told my sister the story of her birth, her adoption, her life, and of course, her death. I left out the grisly details, half because she already knew those, and half because the baseball diamond seemed even more chilling than the last time I was there. I remember that night, three months ago, like it was three hours ago. And I knew I would remember the events of this past summer for the rest of my life. A summer of tornadoes, secrets, lies, murder, and truth.

I awoke the next morning with a soft breeze on my face, after a night of talking to my sister Mary McCann for the first and last time. And then I left Mary's prairie for good, on my way to Enid. A new life.

epilogue

It's November, now, and Mikey's roaming the haunted hallways of Roosevelt High School once again. Me, I've started attending a much larger school in Enid, where I've been staying with Nelda. Mikey came up the first few weekends of school and helped me finish the shed. It started as a ghost project Nelda conjured up to keep me near her and ward off her demons. Then, over time, part of me realized I was intended to live in this house. When we finished roughing-in the shed, Nelda and me moved all of Mary's things in there. The dresser in her closet, all her old clothes, records, letters from Nash and all of his secret wood carvings with his initials on the bottom. I made a special shelf for those. But her book collection, at my specific request, remained in the house.

I sleep in Mary's old room now. We bought a used twin bed at a garage sale in town and Mikey and me started building a dresser. In the meantime, Nelda let me use one of her old ones that had been stuck in the basement for the past ten years.

Lots of things changed in ten years. And the thing about change is that you never really know which direction you might go. You can change back, and revert, like Nelda did after Mary died. But sometimes, if enough time goes by and the right sequence of events occurs, things turn around. They turn slowly, for sure—my own life is evidence of that; but changing forward, sure enough, can happen just as well.

I still call Mama and talk to her every night. Daddy and I haven't spoken in two months and I have a feeling Mama hasn't spoken to him either. I don't know what will happen with them, or if maybe it happened a long time ago. Mama restrained her protestations about my being here, in Enid, long enough for me to take care of those most important to me. She seems to understand I'll come home eventually, when all the dust and baggage finally settles down. Or maybe she just understands that this house, Nelda's house, is home to me as well.

Turns out that Roman Laszlo has family in Enid and he and Lewella and baby Faith have already come up here to visit twice. I introduced them to Nelda, and they came inside and sat in the living room, quietly wondering about her, and this place, and what the hell I was doing up here. But Lewella has a spiritual side to her and seemed to easily comprehend my need to connect with the life I was supposed to have, or maybe the life Mary wasn't. What would have happened if Mama and PJ kept Mary, and raised her as her and Daddy's daughter? What if I'd grown up with not one but two sisters in the same house? Would she have ended up with Nash Farrell, and lived her crazy rebellious lifestyle always on the verge of either insanity or destruction? I knew she would have. I'd never met Mary McCann, but we shared a common lineage, and more than that, we were a part of each other. I know it, I know for sure that Mary knows it, even Nelda does. When I'm sitting in my new bedroom, Mary's old room, late at night, just staring out the window from my bed, Nelda walks by in the hallway and quietly looks the other way, knowing I'm entranced by some ghostly vigil. I call them our secret talks. Mary has a voice, you know—I've heard it, and not just that first night in the baseball diamond. Sometimes I think it's a gift, this telepathy of sorts, of which even Nelda was capable those times last summer when I caught her talking to ghosts. Every prairie has them. Every piece of open land, once inhabited by powerful souls, is a place where they return at night, from their new dimension, to both remember and forget.

Though Mary likes my being here in her home, I can tell she wants me to go back to Grady. Our secret talks, though often one-sided, sometimes leave me with an overwhelming thought or feeling. This is how she communicates—implanting the seeds of change by tiny thought fragments in my tired brain at the end of the day. There's unfinished business there, Mary says. She tells me I need to look after not only Mama, but also Grandma Weaver. And I think I have always known, in some strange way, that it would be my job to take care of all of them.

Janet rides the train to visit me on Saturday mornings. Her parents talked to Mama to get an explanation of why I was up here and when I'd be coming home. I don't know what she told them—I never know what Mama's going to say until she's said it. Nelda cooked dinner for the three of us one night, and even bought a new outfit for the occasion. Before I came up here for good, I thought Nelda was never closer to death. Physiologically she seemed okay—heart beating, eyes open, seemingly drawing air into her lungs. Yet every other part of her, internally, deeper than just skin and blood, had long ceased to exist. But once the shed was finished and we started boxing up Mary's things from her room, Nelda changed forward instead of back. We were on the porch resting after struggling the dresser out to the shed. I poured us glasses of lemonade from the big pitcher and she looked up at me and said, "Thank you." And I knew a part of her frozen soul, maybe the deepest, most fragile part, had begun to thaw. So in just one summer of my life, I saw a homeless man die and learned the truth about my dead sister, but I believe in the darkest folds of my heart that I have saved two lives: Nelda's and my own. Family, I always thought, was something you could not choose to either have or will away. I still had my own family—Mama, Daddy, Lewella, and Weaver. But Nelda McCann, snoring in the room next to mine right now, was besides Mary the only real "kin" I would ever recognize as my own.

The fall nights have been cool lately in Enid. I sleep with the window partially open, and there were two nights up here so far when I slept on the open ground in Nelda's backyard. Maybe I wanted to remember the baseball diamond and how terrified I had felt at my exposure. Connections, I now realized, were what I lived for.

Tonight I'm too jumpy to sleep. So I wander through Mary's voluminous book collection, and both smile and cry when I wander upon an old, faded stack of Superman comic books.